T5-AFR-473

CRIME SCENE AT "O" STREET

CRIME SCENE AT "O" STREET

A NOVEL

PAUL W. VALENTINE

St. Martin's Press
New York

This is a work of fiction. All of the events, characters, names and places depicted in this novel are entirely fictitious or are used fictitiously. No representation that any statement made in this novel is true or that any incident depicted in this novel actually occurred is intended or should be inferred by the reader.

Editor: Jared Kieling
Copyedited by Eva Galan Salmieri
Design by Debby Jay

Library of Congress Cataloging-in-Publication Data

Valentine, Paul W.
Crime scene at "O" Street.

I. Title.
PS3572.A396C7 1989 813'.54 88-30574
ISBN 0-312-02563-7

First Edition

10 9 8 7 6 5 4 3 2 1

For Elizabeth

Crime Scene At "O" Street

Florian Boldt had known few surprises in his life. It was his mother's wish, sensible woman. Her world had never encompassed much beyond what was immediately certain, and she had labored with quiet fervor, even in her final years, to preserve some small island of that certainty in the darkening waters around them.

Had she been with him, she would have concurred in his shock when he saw the body. He staggered back in his apartment doorway, a quick gasp at his lips. He regained his balance, then raised his eyes and looked more closely in the waning light. It was Frank, grotesquely animate, yet—

He stared fascinated at the dim form on the foyer floor. The muffled brool of early evening traffic outside, like the drone of a distant organ, filtered through the building. Strangely, he did not want to move, his gaze fixed on the floor. With reluctance, he roused himself. Stepping carefully, he tiptoed into the living room and looked. He could see now that the eyes were open. They had an unfocused neutral look, not like Frank's at all. He started toward the body, wondering if he should check for vital signs. Instead, he stooped from a distance and peered cautiously. No blood, no punctures. Perhaps a heart attack or stroke, he thought almost with relief. Then he noticed, scattered wantonly about the floor near the body, his collection of prize antique Gorham and Whiting pickle forks. They had been knocked from their shelf in the foyer. Next he noticed the shelf itself was broken, and the tines of one of the forks had pierced a lamp shade. A black Windsor chair in the living room lay on its side. He stood up abruptly. A new uneasiness, like a cold draft, came across him. The shadows of the room seemed to darken. He glanced at his watch: 7:25. He thought: Get hold of yourself, Old Thing. Time to focus. The police? Yes, the police. He scurried to the telephone, remembering the building security instructions about dialing the emergency number.

"Hello? My name is Boldt, B-O-L-D-T. Florian Boldt. . . . Yes, Seventeen sixteen L'Enfant Court Northwest. . . . No, not L'Enfant Plaza. That's Southwest. This is a little place. Just off O Street. . . . An apartment? Yes, One-B."

He hesitated. "I'd like to report a. . . . There's a. . . . When I came home just now, I found my apartment mate on the floor and he appears to . . . . I think he may be unconscious or possibly something. . . . Yes? A few minutes? . . . Certainly, I'll be here."

Boldt heard the Roxbury clock in the living room strike the half-hour. As he waited, he decided to turn on the overhead lights. The body suddenly loomed much larger. The hair was mussed, but the body retained a certain neatness, even in these circumstances. Just like Frank. And while the narrow shoulders and slender feet were unmistakably Frank's, their utter stillness gave the body an alien air. Boldt looked away. He busied himself going through his wallet, assembling his driver's license and Interior Department employee pass. Surely the kind of thing they'll want to see. He looked about the living room. The windows and their locks appeared in proper order and secure. The front door, he remembered, had responded to his key in its usual cantankerous way, taking several seconds of jollying to open. Nothing suspicious there. For an electrifying moment, he thought someone might still be in the apartment. Hesitantly, he sidled down the hall past the kitchen on the left to the first bedroom, reached around the doorway and switched the light on. He looked in. All appeared normal. He went to the second bedroom. The same. Should he look under the bed? Don't be absurd, he thought uncertainly. He glanced at the hem of the bedspread. It was moving slightly. The air conditioning vent, of course. He walked back to the living room, and as he surveyed the tiny silver forks strewn on the floor, he heard a car brake sharply in front of the apartment building. With relief he saw through the front window a cream and blue police scout car double-parked under the sycamore tree across the street. Two uniformed officers clambered out. One was black, one white. Funny, he thought, how we always notice such things. The red emergency lights on top of the car continued to turn lazily. Moments later, Boldt heard the whine of a siren ricocheting off the buildings across the street and saw an ambulance enter the street and stop abruptly behind the scout car. Two blue-clad medics jumped from the ambulance. Boldt marveled at how his single telephone call had set this extraordinary series of responses in train.

There was a loud rap on the main doors of the building. Boldt walked out into the lobby and admitted the four men. The medics entered first and, after nodding, headed for the open apartment door to which Boldt pointed. The uniformed officers, holding their nightsticks awkwardly, followed. They filed into the living room without a word, then turned and formed a half circle around the body on the floor.

One of the medics knelt over the head, examining the eyes and neck. The body lay on its chest, rump thrust in the air, a knee pulled up under the stomach. The face was turned to the side with the corner of the mouth pressed against the floor. The medic stood up after a moment.

"No signs." They were the first words uttered since the men had entered the building.

"Call downtown," one of the uniformed officers said. The other raised a handset radio to his lips and mumbled into it. The radio sputtered back. He spoke a second time and then lowered the radio.

“See you guys later,” said the medic. He and his partner turned and left the room. Moments later, Boldt heard the ambulance pull away from the building.

More silence. Boldt and the two police officers continued their vigil. Boldt fussed at the buttons on his suit jacket.

“I don’t quite understand,” he said at length. His voice seemed unnecessarily loud. “The ambulance people came and then—”

“They responded over here when Communications got your call, is all,” said one of the officers.

“So why did they leave?”

“Routine. Check to see if the person is unconscious or what.”

“But why—”

“If they’re dead, the ambulance leaves.”

“Leaves?”

The officer looked incredulous. “Yeah, leaves.”

“But—”

“Then we call downtown. Homicide responds to the ones like this.”

“Like this?”

“Yeah, unattended.”

“So who’ll pick up the body now?”

The officer glanced bleakly at Boldt. “Tag ’n’ Bag.”

“Tag and—?”

“The M.E., medical examiner. Later.”

Another silence followed. The two uniformed men stood motionless in the living room. Boldt continued to fuss at his buttons.

“Oh, by the way, I’m . . . I’m Florian Boldt,” he said, attempting a smile. “I live here and I—”

“Who’s this here?” asked one of the officers, pointing to the floor.

“Oh. That’s Mr. Kadinsky. Franklin Kadinsky. He also lives here, or, I guess, lived here.”

The officer walked over to the body and knelt down. “How do you spell it?” he asked. He shined a flashlight across the pallid face. The body, dressed in trousers and pink striped shirt, lay in formal rigidity.

"K-A-D-I-N-S-K-Y," said Boldt. "He works on the Hill, House side."

The policeman stood up again and pulled a tattered notebook from his hip pocket.

"K-E, what?"

"No, K-A-D-I-N-S-K-Y. First name Franklin." The officer slowly penciled an entry in the notebook.

"Married?"

"No."

"N.O.K.?"

"Beg pardon?"

"N.O.K. Parents, relative, something."

"Well, there's no one here in Washington. His mother and father live in Chicago. I'm sure I can get their phone number and address in Frank's room." Boldt started to walk toward the rear of the apartment.

"Don't go nowhere," ordered the officer. "Homicide'll do it."

"I was just trying to—"

"It's our job to secure the scene. Just stand by."

"Look, if you don't mind," blurted Boldt, "this is all a little strange to me." The officer looked at him vacantly. "I just want you to know that the last time I saw Frank—Mr. Kadinsky—was this morning. We always get up about the same time, but I usually leave for work before he does. It was the same today. I left about eight-fifteen. He was still here, dressed just the way he is now. He reads a great deal and—"

"What's this here?" asked the officer, pointing to the forks scattered on the floor.

"Oh, those," Boldt said. "Those are antique silver. They seem to have been knocked down." He stepped toward them. "Maybe if I got them out of the—"

"Don't touch nothing," the officer ordered again. "This scene has to be maintained in a secure manner." Boldt stepped back carefully.

“Mr. Bell,” said the officer.

“Boldt.”

“If you don’t mind, I’m going to have to ask you to come downtown.”

“But—”

“My partner’ll stay here and maintain the scene.”

“But why can’t I stay?”

“Routine. Any case like this, you go to Homicide. You may be there a while.”

Boldt looked around the living room, feeling vaguely helpless. He glanced out the front window and saw an unmarked car pull up and double park where the ambulance had been. A short dark man emerged from the driver’s seat and started toward the apartment building. He was struggling to fasten a clip-on necktie to his collar as he bounded up the stairs and rapped on the outer doors.

“That’s Homicide,” said the officer.

He opened the doors. The detective, with an investigator’s badge dangling from his breast pocket, entered the lobby. “Hi,” he said to the two uniformed men. “I’m Nestor Skoda.” He glanced briefly at Florian Boldt and walked into the apartment. Boldt watched his eyes make a cursory sweep of the living room, taking in the Roxbury clock, a heraldic tapestry on the wall, the primly rumpled figure on the floor. The eyes paused at a corner table where a framed photograph showed Franklin Kadinsky shaking hands with the President.

“Mr. Bell,” announced the uniformed officer, “Homicide’ll be taking charge of the scene now.” He placed a clumsy but gentle hand on Boldt’s arm, and the two men left the building.

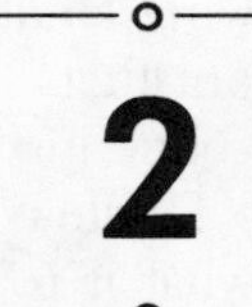

"Dadlemit," swore Captain Hubert Stohlbach at his secretary. "Find me Hudlow and Johnson. I don't care if they're on the back of Mars. This here's a high slope problem."

Captain Stohlbach spat unhappily into his handkerchief and looked at J. T. Greene, his secretary. The secretary wore a pale pink golf shirt with a leatherette bow tie suspended from the collar. Graying, closely shorn hair framed a dyspeptic face. Debate had raged for a decade in Homicide over J. T. Greene's gender, but prevailing sentiment in recent times tended toward a broadly defined midpoint between extremes.

"Done everything I could, el Jefe," croaked Greene. "Skoda's on his way in; he's only twenty minutes. But Hudlow and Johnson, I can't find them. Both of them took a couple days' annual leave."

"We got the preliminaries from the M.E.?"

"S'pose to be up here later this morning. Technicians squawking about the stuff being ordered so soon. They're swamped. Got three more cooking and a couple of new ones on the way."

"This is a negatory situation," said Captain Stohlbach. "Deputy Chief Freeman, the new acting CID commander, is coming down here in a few minutes for a briefing on this thing at the Fruit Loop last night. Says Field Ops getting a ration from the L'Enfant Citizens and wants Hudlow and Johnson put on it, right now. I got it right here in writing. Plus Skoda, since he took the initial report. Three men. You imagine that?"

"Send in the Marines. Skoda's cub scout."

"Yeah, I know. But throwing Hudlow and Johnson together. You think they thought about that?"

"Field Ops don't think. They just look at the closure rates. They don't even know who Hudlow and Johnson are."

"Jacking me around, is what it is. Splitting up regular partners and having them report directly to me, leapfrogging the lieutenant and the section chiefs. I tell you, J. T., it's against the chain of command."

"Look at it this way, el Jefe. At least you got Nestor Skoda to keep Hudlow and Johnson from slam-dunking each other."

"That's true, praise the Lord. Hudlow and Johnson not exactly Romeo and Juliet, are they?" Captain Stohlbach reflected a moment. "But you know, another thing worries me: Hudlow ain't too big on them . . . them whatchacallums, regardless of race, color or creed—"

"Faggots? In the Kadinsky thing? How you figure, el Jefe?"

"Well, you know, a Hill guy on Dupont Circle with a little ring-around-the-roses roommate and his-and-his matching towel sets? What can I say?"

"Bet it's dope," said Greene. "Lots of dope up there."

"How was he killed? Gimme Skoda's paper." Greene handed Stohlbach a file folder. "Says here, contusions to the neck. No wounds." Stohlbach dropped the folder on his desk. "Strangulation, be my guess. Wish Tag 'n' Bag would hurry up."

Stohlbach began clearing his already immaculately neat desk for the arrival of the new acting commander of the Criminal Investigation Division. A wire basket containing two sheets of unused bond paper was placed squarely at the outer left corner of the desk. At the center stood a calendar displaying a paschal lamb clutching a spray of lilies, its mouth fixed in a devout leer. On the right corner rested a photograph of Stohlbach's wife, a large melancholy woman peering through thick glasses and holding a pale open-mouthed child. The remainder of the desktop was bare.

"Get another cup for the acting commander," Stohlbach ordered Greene. Stohlbach pulled an extra chair in front of his desk, dusting it with his handkerchief. He then sat down again in his own chair and rapped a leaden drum roll with his fingers on the desktop.

In strode the acting commander.

"Good morning, sir," said Stohlbach, standing stiffly. "Captain Stohlbach here, chief of Homicide Branch."

"Right," answered the acting commander. "I'm John Freeman." He waved to Stohlbach to sit down. "Sorry we hadn't met before this. How we doing?"

"Be advised, sir," answered Stohlbach, "we are expediting the Kadinsky case in a timely and immediate manner."

"Are the detectives here?"

"That's a roger, sir, or at least one is on the way. As far as response-wise, my secretary placed telephone calls to Detective Hudlow and Detective Johnson, but with negative success. Detective Skoda, however, is reported on his way. Get the commander a cup of coffee, J. T."

"What you got so far?"

"Mobile Crime Lab has completed their examination at the location of the scene, which they will submit a written report, also eight-by-ten glossies and physical evidence. The deceased complainant was bagged and taken to the medical examiner last night, and we should be in receipt of preliminary findings this date, as per your request, in writing or telephonically if you require prioritized service. Being as this maybe was a homosexual case, I requested swabs of the—" Stohlbach hesitated—"anus and mouth. Also scrapings under the fingernails. A full post and toxicology will be forwarded in three to four days on an expedited basis, and et cetera."

Freeman sat down heavily in the chair prepared by Captain Stohlbach. "Christ, I don't need this my first week," he said. "Who's this bitch Evelyn Farnham with the L'Enfant Citizens? She own half of D.C. or what?"

"Yessir," said Stohlbach. "She is the president of the L'Enfant Citizens Association, which she manages several apartment buildings in that neighborhood. It's an area that's come back since the riots, and they're very picky about keeping it nice. Couple of congressmen own property in there."

"Well, she's been whispering in Assistant Chief Flynn's ear already this morning, telling him to get this thing out of the way and meantime put the word out that the neighborhood is perfectly safe and it was some kind of fluky thing and not just another hopped up tomcat from Fourteenth Street. Wants me to tell the newspapers and TV some business about it's a 'aberration' or whatever and couldn't happen for another hundred years. What she got with Flynn that he listens to that stuff?"

"Sir, Evelyn Farnham helps out with the Metropolitan Police Boys Clubs every year, and as you know, the clubs fall in the parameters of Field Operations, being tasked to the Youth Division. She's also buddy-buddy with Lem Stafford in the mayor's office and got him and Flynn doing a hat trick on us."

"She run the White House and breast-feed Doberman pinschers, too?"

"Yessir, seems like that," said Stohlbach, wincing. "Every year, she gets all them . . . them gays that live up around her to contribute to the Boys Clubs, and I mean they contribute. Not just money, but volunteer time and work and job skills and everything but the Empire State Building. Say what you want, they know how to turn a dollar, them boys. Also, she always gets a congressman or two to put their name on the board of directors and the Boys Club letterhead."

"In the meantime," snapped Freeman, "we're short on men. I see on the morning report you got six new homicides working. You're down to a sixty-five percent closure rate. Four investigators been detailed to Two-D, and now we got to put three men to work just on this one. That leaves me with Mother Goose and the Camp Fire Girls to run the rest of the city."

"Yessir, it's highly unusual to stack three men. But when the brass plays," Stohlbach shrugged feebly—"the orchestra jumps."

"Let's face it," said Freeman. "It was actually Evelyn Farnham that got the three detectives. That's how this city's run. Citizens associations and business clubs. If the Russians knew that, they could take over tomorrow. Just roll down Pennsylvania Avenue with a couple of tanks and a membership in the Board of Trade."

"Any luck with Hudlow and Johnson?" Stohlbach turned to J. T. Greene.

"Still negative, el Jefe."

At that moment, Detective Skoda entered the office. A ferocious mustache crowded his small face. "Hi, Chief . . . J. T.," he said, nodding uncertainly at Freeman. "What's up?"

"That one you got last night," said Stohlbach. "He's one of Evelyn's boys. Big-ticket item. Field Ops dancing in the end zone without a touchdown. We're waiting for Hudlow and Johnson now."

"Figured you get reinforcements," said Skoda.

The Homicide chief turned to Freeman. "Sir, this is Detective Nestor Skoda, which he responded to the scene last night. Nestor, this is Deputy Chief Freeman of CID."

The two men nodded and shook hands.

"I see on the summaries you didn't find much of anybody at home last night, Nestor," said Stohlbach.

"That's right. Seemed like everybody in Kadinsky's building was out, except the building engineer, and he wasn't much use. Rest of them were at a zoning hearing or something downtown, according to the engineer. One thing's in our favor: There's only eight or nine units in the building."

"How about the roommate, Florian Boldt? How'd he hold up?"

"Solid citizen on the initial interview. Says he was at work. Couldn't raise his boss, but we'll check it today."

"Pair of butterflies fighting over their nest, wasn't it, Nestor?" said Stohlbach.

"Could be."

"Got any idea where Hudlow and Johnson are?"

"I don't know about Hudlow. Johnson's probably at the cemetery. He always goes there Fridays."

“Who are these other two men?” asked Deputy Chief Freeman. “Batman and Robin?”

“Who? Hudlow and Johnson? More like Paul Bunyan and the Lone Ranger, if you ask me. My two best men, even if they don’t usually work together. Hudlow, he’s a ol’ boy raised up in the country, other side of Hagerstown. Real roof-and-alley man. Got a memory like a elephant, and the body to go with it. Never forgets nothing, car tags, DOBs, serial numbers, you name it. I seen him spot a tag from fifty yards and tell it was from Saskatchewan. Saskatchewan, for land’s sake. How many times you seen a car from Saskatchewan, Chief? Ain’t that up around Greenland somewheres? Hud’s got good snitches, too, best network in town. Knows how to talk to them, how to keep the pressure on. Most of them’s black, you know, but Hud somehow he gets on with them real good. Don’t ask me how. Sucker’s ’bout half peckerwood. Ain’t afraid of nothing hardly, ’cept high buildings. Yessir, high buildings. He was working a jumper one time. The Gramercy Building down on G Street. Talked him off a ledge; got him into a rope sling, but the sling snapped and the jumper went down. Hudlow wouldn’t go near the edge of a building for a year after that.”

“What about the Lone Ranger?”

“Johnson? Magnus Johnson. Now he’s different. Magnus, he’s what you might call, well, what would you call him, Nestor, like very intellectual? I’m not throwing off on him. He’s just very serious. Reads books.”

“Renaissance man?”

“No, sir, he’s black. See, what I’m saying, his wife she died about twelve years back, just after he come on the department, and it seemed to tore him up pretty bad. She wasn’t but about twenty-three years old. Had some kind of cancer. They didn’t have any children, and Mag didn’t have much family left, and for months he just moped around, mostly tending this garden his wife kept out back of their house in Prince George’s County. He kept the house just like she had it, clean as cat gut, except he moved out of the bedroom. Then all of a sudden he took up reading, started taking out stuff from the library, buying encyclopedias and government manuals and like that. Spent all his spare time soaking it up, just jamming information."

"Getting his mind off his wife?"

"Got to where he knew all this weird stuff like the solar system and medicine and weather and archaeology. There wasn't much you could trip him on. Even closed some cases with it. Remember the ol' Clampton homicide back about six years ago? Mag put a trace on a piece of cloth they found in the grip of this stage-show actress that had been strangled and raped—Dorothy Clampton was her name—and Mag found it matched this unusual cross-stitch muslin made only for the robes of a monastery full of off-brand Episcopal priests down in Charles County somewheres. Mag ended up arresting the head priest of the joint. You imagine that? Mag's probably the only man in the free world that knew that particular weave of cloth."

"Maybe a good thing you got men like that," said Freeman.

"Yessir. Of all the branches in CID, sir, Homicide has always had the most strongest type men. Well, dadlemit, women, too. We're getting them now, too, Lord knows. It takes a unusual psycho-amplitude profile matrix type person for this kind of work. I read that somewhere. Men like Hudlow and Johnson are not your regular police. Well, and Skoda, too. Their motor runs to a different tune."

Skoda turned to Stohlbach. "Appreciate all the pretty words, Chief, but are you sure about putting Hudlow and Johnson together?"

"What's the problem?" interrupted Chief Freeman, turning to Stohlbach. "I thought you said they're your two best men."

"They are, alone and by theirselves. But I'm not too sure about together."

"They've never been assigned together?" Freeman said.

"Not since uniform days. All these years, they been like oil and water. They work different, see. Johnson got his office in his skull. Hudlow keeps his in his stomach. Know what I mean?"

"That shouldn't spoil it."

"Yeah, but it makes for a trust situation that isn't there. Even with good officers."

"Good but independent. Maybe they need each other and don't know it."

"Well, we got to run them together anyway. Orders from on high. I don't have no control over it." Stohlbach shrugged resignedly. "You reap the bed you lie in."

3

Dewey Thigpen Hudlow, detective, Metropolitan Police Department, brushed back a loose shock of alfalfa hair from his forehead and turned on his side. He looked at the Reverend Quovadis Logan, pastor of the Fifth Rising New Day in the Morning Church (Independent). Her breathing came in slow peaceful drafts as she slept. Her oval face was in repose, free of the scowl that crouched above her brow in waking hours. A faint glow suffused her cheeks. The only movement in her face were her violet eyelids, quivering gently from time to time as if brushed by a passing dream. Her left hand lay like an innocent child's across the sheet, periodically curling into a half-fist and then relaxing. A cat's tooth on a thin gold chain lay at her neck.

Bitch is flat beautiful, Hudlow thought. How can something so beautiful when it's asleep be so hound dog mean awake? He slumped back onto the pillow and stared at the ceiling. The radio in Quovadis' room was on. The moist crump of disco music beat softly with determined monotony. "I'm your lollipop, baby," babbled a high-pitched voice. "Lick me, lick me anywhere. . . ." On a chair partially concealed by Quovadis' clothing lay a record album emblazoned with a woman singer shuddering over the bulbous rod of her microphone. Hudlow always felt vaguely uncomfortable with Quovadis' music, as if it pulled away a cloak of sanctity around them. Like a goddamn spectator sport, he mused. Why I always got to have some boogiewump hollering at me like the Christopher Columbus of poontang?

He snapped the radio off. Quovadis stirred. Slowly her eyes opened and focused on Hudlow. The midmorning light filtered through the windows of the room, and the scowl returned to her face. Hudlow stood up, his bulky frame filling much of the room, and pulled on his trousers and shirt.

"Got to run, Buckra?" Quovadis asked dreamily.

"Yessir, ma'am," said Hudlow. The thick warp of his western Maryland speech filled the room.

"You always running."

"Keeps me skinny."

"What's to run?"

"Bidness, I got bidness."

"Don't you want to finish some business with me right here?"

"Vadis, the flag is down. Time to run."

"You not running to work. You off this week. Running back to Fronie, ain't you?"

"You leave Fronie out of this."

"She want you to jump and fetch at home?"

"Shitjimpiss, Vadis, leave off."

"Same old jive. That cracker bitch got a holt of you like a catfish on a silver spinner, even if you are separated."

"I'm warning you, Vadis, you getting close."

"Who close?"

"You, bitch. You been talking too much like this lately. Here you got your little chump-change church, sucking all these ol' niggers dry round here. Got your numbers and your after-hours dog juice. And you got me, Deputy Do-Right, making sure it all goes down okay. And what's your end of the deal? Just drop the dime once in a while, that's all, not much, just enough to keep Burglary and Auto Theft going and you don't get burned. Now you tell me what Fronie got to do with all that?"

"You lef' out one thing. Fronie at home, working her sagging butt off, kids hanging on her, bills stacking up, roof leaking, grass need cutting, and you yodeling in the canyon down here on Ninth Street. Think she like to know about that?"

"You forgetting the other half, Reverend Quovadis Goddamn Logan. You deliver for the city and I keep them out of here. If I wanted to, I could have them come down on you like a horny gorilla on a tree toad. You want that?"

"Okay, Huddy-buddy, and you wouldn't have no more black oak to split."

The two glared at each other in stalemate, both panting wearily. Hudlow finally wrenched his gaze from her magnificent stormy face. What the hell's going on here, he thought desperately. He fell back onto the bed in silence. How'd I ever get in with ol' Vadis? Most complicatedest bitch ever was. Going in about ten directions at once. Church, numbers, liquor, little dope, saving souls and pussy-whipping the po-leece, and never signed a Form 1040 in her life. Don't keep no books. Got it all in her head, phone numbers, track odds, addresses. Give me the tag number on ever' damn popcorn pimp east of Fifteenth Street and throwed in the color of the cars for good measure. And that's on a slow Thursday, I clue you.

Hudlow lay motionless. Through the partially open window facing onto the alley behind Ninth Street, he could hear the sounds of two children fighting over a tricycle. One child had a high stutter. That must be Teepo, Jesse Stoddard's eight-year-old boy by Swampy Smith. The other child's voice had a deeper, more commanding tone. That was Juan Freddie Wimbush. His mama from Panama was in Alderson for killing Juan's daddy. Juan lived with a grandmother next to Quovadis' storefront church on Ninth Street.

There was a sudden clatter of metal scraping concrete followed by Teepo's high agonized wail. Juan Freddie apparently had wrested the tricycle for himself and dragged it off, hooting with victory. Beyond the children's sounds, Hudlow now heard grown men talking, soft, raspy Negro voices in the morning air, punctuated occasionally by low chortles and guffaws. He caught only a word here or there, talk of work and wages, borrowing a car, a sickness in the family, paying the rent, a cousin in the service. He could hear the drone of Galley Brown's voice. My God, is he out again, thought Hudlow. Wonder if he went back with his ol' lady or did she finally think better? Hudlow could hear Colie Inabinet, the South Carolina geechie, his rapid chatter indecipherable. The other men in the group grunted noncommittally at his declarations. Soon, Douglas MacArthur Cheek joined the men, his clear tenor voice rising above the others. Hudlow hadn't seen Cheek in months and wondered how he was recovering from his leg amputation. His voice was certainly still strong, and he laughed genially when the other men joshed him for being slow afoot now. In better times, Hudlow had known Douglas MacArthur Cheek as a constant companion in the piney woods of Prince William County near Hudlow's home where the two men trapped foxes as a winter weekend enterprise, days baiting the traps, nights waiting in the bitter chill, crouched in the ditches, their hearts close to the earth. They laughed softly at their tiny victories and miseries. The cold and the smells and the frozen dirt were in their nostrils as they listened for the thin distant bark of a vixen with her pups in the brittle night.

A woman's voice unfamiliar to Hudlow floated through Quovadis Logan's window. The men's voices dropped momentarily in apparent deference. She spoke insistently, something about a lost dog. The men murmured among themselves. The woman left. The voices of the men picked up again. The cadence of sounds was comforting to Hudlow. The city was at peace.

Hudlow stepped to the bathroom and urinated noisily. He returned to the bedroom, picked up Quovadis' telephone and called Homicide.

"Hey, J. T., this here's Dewey Thigpen Hudlow the Fourteenth. Anything working?" He stood restlessly, shifting from one foot to the other. He was a man of immense size, part muscle, part flab. Powerful shoulders sloped into a thickening waist, and his belly pressed heavily over his belt. Yet he walked with a surprisingly light tread, his frame balanced on small nimble feet. His mouth, hanging open slightly, and his eyes in a fixed somnolent stare suggested an inclination to avarice without the volition to act upon it.

"Hey," he said into the telephone, his face brightening. "That sounds like a genuine white-wall, fire-dome booger. . . . I'll be there shortly."

He put the telephone down. "They got one at the Fruit Loop last night," he said to Quovadis. "White man. Some guy on the Hill. They want me and Mag Johnson to do it."

"Mag Johnson? Since when you work with him?"

"Somebody's goosing Homicide." Hudlow shook his head incredulously. "Me and Mag. Whoo-ee! Must've killed the goddamn queen of the Fire Island fireflies."

The earth, nearly matching the color of his skin, trickled through Magnus Johnson's fingers and onto the ground. He surveyed the garden with immense dissatisfaction. The early June heat had not been kind. The tulip stalks and weakling ratoons of yellow lupine stood in uneven rows. Arcs of new blue-violet jewelweed struggled for life, casting a pale mantle of color along the garden rim. There was some hope there. But the long summer lay ahead. From the willow oak above, a warbler with flaming orange throat importuned Johnson with its high slurred whistle. In the distance, Johnson heard the pensive song of a veery venturing from its forest habitat.

Returning from the cemetery was always difficult. Johnson customarily went from his parked car into the neat clapboard house and then to his garden for solace. Inside the house this time he had stopped briefly at the doorway to the bedroom and peered through his thick glasses. The tufted quilt was pulled taut across the double bed. A small red book lay on the pillow. White fur slippers rested on the worn rug at the side of the bed. Everything appeared in order, though the vanity needed fresh flowers. He passed his study, straightened a few books, walked through the kitchen and out to the garden.

He knelt in the brown earth. He tried digging and weeding for a while, pulverizing the clods with his fingers. The dry soil sifted through his fingers, forming delicate pillars of dust. The pillars swayed and shifted gently in the morning air, then dissipated. The dust of a thousand ages, Johnson mused, blinking through his glasses, dust crushed and hurtled and reordered a hundred thousand times, yet always remaining, rarely transported as in other latitudes by migrant rivers and glaciers; dust that in the dark millennia past was pounded, kicked and mixed first with the ordures of the tapir, the cats and great bears that roamed the Potomac wilderness, then trod by the leathered foot of the Piscataways and Nanjemoys, the bare soles of plantation bucks, the boot of their owners and, today, the great earth-moving machines, clawing and digging, transmogrifying the land. He peered through the dust filtering from his fingers. At first he saw nothing. Then presently there emerged a pale glow. He was drawn to it, seeking the unfocused light beyond the curtains of rose-brown dust. He passed through and found himself floating eaglelike over a dark silent plain illumined by dull streaks of dun and amethyst on the horizon. Across the plain, shimmering faintly, was a winding road. It undulated and vanished in the distance among hills. The smell of wood smoke was on the land. From far away came the whispering flutter of an engine. It gradually grew louder, and a pickup truck, canting to one side, appeared. It jounced along the dirt road in the dawn, passing dew-wet fields and dark unpainted houses. Chinaberry trees and palmettos crouched on the bare sand in front of the houses. A solemn Negro man in his forties was driving the truck. He looked straight ahead, a toothpick in his mouth. Deep gullies formed between the cords of his throat. His hands vibrated on the steering wheel. Next to him sat a boy of twelve, holding on to the window frame of the door as the truck bounced and weaved. The boy's eyes were filled with wonder and fear. "Yes, Mag, we going to see your uncle," said the father of the boy. "I want you to see it." The truck purred along and finally came up onto the big main road. It was wide and paved smooth. The boy looked down the road, and after a while, far, far away under the nacre sky he saw a mighty city, its gray-blue towers pushing up toward the clouds. They drew closer, crossing the silent Congaree River and entered the city. The truck made a turn and soon slowed as it traveled along the base of an immense stone wall. The truck came to a halt, and the boy and the father got out. Thin mist floated around a tower where men with shotguns stood and looked down. Figures half hidden in the mist moved silently toward a gate under the tower. The boy and his father walked through the gate where a large sleepy man in a khaki uniform searched them perfunctorily. "You here for Caleb Johnson?" he asked. "Yessuh," said the father, holding the boy's hand. "It's my brother." "Go on in, Sambo," the guard said softly. "It don't take long." The boy held his father's hand tighter. They walked down a long corridor and then entered a small low-ceilinged room already crowded with spectators. The boy had never seen them before. They were all white. Two lightbulbs with green tin shades hung from the center of the ceiling, and beneath them stood a massive oaken chair. The chair was severely simple, bolted to the concrete floor, its rigid back thrusting toward the ceiling. The chair was empty. It stood alone, separated from the spectators by a low balustrade. A guard stood to one side next to a panel of switches and dials. He had pushed his officer's hat back on his head and worked a plug of glistening brown tobacco with his mouth. A physician twirling a stethoscope stood to the other side, chatting quietly with two other guards. From time to time, the guards looked expectantly toward a darkened doorway at the rear of the room. The boy had worked his way to the balustrade now and nuzzled against his father's hip as he peered at the immense chair. Presently, silence fell upon the room. The only sound was the throb of a distant generator. The physician and the guards ceased their activity and stood at awkward attention around the chair. A moment passed, and then from the darkened doorway a small reedlike man emerged, manacled on each side to a uniformed guard. He was barefooted and shaved of head and seemed even smaller than the boy had remembered him. His eyes were clouded with confused terror. Quickly and efficiently the guards placed the man in the chair, binding him with leather straps across his legs, arms and waist. His left pant leg was rolled up and a steel cuff attached to his shin. A dripping metal cap soaked in brine was set on his head. The brine trickled down his quivering face and wet his clothing. The physician asked the man if he had any statement to make. The man's eyes fluttered over the sea of anonymous faces before him, heedless of the two black faces among them, and he shook his head, almost apologetically. The boy looked at his uncle again, and in his eyes he saw the same confused terror. But also somewhere deep in the tiny man there was a final gather of resignation overrunning the shreds of desperation, and the man was able to face the spectators with a sort of dumb calm. A guard adjusted the electrodes on the man's leg and skull, then quickly tied a black rubber mask over his eyes and nose. The spectators pressed against the balustrade. The man sat quietly in the chair. The physician watched him carefully, counting his breaths. A few seconds passed, and then the physician gave a slight, quick nod of his head. The guard at the dials threw a black-handled switch, and a grinding charge leaped across the electrodes and pierced deep into the man. He arched into a fantastic seizure, pressing heedlessly against the leather straps. A sudden surprised intake of breath was instantaneously cut off. Bolts of mucus shot from his nostrils and ran out from under the mask onto his face. His straining neck rippled in furious silence; his fingers drew up into a final protective contortion, and he was throttled into irrevocable stillness. The boy looked on with incomprehension. Minutes passed. The dry rasp of electricity feeding into the rigid body was the only sound in the chamber. Gradually the body lost its tension and slumped jerkily back into the chair. A pall of gray smoke rose from the man's neck and drifted slowly over the room. The physician stepped forward and applied his stethoscope. The crowd began to disperse. The boy felt his father grip his hand and lead him from the room. "They say he might not have done it," the father said softly. "S'posed to been some gray boys up there done it or put Uncle Caleb up to it, one. Uncle Caleb never was quite right, you know. Whichever way it was, he never meant no harm. But to take and do this to him now—" The father's voice broke off, and the boy saw rings of water around his eyes. "When you grow up," the father began again, "don't let this happen to nobody you know. Don't let it ever happen." The boy pulled his hand from his father's and fled down the corridor. . . .

o

The telephone was ringing. Johnson roused himself and stood up dizzily in the garden. The house seemed miles away. The telephone continued ringing. Slowly he walked toward the back steps. He mounted the porch, entered the kitchen and picked up the receiver. It was Homicide.

As Dewey Hudlow trotted into Homicide, the telephone was ringing. J. T. Greene picked up the receiver, spoke briefly and shoved a thin medical examiner's report toward Hudlow.

"Six-three for you, el Jefe," Greene squawked to Captain Stohlbach. "It's Friendly at Tag 'n' Bag again."

Hudlow opened the report: Kadinsky, Franklin R., deceased, white male, 37 years old, 5′ 9″, 167 pounds, no distinguishing marks; cause of death: asphyxia by manual strangulation. N.O.K.: Jerome and Alba Kadinsky, parents, Chicago.

It was an odd report. A hastily prepared draft copy, delivered to the captain's desk in less than twenty-four hours. Who's goosing who, wondered Hudlow. Usually this stuff takes days. He read on: Contusions both sides anterior neck; hyoid bone fractured; anal and oral swabs: no sperm identified; fingernail scrapings negative; petechial hemorrhages of the eyes, pinpoint bleeding lower portion of eyeballs and inside lower lid; full rigor when examined at scene, 2030 hours.

Hudlow dropped the file and scanned Detective Skoda's summary and an incident report by the uniformed officers. More boiler plate: Deceased complainant resided 1716 L'Enfant Ct., NW, apartment 1-B; professional staff member, House Public Works and Transportation Committee, surface transportation subcommittee. Apartment mate, Florian Boldt, white male, 35, administrative officer, Bureau of Reclamation, Main Interior, reported last seeing deceased alive at 0815 hours Thursday at above address upon leaving for work and discovering the body at approximately 1925 hours same date upon returning home from work. Estimated time of death: between 0815 hours and 1430 hours, allowing for onset of maximum rigor. No sign of forced entry. Nothing taken. Boldt downtown for questioning; preliminary: uninvolved. No other witnesses available, except building engineer; negative results.

"No one else interviewed?" Hudlow exclaimed to J. T. Greene. "Sumbitch been dead twenty-four hours and Skoda and them ain't talked to nobody but the guy's sorority sister and the building engineer?"

"Skoda notified the family in Chicago and talked to them, too," said Greene.

"He get anything?"

"Not much. The old lady was a basket case, and the father didn't seem to know much. Couldn't name any other friends or connections, except Boldt. Said they haven't seen much of their son the last few years."

"How 'bout brothers and sisters?"

"Just one brother, and he was killed in some kind of accident ten years ago. That's why the old lady's so messed up."

"What's the father do?"

"Investment banker. Big bucks."

Hudlow's jowls tightened. "We got a weekend coming up. Where in hell were all the tenants in that building last night?"

"All out at some zoning thing. El Jefe said we didn't have anybody else to cut loose to help Nestor. It was wall-to-wall homicides. Two in Six-D, one in Five, plus this one."

"Yeah, but this one was uptown. Usually the response is faster."

"We got the response this morning. Ol' Evelyn Farnham started calling Assistant Chief Flynn and Lem Stafford over at the mayor's office. Gave them the Boys Club routine. That's why you and Johnson on it now."

J. T. Greene watched for a reaction. Hudlow stared stonily at the floor. "Well, what are we waiting for, the next solar eclipse?" he asked.

"Waiting on Mag Johnson. I just reached him a minute ago. He's on his way."

Hudlow wrinkled his nose. "What about this guy Kadinsky's work place on the Hill? Hadn't nobody been there either, right?"

Captain Stohlbach emerged from his office. "The M.E. blanked on the tox," he announced. "Looks like a straight asphyxiation. No booze, no dope."

"Goody goody," said Hudlow. "What about all these tenants nobody said boo to?"

"Right, Hud. Would you start lining them up? It's a small building. Only about eight units. The management is S&N Realty down on K Street. Get the list from them. You can work the tenants tonight after they get home."

"Me and Mag Johnson together?" Hudlow asked.

"Well, and Nestor, too," said Stohlbach. "I know he's second string, Hud. But he took the initial report, and at least he can play mother hen for you and Mag. He'll be your constant companion."

"'Cept Sundays. Sumbitch goes to church. I mean, goes to church."

"Sunday is the sabbath, Hud," said Stohlbach, recoiling. "S'posed to be a day of rest, like the Lord said—"

"Goes to some banjo-slapping folk thing at this Catholic church in Arlington. Guitars, clavicles, women flopping around dancing."

"They say music often smoothes the savage feathers."

"More like Spike Jones, if you ask me. Nestor says he digs the stringed instruments. Gets up real close. I bet. Prob'ly shooting the squirrels on them hippie nuns they got over there."

"Ain't we getting off the subject, Hud? We were talking about the tenants."

"Yeah, the tenants." Hudlow looked at the ceiling. "What'd this here Florian Boldt have to say for himself last night?"

"Seemed pretty solid, according to Nestor. I figure a honey bee case. Check with Main Interior where Boldt works, would you? Nestor's busy. He'll meet you at the apartments tonight. Meantime, you and Mag hit that committee on the Hill where Kadinsky was. What was it? Public Works? S'pose they willy-diddle with our budget, too? Everybody else on the Hill does."

The dull green departmental Plymouth Reliant stopped at a No Parking sign on K Street. Hudlow and Johnson got out, staring ahead in silence. Hudlow towered over the bespectacled Johnson. The two men went into the Eureka Building and boarded an elevator. At suite 750, they entered S&N Realty. A clerk asked them to wait. A moment later a large handsome woman with tightly cropped hair came from an inner office.

"Hi, I'm Mary Davis. Why did it have to be our building?"

"If we could answer that," said Hudlow, identifying himself and Johnson, "our job be mostly done."

"The news didn't have much this morning," said Mary Davis. "I mean, you haven't made an arrest or anything?"

"No, ma'am," said Hudlow. "That's where we thought you might could help. We were wondering if you could give us the tenants."

"You think it was one of the tenants?" the woman asked.

"We don't think much of anything right now. It just might be helpful to have the tenants."

"They're all very nice, quiet people, I assure you. Some have lived there for years. It's a very solid neighborhood."

"Yes, ma'am, we understand that."

"I mean, it had to be an outsider, somebody from somewhere very far off."

“Yes, ma’am, but if it’s not too much trouble, we’d like to have the tenants.”

“I said it’s inconceivable any of them could be involved.”

“And I’m saying we need the list.” Hudlow’s voice had begun to rise. “You ought—”

Magnus Johnson raised his hand, cutting off Hudlow. “We’re not suggesting anything, ma’am,” Johnson said softly. “This is just routine. Some of the tenants may have heard something or seen something that could be helpful to us. Maybe not. But we won’t know until we talk to them.”

Hudlow scowled at Johnson.

“Well, obviously,” said the woman, “I can’t stop you from going in there and interrogating them and frightening them and making them feel as if they’re in an unsafe neighborhood.” Hudlow shrugged heavily. She continued. “I would not be at all happy if any of them moved out as a result of your official conduct. Why do you need a list of tenants? You’re going in there and knock on their doors anyway, aren’t you? You’re pointing your finger at them, I don’t care what you say.”

“Ma’am,” said Johnson, “we just came here as a matter of courtesy to let you know what we would be doing. We don’t want any misunderstanding. The tenant list will help us familiarize ourselves with their names and assist us in making contact with their employment if they are not at home. Is that a little clearer?”

“Well, I want to cooperate,” she said, relaxing slightly. “I can’t really stop you anyway.” The woman retreated into her office.

She returned with a handful of index cards. “You’re lucky,” she said. “We had an extra set.” She handed the cards to Johnson.

The two detectives left, riding down the crowded elevator in silence.

“Cast-iron bitch,” muttered Hudlow outside.

“Yeah, but did you dig her legs?” said Johnson.

“Who the hell is she, nickel-diming us about the tenants. We had an absolute right to them?”

"There's two ways to get something like that, Hud."
"Yeah, I know. But I say when it's ours by rights, we take it. Fuck the explanations."
"Well, she gave us the—"
"She ain't some fourth-class moron, Mag. She knows the rules."
"Look, she's a mouse, and you're the big bad cat. Do you bat her around a little and keep her in the cage, or do you gobble her up in one gulp and get indigestion?"
"Stomachache wouldn't last ten seconds."

At Main Interior, Manfred Sorensen was waiting for them.

"As Mr. Boldt's supervisor," he said, "I must tell you Florian is always punctual and always punctilious."

"Yeah, but did he show up on time yesterday?" asked Hudlow.

"Of course. He came in about eight forty-five in the morning, the same time as myself. He had lunch at his desk. Never left the building. That's his regular habit. Then he went home about six. He works a long day. Very conscientious man."

"How does he get to work?"

"Walks. He says it takes him twenty minutes to a half-hour. He could do it faster straight, but he takes a roundabout way for the exercise."

"How did he seem yesterday?"

"Entirely normal," said Sorensen. "Amiable, chatty. He has a very even personality."

"The deceased, Franklin Kadinsky, did he know anybody in this office besides Florian Boldt?" Hudlow asked.

"I don't believe so," said Sorensen. "Mr. Kadinsky worked on the Hill, House Public Works Committee, isn't it? That committee has no oversight over this bureau. Socially, I'm not aware of anyone he knew here, either, except of course Mr. Boldt."

“Any problems between the two of them?” Hudlow asked.

“No. What kind of problems?”

“You know, money, boyfriend-girlfriend, like that?”

“No. From what Florian has told me, they appeared to be very compatible. They’ve lived together for several years— Oh.” Sorensen stopped abruptly, his hand to his mouth. “Oh,” he repeated. “I didn’t mean to give the wrong impression. He . . . they. Well, I’m just not sure what their . . . their arrangement was. But Florian has never spoken negatively of Mr. Kadinsky.”

There was a pause. “That about it for you, Mag?” Hudlow turned to his partner. Johnson nodded.

The two detectives left the office and headed east toward Capitol Hill. “See anything there?” Johnson asked Hudlow.

“Nothing worth a pinch of beaver shit.”

8

In a small windowless room of the House Public Works and Transportation Committee, the detectives saw two desks. One was unoccupied. On it lay several thick gray reports and in the center a black-and-white nameplate that read Franklin R. Kadinsky. The other desk was strewn with newspapers, manila folders, books, calendars and boxes of paper clips. Behind it sat a waxen-faced man. He appeared to be in his sixties, a frail white-haired wraith draped in a blue shirt and paisley necktie knotted loosely at the collar.

"I am John Hero Smith," said the man, extending a trembling hand without rising. He was seated in a wheelchair. "You're here about Franklin."

"Yessir," said Hudlow. "The staff director says you worked with him."

"I did," said the man, shaking his head slowly. "An awful tragedy. I suppose you know his only brother died accidentally ten years ago?"

"Yessir, we were told. Do you know how it happened exactly?"

"No, Franklin rarely spoke of it." Smith surveyed the two detectives for a moment. "I don't imagine this is your ordinary case, is it?"

"No, sir," said Hudlow. "We don't get too many asphyxiations. Mostly shootings and cuttings. Now and then a shod foot."

"No, I mean the murder of a man of some considerable skill and credentials, an educated man with a respected reputation in the field of transport legislation."

"Oh, yessir," said Hudlow. "Most of our homicides are just domestics, ol'-lady-ol'-man, jitterbug stuff. Mr. Kadinsky wasn't no jitterbug."

"Exactly," said Smith. "And hence, because the circumstances of his life do not conform to your more common experience, the explanation of his death may not conform, either, and your investigation may be prolonged. I hope I may help you make it shorter."

"Sound like you maybe already got it solved," said Hudlow.

"No, certainly not." Smith smiled weakly. "But I knew Franklin well enough perhaps to give you some insights that may be helpful, if you ask the right questions."

"Well, we can start right here," said Hudlow. "Like, did you do anything when he didn't show up for work yesterday?"

"No."

"Didn't you think it was odd?"

"Not really. He occasionally went to outside meetings during the day. Agencies."

"Agencies?"

"Regulatory agencies dealing with our subcommittee. Federal Highway Administration. Things like that."

"All day long?"

"Sometimes. He'd even go straight from home in the morning. Ordinarily, he was supposed to leave word and call in for messages during the day."

"Did he call in Thursday morning?"

"No. I checked with the staff assistants."

"Didn't that concern you?"

"Not at the time. That was like Franklin. He'd get so involved, he'd forget."

"You got a time and attendance clerk here?"

"No. We're fairly informal. As a professional staff member, Franklin could exercise a great deal of flexibility. His absence for a day was no cause for alarm."

"Did he have any problems with anyone here? You know, money, debts, boyfriend-girlfriend?"

"That's what I mean by your not asking the right kinds of questions," said Smith, peering at Hudlow with pale rheumy eyes. "Franklin's life was not enmeshed in debts and random sex."

"If you'll pardon me, sir," said Hudlow, "I don't know a whole heap of people in this world that their nose isn't stuck slap-dad in the middle of it—bucks or booty, one or other. What's to stop ol' Frank Kadinsky from getting up to the trough with ever'body else?"

"What Detective Hudlow means to say," interjected Johnson, seeing Smith recoil, "is that as investigators, we don't yet know the principals in this case and can't make any assumptions. We cannot assume that Mr. Kadinsky was one way or another."

Hudlow ignored his partner. "You get my drift about Frank Kadinsky, Mr. Smith?"

"Of course I do," joined Smith quickly, eyeing Hudlow. "All I am suggesting is that you look a little beyond your normal experience. I trust you can do that?"

"We try harder," mumbled Hudlow.

"Now that we have the preliminaries out of the way," said Smith, "let me be candid. Despite what I've already said about him, in recent months, I sensed a change in Franklin, a change I find difficult to describe. But I cannot stop thinking that the change, in some way none of us yet understands, may be connected with his death."

"How was he changed?" asked Hudlow.

"Two things seemed to have happened. One was he had become much more excitable. That was not like him. He normally took all his ups and downs with great calm. But in recent months he had become oddly manic. The second thing was that, around me at least, he had become secretive. He would not discuss whatever it was that was exciting him. It seemed to be related in some way to his work here. We had always shared thoughts and ideas in our work, but there were times recently when he would keep to himself, even go to another room to do things, perhaps phone calls or research, I'm not sure."

"How you know he wasn't just calling a private friend?" said Hudlow.

"Yes, that's the easy answer again," said Smith. "What I'm telling you is that each time he did this, it appeared to have something to do with the work on his desk—reports, correspondence, other papers that he would pick up and take with him into another office."

Hudlow drew closer to Smith's desk. "What kind of work?"

"I don't know," said Smith. "He never volunteered anything to me, and of course I would never ask."

"Didn't you look on his desk to see what was there?"

"No, I, uh, am somewhat limited, as you can see. And besides, I would never go pawing through his desk without his consent."

"What was he working on?"

"A number of highway amendments, and some committee hearings on funding standards. He was helping draft some of the language and dealing with the Federal Highway Admin—"

"Anything unusual about the people he was dealing with?"

"My word, no. Utterly routine. More important, he talked to me frequently and at great length about it. There was nothing there that he seemed to be holding back. In fact, we got into several long discussions—"

"How did he get on with other people in the office?" asked Hudlow.

"There you go again," said Smith. "Of course he got on well with the others in the office. There were the usual little conflicts. He didn't particularly like Fitzloyd in the front office because of his cigars or the receptionist because of her habit of saying 'you know what I'm saying?' at the end of every sentence. But that is not the stuff of murder, is it?"

"You sure he didn't maybe have something going with somebody in the office and it went sour?" Hudlow insisted.

"No, I'm sure." Smith spoke impatiently. "Nothing of that magnitude."

"How 'bout a boyfriend?"

"I beg your pardon?"

"You know, a little boy blue under the haystack?"

"Good heavens, no," said Smith almost wearily. "Look, what I suggest is this. Give me your card or a telephone number and we'll keep in touch. The staff director has asked me to go through Franklin's files and help parcel out his assignments. I will take the liberty of seeing if he left any letters or other documents that don't seem to fit the routine. I'm sure the staff director will authorize—"

"Normal procedure is for us to do that type thing," interrupted Hudlow, "not somebody that worked with the deceased."

"Well," said Smith, "in the first place, the papers are voluminous. Boxes and boxes. I'm not sure you'd know quite where to begin. And in the second pl—"

"You suggesting—?"

"He's suggesting we may need an interpreter, Hud." It was Magnus Johnson again. "He can tell what looks funny in all that technical stuff a lot better than we can. Trust him."

"Thank you," said John Hero Smith.

o

Outside, Hudlow turned on Johnson. "Goddamn it, Mag. I kept my tongue in there, but you know damn well those papers are our jurisdiction. He shouldn't be fishing through them."

"He's doing us a favor, saving us time. If we raise a stink, some member of the committee might decide to hold up on the papers. You know, congressional privilege and all that. Smith can make them available to us on an informal basis."

"Yeah, but when he's done, the papers ain't virgin. We want original stuff."

"What's he going to do to them—delete the name of Kadinsky's killer?"

"Something, whatever."

"Get serious. If the papers had stuff he didn't want us to see, he wouldn't have told us about them in the first place."

"You're going on him too easy."

"Easy, hard . . . your choice, Hud. Look, we're making progress, little as it is. Lighten up. We may be in this together for a while."

"I'll lighten up when all them papers are in our property office," said Hudlow.

9

They were starting to grapple with the afternoon rush hour as the Plymouth headed toward Dupont Circle. After searching for ten minutes, they found an open space by a fire hydrant and parked. The engine gave several wet coughs as Hudlow turned the key off.

"Goddamn points or air filter, one," he muttered. "Just got this cruiser out of the Northeast Shop. What those jerkoffs do down there all day, pick their nose and patch tires with it?"

They scrambled out and walked in silence toward L'Enfant Court, passing rows of stolid Edwardian brownstone townhouses, once busy family homes brimming with children and servants, now the staid, sad refuge of law firms and think tanks interspersed with warrenlike apartments tenanted by Washington's vast new population of middle class drifters: singles, anonymous gays, senescent hippies, ramrod professionals, even a few flinty sectarian radicals, all in their own way seeking romance with bureaucracy.

As Hudlow and Johnson approached Florian Boldt's apartment building, they encountered Nestor Skoda on the steps.

"We got the tenants here from the management," said Hudlow, pulling the stack of index cards from his pocket.

Hudlow and Johnson stood distantly from each other, like two schoolboys who have been ordered to stop fighting.

"I talked to Boldt again just now while I was waiting for you two," said Skoda.

"How'd he check out this time?"

"Still solid. Swears he and Frank were not lovers."

"Score one for Pinocchio."

"He didn't flinch. I asked him up front. Said Frank even had a girlfriend, but he can't remember her name. Works for the World Bank."

"You do good work, Nestor. What else didn't he tell you?"

"Said Frank played tennis with a couple of guys on the Hill. I got their names. That's about it for friends. He didn't hang out much."

"How 'bout his story yesterday morning? Still the same?"

"Basically. He only quivered a little when I pushed him. Says he left the apartment about eight-fifteen in the morning, and it was Kadinsky's habit to leave about fifteen minutes later at eight-thirty. That's a little close."

"Well, hold on a minute," interjected Hudlow. "The M.E. says Kadinsky died six hours or more before the technicians picked him up at eight-thirty Thursday night. That means Kadinsky died anywhere between when he got up in the morning and two-thirty in the afternoon. That's a big margin. Don't be breathing on Boldt so hard, Nestor."

"I'm not breathing on Boldt. I already told you I think he's solid. But if it wasn't him, it had to be somebody that got in there between eight-fifteen when Boldt left and eight-thirty when Kadinsky ordinarily would have left, not at noon or two-thirty or sometime later in the day. It's just that whoever got to him must have done it early and quick, somebody that knew his habits. Don't forget also, there was no forced entry. Kadinsky probably let the person in."

"Like maybe one of the other tenants," said Hudlow, holding up the index cards. "Time to play peek-a-boo."

Skoda took the cards from Hudlow with a peremptory sweep. "I'm den mother here tonight," he said. "You two look like Ken and Barbie after an argument over the slipcovers. Hud, why don't you work solo this time, okay? Mag and I will go together. Do we understand each other, girls?"

"Junior man giving orders these days?" Hudlow grunted.

Johnson was silent. Then he said, "I saw on the reports that Kadinsky was from Chicago. His mother has an unusual name: Alba."

"Alba?" Hudlow looked at Johnson. "So?"

"It means 'white' in Latin."

"What you trying to say, Mag?"

"Just that. It's unusual. I think I might remember it."

Skoda began sorting through the tenant cards. "Counting Boldt and Kadinsky's, there's eight units," he said. "Two each on the first and second floors and what looks like three smaller ones on the third floor. Plus the basement unit. That's the building engineer. Name of Jae El Quaver. He'll let us in."

The three men mounted the steps of the building and opened the glass doors to the lobby. Inside, a row of recessed metal mailboxes lined one wall. At the far end of the lobby, Skoda pushed a button on the locked door leading to the interior of the building. Moments later through the glass panels they saw a small figure approaching them, a man shuffling in plastic sandals and wearing what appeared to be loose pajamas. He opened one of the doors and squinted at Skoda.

"Yi?" he asked.

"Mr. Quaver, it's me again," said Skoda. "Remember me? This is Detective Hudlow, also from the Metropolitan Police, and Detective Johnson. Mind if we come in again? Just to look around and maybe talk with some of the tenants?"

Quaver was momentarily mystified. Then: "Okay, you back." He spoke in a heavily accented rasp. Tufts of black hair sprouted from the cheekbones of his olive face. His ancient eyes conveyed nothing.

The detectives stepped into the inner hallway of the building. The high ceiling was lit dimly by a small chandelier. There were apartment doors on either side of the hallway, and a dark curved stairway disappeared toward the second floor at the rear of the hall.

"If you don't mind doing this again, can you tell us what you were doing yesterday morning, early?" Skoda asked Quaver, speaking in slow measured syllables.

---o---

The little man looked up at Skoda and paused, as though waiting for some internal organ to decode the detective's words. At length, a faint movement animated his face.

"At eight o'clock, yes?" he said. "Like I tell soon before, I in apartment Two-A with Mr. Finger. Fix sink."

Skoda looked at the index cards. "Yeah, Two-A. There's two people in there. Name of Finger. Ira Finger and Jared Finger. Did you hear anything or see anything unusual, anything you haven't told me before?"

Quaver pondered. A look of recognition finally came into his face. "I in apartment Two-A. See pipe and apartment wall. Hear water. Water in sink. Sink fix. You want see?"

The detectives looked at each other resignedly.

"Feather merchant," muttered Hudlow.

"Thank you, Mr. Quaver," said Skoda. After a brief hesitation, the little man bowed perceptibly and receded toward the basement.

"Here, Hud, take these," said Skoda, handing him two of the index cards. "You get Ira and Jared Finger in Two-A and this other guy, Ambrose Fairlyte, in One-A. Mag and I'll do the rest."

Hudlow disappeared down the hall toward 1-A as Skoda and Johnson climbed the curved staircase to the second floor. They stopped at 2-B. The small brass frame under the doorbell for a name was blank. Skoda looked at his cards.

"It says Jeffrey Stanton for Two-B." He held the card to the hallway light and pushed the bell. A faint chime echoed inside. No answer.

"Odd there's no nameplate," said Johnson. "Thinks he's Mr. Nobody."

"Says he works for the Government Printing Office, GPO," said Skoda, looking again at the card. "Proofreader." The two detectives waited another moment, then moved down the hall toward the stairs to the third floor.

At 3-A, the name Shirley Diaz-Diaz was printed neatly below the bell. It matched the index card. Johnson pushed the bell, and there was the clipped sound of high heels on hardwood floor. They stopped and a voice said, "Yes, who is it?"

"Police, ma'am," said Johnson. "Metropolitan Police."

There were some muffled sounds and then the dark paneled door opened an inch, a security chain pulled tight across the gap. Portions of a woman's face filled the space. "Yes?" said the voice.

"I'm Detective Johnson, Magnus Johnson, from the Metropolitan Police." Johnson displayed his card case. "This is Detective Skoda. You Miss Diaz?"

"Diaz-Diaz," the woman said.

"Like to ask you some questions."

The woman closed the door, released the security chain and then opened the door fully. She was a short, full-bodied woman, her dark face sprinkled with freckles. She held a squirming brown Chihuahua in her arms. Its head shook in delicate tremors as it stared disapprovingly at the visitors.

"You're here about the man downstairs?" she asked.

"Yes, ma'am," said Johnson.

She looked greatly relieved. "I couldn't imagine who you were at first," she said, her speech filigreed with a faint trace of Spanish. "You did not have uniforms. The only people I ever see in this hall are other tenants."

"Yes, ma'am," said Johnson. "Did you know Mr. Kadinsky?"

"Yes, just as another tenant. We used to meet occasionally in the hall downstairs or once in a while on the street, just to say hello."

"Were you here yesterday at all?"

"Yes."

"When?"

"Well, in the morning and then again late in the evening. I went to a zoning meeting with the other tenants. It ran very late."

"Tell us about the morning, what you did from when you got up, if you would, ma'am."

"Yes, I woke up about seven-twenty. I got dressed, had a little breakfast. Then it was about eight o'clock. I was running late. I remember that. I am a projects officer at the Mayor's Office of Latino Affairs, and I was late for a staff meeting. I left about eight-fifteen."

"Did you hear or see anything unusual around the time you left?"

"No, I don't think so. This building is very quiet. If I had heard anything unusual, I would remember it. Of course, Mr. Kadinsky was on the first floor. This is the third, and maybe I wouldn't hear if something unusual happened down there."

"Well, did you hear anything at all?"

"Not really. I mean, well, I heard somebody walking past my door toward Miss Edwards' down the hall. But there's nothing unusual about that. Besides, that was much earlier in the morning."

"How much earlier?"

"Oh, I don't know. Maybe seven-thirty, quarter to eight."

"What do you mean there's nothing unusual about that?"

"She has a couple of girlfriends where she works at Roper's Department store, and they come by in the morning sometimes to take her to work. I think they have breakfast first and then go."

"They have keys to get in the main door downstairs?"

"They must. You can't buzz people in here."

Johnson stepped closer to the woman. "You say you knew Mr. Kadinsky just to say hello?"

"Yes, that's all."

"You sure no other way?"

"Of course I'm sure." Her eyes opened wide. "Well, I forgot. I've met him a few times at our building security meetings."

"Building security meetings?"

"They're just building security meetings. Once every two months or so. We discuss ways of keeping the building safe. We exchange phone numbers and get to know each other in case there is an emergency."

"Everybody's got everybody else's phone number?"

"Except Mr. Stanton. He doesn't have a phone."

"No phone?"

"That's right. Don't ask me why."

"Stanton." Johnson turned to Skoda. "That's the one downstairs that doesn't have a nameplate, either." Johnson turned back to the woman. "So why do you have everybody's phone number?"

"Oh, that's in case we need each other. Or to just let someone know we are coming to visit or something like that. So it's not a surprise, like when you came to my door just now."

"Visit each other? You ever visit Mr. Kadinsky?"

"I beg your pardon. Of course not." She gave Johnson a sharp look. "I do visit other people, though, like Miss Edwards down the hall."

Shirley Diaz-Diaz scratched the Chihuahua's head for a moment, then set the dog down on the floor. It clung to her ankles, still looking reprovingly at the two detectives.

"Pilar, *vete*," she snapped at the dog. It refused to move.

"One last question," said Magnus Johnson. "This Mr. Stanton in apartment Two-B, do you know him?"

"Yes, about like the others. Just to say hello."

"He's not in just now. Any idea where he might be?"

"Well, he works at night at the GPO. He may be there. I'm not sure of his hours. They seem to change around a lot."

"How do you know he works nights?"

"Oh, that came out at the building security meetings. He told us that was his job. We like it, because it means he's here in the building during the daytime when the rest of us are away."

"What kind of person is he? Friendly, unfriendly?"

"Well, I don't know how to say—" The woman stopped. "He's strange, yes, in a way. But perhaps it is not for me to say. I don't know him well at all."

"How is he strange?"

A faint line of distress came across her face. "Just strange. How else can I say? I do not know him."

"Yes, ma'am," said Johnson softly. He looked at Skoda. "That about it?"

"Yep."

"You've been most helpful, Miss Diaz," said Johnson. "Thanks again." The door shut.

"So much for the lady with the Spanish-speaking dog," muttered Skoda. "We can check her work hours when the Latino office opens Monday."

"Yeah, but what about the way she reacted to Stanton," said Johnson. "What do you make of that?"

"Typical Latin overreaction. The guy probably looks like a used car salesman."

"Reason enough."

The detectives approached apartment 3-B. The nameplate on the door bore a series of Oriental glyphs and under them the name McHenry Goon. Before Johnson or Skoda could ring the bell, the door opened, and a sallow, smiling man of fifty stood before them.

"Can I help you? I am McHenry Goon," he said in crisp English. "I overheard you when you announced yourselves to Miss Diaz. You are canvassing the building about Mr. Kadinsky?"

"Yes, sir," said Johnson.

"Well, I did not know Mr. Kadinsky, except to nod to in the hallway," said Goon.

"Were you here yesterday morning?" asked Johnson.

"Yes, but only briefly."

"Tell us about it."

"I got up at seven-thirty and almost immediately went out. I never have breakfast."

"Where did you go?"

"To Dupont Circle, to play chess with an old friend."

"Chess?"

"We play every Wednesday and Thursday. Then I walk to school. I teach mathematics at Cardozo High. I also do free-lance Vietnamese and Laotian translation work for some of the embassies here so that I can pay the exorbitant rent for this apartment."

"Exactly when did you go to the circle and then leave for school?"

"Promptly at seven forty-five I was at the circle. My friend is very punctual and expects me to be there. We always play for forty-five minutes, and then I leave for school."

"Who is your friend?"

"His name is Bek, a Yugoslavian."

"Does he live near here?"

"Right on this street, at Seventeen forty-four."

"What apartment?"

"Four-twenty-three, I believe."

Johnson studied the man for a moment. "Who won the game yesterday, Mr. Goon?"

"Oh, he did. He's a very accomplished chess player."

"How many moves?"

"Sixteen." McHenry Goon looked closely at the detectives as Johnson wrote down Bek's name and address. "Of course, he will verify my account," he said with a faint smile.

"Thank you, sir."

"I am at your disposal," said the man as he disappeared behind his door.

"One more to go," said Skoda, looking at the index cards. "Ms. Rula Edwards, buyer for Roper's Department Store."

As they approached 3-C, the two men could hear the low murmur of television voices beyond the door. "Evening news or reruns of 'The Flying Nun,' your pick," said Skoda. He pushed the bell above Rula Edwards' nameplate. The television voices stopped abruptly and steps approached the door.

"Just a moment," said a low female voice. The detectives heard two locks snap back, and the door opened on the security chain. Small blinking eyes examined them for a moment. Then the chain was loosened and the door swung open.

"Miss Diaz called me a few minutes ago and said you might be coming," said the woman. "I'm Rula Edwards." Dressed in a severe gray dress with a choke collar, she examined the detectives again. She had the weak squinting eyes of an opossum. Her graying hair was pulled back into a tight chignon, revealing large pink ears. Trimly built, she possessed a narrow waist dominated by a sharply defined bosom. Her nostrils quivered as though detecting a scent. She invited the two men into her living room, a dark elegant space furnished with a voluptuous flowered sofa, Queen Anne end tables and delicate high-backed Hepplewhite chairs. The walls were decorated with old English woodcuts and an array of braided quirts. Against one wall stood a tall Sheraton secretary with a labyrinth of pigeonholes. A miscellany of leather-bound books was tossed on the shelves above. On the mantel over a closed fireplace sat several large pieces of Wedgewood, a cluster of family photographs and a flat, heavily chased silver case. She did not ask the detectives to sit down.

"The Roper store do this for you?" asked Johnson, circumnavigating the room. He stopping briefly at the mantel, picked up the silver case and put it down again.

"Why, yes," said Rula Edwards. "I'm a furniture and accessories buyer there. We occasionally entertain factory reps. It helps."

"About Mr. Kadinsky downstairs," said Johnson. "Did you know him at all?"

"Only slightly. I knew he worked on Capitol Hill. I used to see him in the main hall downstairs."

"How long have you known him?"

"Ever since he moved to this building about four years ago. I was already here."

"When was the last time you saw Mr. Kadinsky?"

"Maybe three days ago."

"How did he seem? Was there anything unusual about him?"

"No, I don't think so. He seemed pretty normal. He just said good morning to me. We were leaving the building at the same time, and he opened the main door for me."

"Did you know any of his friends, the people he socialized with?"

"No, not that I can remember."

"Were you here yesterday morning after eight o'clock?"

"Let's see. No, actually, I wasn't. I left unusually early. I had a doctor's appointment."

"When?"

"At eight-thirty. I had to leave about seven-thirty. The doctor's office is in Bethesda. I had to take the Metro. My car's in the shop. I got some breakfast and then took the subway—about a twenty-minute ride. After the subway, it's a ten-minute walk to his office in Bethesda."

"What kind of doctor?"

"OB/GYN. Dr. Egger."

Johnson leaned slightly toward the woman. "Ma'am, Miss Diaz next door says she heard someone walking by her apartment toward yours at just about that time, seven-thirty. Did you have a visitor?"

The woman looked directly back at Johnson. "Oh, Miss Diaz told me about that when she called a few minutes ago. About the footsteps. No, there wasn't any visitor. What happened was it was my own footsteps she heard. I left my apartment, and when I got downstairs, I remembered I had a leftover subway fare card with about two dollars still on it in the apartment. So I came back upstairs and got it for my ride to Bethesda. What she heard was my own footsteps."

"Got any of the fare card left?"

"No, I used it all, plus some."

There was a pause. The woman squinted. Her nostrils dilated rapidly as she waited for Johnson or Skoda to speak.

"I think that will be it for now," said Johnson.

"Yes, certainly." She escorted the two detectives to the door, closing it gently behind them.

Johnson and Skoda headed for the stairway. "Did you dig the shirtful of goodies?" marveled Skoda.

"You horny little Catholic schoolboy," said Johnson. "How can you be so preoccupied when we have a liar on our hands?"

"Liar? How so?"

"Rula Edwards was lying. There was a man in her apartment Thursday morning at seven-thirty, and she never went to her OB/GYN appointment in Bethesda."

"How you figure?"

"In the middle of all that elaborate English period furniture and bric-a-brac in her living room, did you see that silver case on the mantel? That was a man's cigar case. Beautiful hammered silver. Expensive and all that, but completely out of time and place with everything else."

"She got it at K mart."

"It had a very distinct coat of arms on it. South American: a llama, cornucopia and a tree, the cinchona. That's Peruvian. Probably early twentieth century."

"So, maybe Rula Edwards smokes cigars. Everybody's got something."

"Maybe it's her boyfriend's and he left it there on the mantel after their little dalliance."

"Maybe it's her father's and it's been there for ten years."

"Not in that self-consciously furnished room."

"Why not?"

"Always the devil's advocate, aren't you, Nestor. No wonder you never make any cases. It's a boyfriend, I'm telling you, probably somebody in her line of work, with a cigar case like that. Maybe even somebody at Roper's. You don't see many cigar cases these days, especially hammered silver."

"So why would she want to shield the boyfriend? Isn't this the new age of let it all hang out?"

"Yeah, but Rula Edwards has some kind of protective instinct working. Maybe he's her boss. Maybe he's a congressman. Maybe—"

"Lemme guess. You're thinking Kadinsky's killer?"

"Well?"

"That's too simple."

"I know. Silly me."

"Still, don't knock it off the list."

"Leave no stone unraveled, as Captain Stohlbach would say."

"So what's next? Check out her doctor's appointment? What did she say his name was? Egger? Eager?"

"Right. Egger. E-G-G-E-R, I guess."

"Great. Then maybe we'll just have to come back and see her again. Love to reexamine her bones."

10

Twilight had fallen like a warm towel over the city when Johnson and Skoda rejoined Hudlow in the main hall of the building and went outside.

"How'd you do, Hud?" asked Johnson. "We hit three zeroes and a possible liar. One tenant wasn't even home."

"My three were all home, okay," said Hudlow, wiping his enormous forehead with a handkerchief, "but didn't any of them come out too ripe."

"Any mention this guy Jeffrey Stanton in Two-B? He wasn't in. One of the other tenants said he was weird or something."

"No, I ain't heard nothing about weird."

"So who'd you find?"

"Well, in Two-A, where Quaver fixed the busted pipe, there's two brothers, the ones named Finger, which I think they're Jewish. They're both twenty-six, twins." Hudlow consulted his notebook. "Jared Finger, he's the redheaded one with freckles and some kind of cleft palate thing which it's hard to understand him. Had a little beanie type cap setting on back of his head. He goes to the University of Maryland, College Park. Graduate student in philandery or something. I didn't press for details. The other one's Ira Finger. He's almost regular. Got light hair near 'bout like a crew cut. He's a bartender at the Brown Study in Georgetown."

"So what did they say?"

"Not a whole hell of a lot. Ol' Ira, the one that's a bartender, he confirmed what Quaver said about the plumbing. Said the trap under the bathroom sink broke loose when they were using the bathroom about eight o'clock Thursday morning. Jared, which is the graduate student, was in a hurry to leave for Maryland, so they called Quaver, and he come right away. Ira said Quaver looked at the problem and left the apartment for a minute or two and come right back with a new piece of pipe for the trap and some packing and a pair of wide-mouth pliers. Had a hell of a time working the old trap off. I mean, here's Quaver 'bout two hundred years old and them two boys setting there watching him work the trap loose, which they couldn't fix it on their own if Jesus Christ himself had give them a gold-plated Stillson wrench. But he finally got it off and put on the new one and tested it to see if it leaked which it didn't, and then ol' Jared could finish brushing his teeth and fix his cleft palate and leave for Maryland, which it was about ten minutes to nine and he was already late and pretty pissed. Least that's what Ira said."

"Didn't either of them say they heard or saw anything unusual?"

"Naw. Said the banging and clanging Quaver was doing on the pipe and the water running kind of drowned out ever'thing else. Said they didn't see nothing, either."

"So who else you talk to?"

"Well, it wasn't but one other tenant, this Ambrose Fairlyte in One-A."

"He has the only other apartment on the ground floor with Kadinsky and Florian Boldt. Did he hear or see anything?"

"Says he wasn't even there at eight-fifteen Thursday morning. He's part owner of some kind of health food joint downtown and had already went there to open the place at seven A.M."

"Anybody at the store to vouch for him?"

"No. Said his partner didn't come in till ten. He was running the place by himself until then."

"Customers?"

"Yeah, well, the customers are a problem, too. He says he knows some of the more regular ones by sight but doesn't know their names or where they live. Besides, he's not sure which ones were there early, you know, before eight or eight-fifteen, and which ones came later. It's hard to tell them apart."

"All these tofu eaters look alike," murmured Johnson.

"What kind of guy was this Ambrose Fairlyte?" asked Skoda.

"Big soft squishy white boy, probably 'bout half queer, be my guess," said Hudlow. "Speaks like a schoolteacher, kind of prissylike. He was all the time correcting me. You imagine that? Here I am asking him about a goddamn homicide that happened fifteen feet from his front parlor, and he's saying I should call him 'mister' and not be running over him with too many questions and like that. Down damn unfuckingbelievable."

"Tmesis," muttered Johnson.

"At one point," continued Hudlow, "I looked that boy in the eye and said, 'Neighbor, if you know what's good for you, you'll answer any damn question I put to you.' He backed down pretty fast, I clue you. I was ready to knock his cock into his watch pocket. 'Course, I would've read him his Miranda rights first."

Magnus Johnson turned slowly to Hudlow. "Weren't you talking a little out of school?"

"Out of school? Mag, don't run that ACLU poodle poop on me. This ain't no lawyers' tea party." Hudlow's cold, unforgiving voice echoed sharply against the apartment building.

"You saying Ambrose Fairlyte knows something about Kadinsky and therefore you should bear down on him?" asked Johnson.

"Ambrose Fairlyte don't know jackshit about Kadinsky. I think he's telling the truth when he says he was at his yogurt stand at seven o'clock in the morning. That ain't the point. The point I'm making is here's this high-wire jelly boy, and there's countless thousands more of them cooped up in these buildings just like Fairlyte and them Finger boys, and it ain't a jack-man among them ever got their left toe dirty down in the sewer here where you and me work day and night, Mag. And he's pulling all this high-and-mighty stuff and correcting my manners. That can piss a man off."

"You let that get in the way of an interview—?"

"I know it's off the line, Mag, but it burns me up how some of these folks so soft and limp-brained they wouldn't know what to do if a real problem hit them in the natural ass. I mean literally they wouldn't know what to do if there was a earthquake or a building fire. Hell, they wouldn't know what to do if the lights went out in their apartment. 'Don't worry,' they say, 'somebody's out there taking care of it.' Somebody'll do it. The city, the phone company, the trash man, the secretary, the office boy and all them other various and sundry niggers like you and me, Mag, that keep them alive. And these same goddamn people with all their airs expect us to adapt to their level and act like them and be all prim and polite when they have the misfortune of having to actually deal with one of us, whereas and instead you would think with all their intelligence they would adapt to us, or at least understand that since we work in a sewer, we going to smell like a sewer and they better damned sight get used to the stink."

Johnson looked steadily at Hudlow. "Hud, you talk like some kind of loose-wired Superman. You think you can get on just fine in this world, don't you, without your trash men and your Mr. Quavers. That's an honest but romantic conceit—"

"Stop slinging those nickel-plated words around, Mag. You sound like Ambrose Fairlyte. You sound ridic'lous."

"Ambrose Fairlyte may be ridiculous," Johnson went on. "But you're skating close to it yourself. All this talk about being down in the sewer and how that somehow makes you more noble and high-minded. Get off it, Hud."

Skoda moved abruptly between the two detectives. "Hey, kids," he scolded. "No breaking each other's toys—"

"Fuck off, Nestor," flared Hudlow. "You don't know nothing. Just look at Mag. Soon as he gets around these people, he acts just like them. You should've seen him today taking up for that building management bimbo downtown and the crip on the Hill that worked with Kadinsky. Make you puke."

"Taking up for them or cleaning up your little messes, Hud?" It was Johnson, his voice small but firm.

"'Cleaning up your little messes,'" mimicked Hudlow. "See what I mean?" Hudlow spat on the pavement.

"Christ," said Johnson, stepping back. "What is this job all about, Hud? It's about gathering information. Just gathering information. Like I told you before, there's two ways to do it: go heavy or light—"

"Go light?" shouted Hudlow. "God amighty, you ain't going light, Mag. You crawling between the sheets with them."

"Come on, fellas," Nestor Skoda inserted himself again. "We're going to get busted for loitering."

Hudlow and Johnson continued to glare at each other, but the looks softened with Skoda's words.

"Shitjimpiss," said Hudlow, turning from Johnson. "What do we do now?"

"Nothing much for the rest of the weekend," said Skoda. "It's Friday. Maybe drop by tomorrow and see our friend Stanton in Two-B. The employment confirmations can wait till Monday. I'm for knocking off."

"Ditto," said Hudlow.

Johnson said nothing and walked away.

11

Skoda sat on the long concrete and oak bench that arced around Dupont Circle, feeling self-conscious in his brown suit and regimental tie. The Saturday afternoon sun sifted through the trees, casting dappled patterns on the walkways. Young wiry men in sneakers and cutoffs tossed a Frisbee on the adjacent grass. Strollers ambled by, talking softly, clad in T-shirts bristling with messages: Solar Power; Free Ayn Rand; Ignore Consciousness. Shrill arpeggios of a flute split the air, blown by a raven-haired woman strutting coolly through the circle in Spandex tights. Nobody seemed to notice but Skoda.

Then Skoda saw Jamie, the tall open-faced youth, now a mature man, he had first met a dozen years ago when he was assigned to Three-D in uniform. Jamie had become Skoda's first snitch, a genial manager of a gay restaurant who plied him with marginally helpful information about local sources of cocaine and butyl nitrite on the disco scene. In exchange, Skoda blinked at a modest garden of marijuana that Jamie maintained in his backyard. Skoda did not particularly want to see Jamie now, but Jamie had spotted him and ran over to his bench.

"What's up, Nestor?" Jamie asked, shaking hands. "Haven't seen you in months."

"Just waiting on a friend."

"Cops don't have friends," said Jamie.

"No, for once this is a real friend."

"Anybody I know?"

"I doubt it. Hey, I thought I was the one to ask the questions around here."

"Just getting curious in my old age."

Skoda was annoyed. Jamie remained perched on the bench. Well, Skoda thought, at least put him to work.

"Jamie," he said, "heard anything about this guy Kadinsky killed Thursday over on L'Enfant Court?"

"Hey, Nestor, you know I'm a specialist. Strictly dope."

"Couple of my brother police officers think it might be a gay lovers' quarrel."

"So what else is new?"

"Well, have you heard anything, like specific?"

"Not a whisper."

"Would you mind listening around and see what the talk is? If you get me something, I'll guarantee you many happy harvests in your backyard."

"You know you don't have to bribe me, even though murder is not my line."

"Now do you think your friends would like to see you here in the middle of Dupont Circle fraternizing with a member of the law enforcement establishment? You know I stand out like a sore thumb. Maybe you should go along."

"Yeah, I noticed your elaborate disguise."

"This is my serious going-to-an-interview suit. Official business, Jamie."

"Got your message, boss. I'm on my way."

Jamie got up. The two men shook hands again, and Jamie trotted off.

Skoda waited alone. In a way he was relieved that Hudlow had not showed up. Perhaps he won't come at all, Skoda thought, and Mag and I'll have the job to ourselves.

The internal competition among members of the Homicide Branch often dictated that partners not miss any steps along the investigative path. Deputy Chief Freeman was right: Even Hud and Mag need each other. But Skoda hoped Hudlow would make an exception this time. Maybe he's out banging that black preacher of his this afternoon, Skoda thought. Snitch-snatch they called her behind his back. Skoda smiled. He had never seen the Reverend Quovadis Logan, nor had many of the other men in the branch. But a faintly ominous mystique had grown around her over the years: a ruttish lioness of extraordinary beauty and unpredictable rages; she hated men, preached against the white devils in her storefront church and was reputed to have slain a city building inspector with a kitchen knife one quiet afternoon as he knelt in adoration before her beckoning mons. Yet she maintained an inexplicable bond with Dewey Hudlow, of all men. Was there something beyond the crude protection he provided and the information she traded? And what of the talk that Hudlow had helped work the building inspector case a decade ago and nothing had come of it? No, that would not be like Hudlow. He was blustery and noisy but oddly scrupulous. There must be some greater inner sustenance holding them together, although neither seemed to the outer world to have the will for it.

Skoda saw Magnus Johnson approaching across the circle. Johnson walked slowly with a slight slump of the shoulders. There was a weary hesitance in his stride that suggested approaching old age. He trudged along the walkway, oblivious to the slow-motion carnival around him, his balding down-turned head glistening in the sunlight.

"Afternoon, Mag," said Skoda. Johnson looked up and stopped.

"Oh, afternoon, Nestor." Johnson looked around briefly. "Hudlow coming?"

"I don't think so. It's way past time."

Johnson relaxed slightly. "Anything new?"

"Not much. I checked out Kadinsky's two tennis partners. One's on vacation. Cape Cod. Been up there since before Kadinsky. The other one's in the hospital. Ruptured disc. He's been there more than two weeks."

"They know any other friends?"

"Not a one. Never even heard of the girlfriend at the World Bank."

The two men walked toward L'Enfant Court east of the circle. They were silent now. Birds rustled noisily in the sparse urban trees of O Street. Johnson heard the grieving whistle of an errant white-throated sparrow. Little guy ought to be in New Hampshire by now, he thought.

He turned to Skoda. "Sorry about last night," he said.

"Why apologize?"

"Hudlow and I kind of forced you to intervene."

"My luck."

"I can't quite get Hudlow's drift. He's not your garden variety freckle belly, that's for sure. But there's something about him I still cannot trust."

"His mouth's too big."

"No, he has a certain rustic eloquence I can almost admire."

"He uses the wrong underarm deodorant."

"Be serious."

"Maybe it's because he's white."

"I would hope I've overcome that barrier by now. After all, I've been dealing with you folk for thirty-some years. I've observed a few hopeful signs along the way."

"Even in Hudlow?"

"I'm not saying that yet. Maybe he dislikes me, not because I'm a . . . a nigger, but because I remind him of those soft squishy people he was fuming about last night. Am I soft and squishy, Nestor?"

"Only in the ego, Mag."

The two men rounded the corner and entered L'Enfant Court. At 1716, a postman was stuffing letters into the mailboxes in the lobby. Johnson looked at the box for Jeffrey Stanton in apartment 2-B. The brass-framed square for the name was blank. Just like his apartment door.

"Anything for Two-B?" the detective asked the mailman, flashing his identification card case. The mailman hesitated, then riffled through a handful of letters. "Just two," he said, handing Johnson a rolled government newsletter and a plain brown envelope. Johnson examined both. The newsletter was a Government Printing Office publication addressed to Jeffrey Stanton. The brown envelope was different. The address, centered in a cellophane window, read: JUBAL SYMCOX, % JEFFREY STANTON, 1716 L'ENFANT CT. NW, APT. 2-B. The postmark was smeared and illegible. There was no return address.

"Jubal Symcox?" The name rolled slowly across Johnson's tongue. Symcox. Jubal. It had a peculiar ring to it—distant, remote.

"What you make of it?" asked Skoda.

Johnson frowned. "Stanton must have company. Odd name. Look at the envelope: address window, metered postage. Business letter, I guess. Too bad the postmark's smeared."

Johnson turned to the mailman. "Delivered any of these here before?"

"Not me. I'm the relief man." Johnson gave the envelope and newsletter back to the mailman. He slid them into the 2-B slot.

Johnson rang the bell for Quaver. The little man came to the heavy glass door and let the detectives in with a bemused smile. They walked up the curved stairway to the second floor and approached 2-B. They looked quizzically at the blank nameplate, and Johnson knocked on the door.

Silence. Skoda shifted from one foot to the other. Johnson stood still, head down, arms folded across his chest. Finally they heard the soft rasp of feet coming across carpet.

"Yes?" said a voice at once calm and breathy.

"Police," said Johnson. "Metropolitan Police."

The door opened slowly. In the entrance stood a man in his mid-thirties, tall, pale, with thin pewter-gray hair. A high rounded forehead dominated his face. Delicate eyebrows arched over the darkened sockets of his eyes, eyes that, within, were a deep lifeless blue. Below them his face fell away to a finely arched nose and thin immobile lips. He said nothing and stared at the two detectives.

"You Jeffrey Stanton?" asked Johnson, looking at the index cards.

"Yes, I am." The voice was suffused with a kind of soft expectancy, outwardly gentle, yet sinewy within. Woven through its textures was a strange lilt, an alien cadence that echoed within itself. The man continued looking at the detectives.

"We've been canvassing the building about Mr. Kadinsky downstairs," said Johnson.

"Yes," said the man. He remained at the doorway, his frame blocking the view to the interior.

"Did you know him at all?"

"Only slightly."

"When's the last time you saw him?"

"Much earlier this week. Probably Sunday."

"You didn't see him during the week?"

"I rarely see anyone."

"Why?"

"I work at night. I'm usually in bed asleep when the other tenants are up and about."

"Oh, that's right. You work at the Government Printing Office. Proofreader?"

"That is correct."

"What shift do you work?"

"It varies, but usually from eleven P.M. to seven A.M."

"So when did you get back Thursday morning?"

"Sometime after seven."

"What did you do?"

"Went to bed."

"You always go right to bed?"

"Always."

"By when?"

"By seven-thirty or seven forty-five."

"No breakfast?"

"That is correct. I do not sleep on a full stomach."

“So did you possibly hear anything unusual Thursday morning? Did anything wake you up?”

“Nothing, sir.”

Johnson looked at Skoda, a tinge of frustration in his eyes. He stepped deliberately toward the tenant and placed his hand on the apartment door. The tenant did not move.

“Sir,” said Johnson, “you don’t have your name on the door here. Any particular reason for that?”

The man looked at the door. “Oh, that. That’s an oversight. I . . . I just keep forgetting to put one on. We actually have very few visitors, but I suppose as a matter of courtesy—”

“You live alone?”

“That is correct.”

“Ever have any friends or relatives stay with you?”

“Well, yes, occasionally.”

“Long enough to receive mail?”

“Occasionally.” A faint tone of wariness had crept into his voice.

Skoda shot Johnson a quick negative glance. Johnson withdrew his hand from the door. “Uh, we’re almost done, Mr. Stanton.”

Skoda spoke quickly. “Sir, do you have any time-and-attendance cards or shift stubs or something to show us your schedule?”

“I’m not certain. But let me look. Could you give me a moment?”

“Yes,” said Johnson, “and while you’re at it, could you bring us a driver’s license or your GPO employee card? Some kind of ID?”

“Of course.” The man stepped back from the entrance and began to close the door. Johnson placed his foot inside the threshold. The door pressed momentarily against his shoe, then sprang back slightly. The man gave Johnson a surprised look.

“That’s all right,” said Johnson. “We’ll be right here.”

“Very well.” The man retreated into the living room, his feet scraping softly over thick gray carpet.

The room, deep and high ceilinged, was dimly lit, but from the rear a beam of light penetrated a hallway leading to the living room. In the hallway stood a table, and on it sat a tall smooth obelisk. Even in the weak light, Johnson and Skoda could see that its surface was a shimmering azure glaze spotted with yellow flecks. The tenant stood in front of it, leaning over and pulling papers from a drawer in the table. As he thumbed through the papers, his right hand rose toward his mouth, and to their astonishment, Johnson and Skoda saw his tongue suddenly flicker from his mouth in a huge darting surge, extending a full three inches beyond his lips to wet his fingers as he went through the papers. The tongue vanished, like a serpent's, as quickly as it had appeared. The man straightened up over the table and turned toward the front of the living room. He walked slowly and deliberately to the apartment entrance and handed the detectives a sheaf of papers. They contained several pay vouchers and a GPO employee's card with a photograph showing his colorless face.

"Oh, uh, thank you," said Johnson abstractedly, staring at the man.

There was an awkward pause. "Thank you," repeated Skoda. "That will be all." He pulled the papers from Johnson's hands and gave them back to the tenant.

The door closed slowly. The two detectives watched the narrow face disappear, the lips parted, betraying the faint dark bulk behind them.

12

"Whereas I told the chief," said Captain Stohlbach, "I said, Chief, if you give me three more men and a civilian clerk, that ain't but sixty-four thousand seven hundred dollars a year not counting the clerk, which is only part-time, and throw him in for another seven thousand nine hundred and no benefits and you're still under seventy-five thousand dollars which is authorized in the budget. And the chief he says, Stohlbach, I told you I need cars, not bodies. And I says, Chief, cars don't raise the closure rate, bodies do. And he says we need cars more'n Kingdom Come. Them old Volarés and Reliants got a average fifty-eight thousand miles on them, running day and night, seven days a week, city traffic. Half of them's in the shop being put together with Super Glue. He says before long your men'll be walking. Then where's your closure rate? And I says, Chief, let's compromise: two men and only four new cars. And the chief, he sets there an instant and then he says: One man and five cars, plus accessories. And I says, Throw in the civilian clerk and some overtime. The chief he kind of nods his head, and I see I wasn't going to get nothing more. The field was getting muddy so I figured I better pull into a safe harbor."

Hudlow yawned, his enormous frame sagging in the office chair. "You come all the way in here on a Saturday just to moan and piss about the budget?"

"Got to prepare my report this weekend for the chief's desk on Monday. Most of it's done, except J. T. ain't here to type it. We need more bodies."

"That why you put three of us on one case, Cap, because of all the bodies you don't have?"

"Doctor's orders," said Stohlbach. "I didn't have nothing to do with it."

"But why me and Mag?"

"Because you're so awesome good."

"Can't you do something to break off the engagement?"

"Too late; wedding's already announced."

Hudlow grimaced.

"Look on the bright side, Hud," said Stohlbach. "You got Nestor on the case. When you and Mag start circling like dogs, he'll be there to pull you apart."

"Goody goody. He's done that already. Last evening. Mag and me was getting a little froggy, and Nestor stepped in like ol' Mother Hubbard."

"That's what he's paid for."

"I don't need no babysitter. Piss me off, I clue you."

"There's worse things in this world."

"Not very damn many. Tell me, Cap, how you peg ol' Mag?"

"Canny sucker."

"Yeah, I know that. I mean what's going on way down inside him?" Hudlow motioned toward his protruding gut.

"You know the man better than I do."

"Yeah, well, I think he's a down lumpacious burrhead that pulled himself out of the swamps of South Carolina or wherever he's from and he come up to dry land. He come up here and shook off all the mud and ticks like a back country bird dog and now he wants to set at the table with all the pedigreed poodles. You should've seen him last night taking sides with this queer-ass faggot bastard I had just run up on in the Kadinsky thing. I told him he was forgetting about the swamp he come out of—I called it a sewer, I think—and he ought to damn sight remember that in this line of work, we're all still down there. It didn't have no effect on him."

"Well, did you kiss and make up?"

"Sumbitch walked off. Skoda wanted him and me, all three of us, to get together again today and hit this one last tenant on L'Enfant Court. But I decided to take a sabbatical." Hudlow yawned again and studied the floor. "I don't know," he said, "maybe I'm being too tough on ol' Mag. Here his wife Rosalie up and died on him ten, twelve years ago, and I swear I don't think he's ever got over it. Funny thing. He really cared 'bout his ol' lady. I didn't see her but once or twice before she died. She was pretty sickly-looking with this sickle cell stuff they get, but even then she kept trying to keep Mag's spirits up, telling him he was the greatest thing since pig's knuckles and ever'thing was all right. He was new on the department and she dying, and here he was juggling all this stuff in the air and trying to come over from uniform to CID and working extra shifts. Not exactly a lay-down-and-sleep jitterbug. But after Rosalie when he started at the books and all, that's when I seen the biggest change happen in him. Seem to me he started showing off with all the new stuff he was picking up. He just had to let you know who the king of goddamn Tasmania was in nineteen-ought-seven, or how far a African jumping frog can spit on Sundays. You've heard him. He knows ever'thing. I got to hand it to him. But at the same time, it seems to me it's made him pull away from the rest of us. He thinks he's getting out of the sewer. And my problem is I just can't relax around a man that's out of the sewer. A man up on dry ground tends to let his guard down. He gets soft. You know, there was a time when me and Mag was first on the force back in uniform and if I had to go into a house in the middle of the night on a man-with-a-knife call and Mag was with me, I trusted him completely. I knew he'd back me up and I would him. That's trust. It's a thing you can't know till you're there, till your sweat's got sweat on top of it wondering what's behind the next door, but your partner is there with you and you know he's not going to split. Ain't nobody outside the po-leece understands that. But that's real trust. Now I ain't sure I got it with Mag anymore."

"Well, you're not playing peekaboo in the haunted house

anymore, either," said Stohlbach. "You a big boy now. Desk work and interviews. No more running the streets."

"Don't make no difference whether it's a haunted house or a garden club meeting, Cap. You want your partner to back you up. Brother officers. That's what we are. Brothers."

"I don't much think anything's going to cure you of ol' Mag." Stohlbach sighed heavily and pushed his chair back. "Trouble is—"

At that moment, Skoda and Johnson walked into the office, and the telephone rang.

"Hi, troops," Skoda said. Stohlbach got up and went to his private office to take the call. Hudlow turned away.

"We talked to the last tenant, Hud," said Skoda, "that guy Stanton in Two-B. Works nights at the GPO and says he was asleep when Kadinsky got it. He lives alone."

"So the yo-yo was asleep."

"But you should have seen him, Hud. Weird silver-colored hair. Dead fish eyes. And this tongue. It hangs about a half a mile out of his mouth. Spookiest dude I've ever seen."

"Tongue? What were you doing with him, French kissing?"

"No, seriously, we asked him for some ID and he was going through his papers and when he went to wet his fingers, out jumped this humongous tongue."

"Catch flies with it, too?"

"He's got a boyfriend that camps out with him sometimes. What's his name, Mag?"

"Symcox. Jubal Symcox."

"Jubal. Sounds like *Gone with the Wind*."

Magnus Johnson nodded. "And the guy's speech. I can't place it. There was something southern about it, or maybe old world, but nothing I've ever heard."

"Sorry I had to slide-tackle you, Mag, when you were pressing him about his mail," said Skoda. "Don't think he'd appreciate knowing we tromped through his mailbox."

Johnson began counting on his fingers. "Let's see now: there's the speech, the face, the tongue, no nameplate on his door, no name on his mailbox and no telephone. Also, I checked MVA. No driver's license and no vehicles registered in his name. What do you make out of that?"

"Just another regular guy at Dupont Circle," grunted Hudlow. "He's no killer. What's in it for him? Gimme a motive."

Johnson was silent.

Stohlbach came out from his inner office. "That was Friendly at Tag 'n' Bag on the phone. Says he's found something strange on Kadinsky's body he hadn't seen before. Thinks you should go over and see him. The sooner the better. He's releasing the body tonight."

13

Dr. John Friendly, Assistant Medical Examiner for the District of Columbia, stood in his freshly starched lab jacket like a waiter in a prime beef house about to uncover the main dish. Gently he pulled back the muslin sheet. Beneath lay exposed the head and shoulders of Franklin R. Kadinsky. The mouth was slightly ajar. A day's growth of stubble covered the chin and jaws. The eyes were open, undisturbed.

"This body is largely unremarkable," said Friendly in his low intimate voice, "except, of course, for the markings on the neck. But within those markings, I believe I may initially have overlooked something of possible significance. Look here."

Friendly turned Kadinsky's head slightly. "Notice along the left anterior neck there are four focal contusions. They are discrete, roughly circular one-centimeter impressions where the fingertips pressed the left side of the larynx. There are no fingernail cuts along the edges of the impressions.

"Now," he said, turning Kadinsky's head the other way, "here on the right side you can see four similar impressions from the fingertips of the other hand. But in this case, each of the impressions has a distinct and very deep fingernail cut, a narrow curvilinear laceration along the anterior edge approximately a half-centimeter in length."

"Nothing unusual about that," said Hudlow. "Lots of times

in the struggle, the guy's nails dig in more on one side of the throat than the other. I seen that before."

"I agree, but let me finish," said Friendly. "It's a little too neat this time. The lacerations don't have the randomness of a struggle. Furthermore," he said, turning Kadinsky's body over partially, exposing the back of the head and neck, "look at these two large bruises on the postero-lateral neck. Those are thumb impressions. The person who administered the strangulation approached Kadinsky from the rear, bracing his thumbs on the posterior neck and compressing Kadinsky's larynx and upper trachea in front with his fingers. Needless to say, that is an unorthodox way to strangle someone."

"Yeah," said Hudlow. "Usually it's from the front. Or if it's from the rear, it's a yoke-type job with the arm. And there wouldn't be any finger marks at all."

"Exactly," continued Friendly. "Also, if you're trying to strangle from the rear with just your hands, it's awkward and difficult to get good leverage, and the victim can resist better. Typically, it takes thirty to sixty seconds for the onset of unconsciousness in a strangulation, so the victim has some time to put up a struggle. Death does not occur for another two to four minutes after that."

"So what does it all add up to?"

"It suggests," said Friendly, "that the person administering the strangulation yoked Kadinsky first, then once he had him on the floor and unconscious, he completed the strangulation with his hands from the rear. Of course there was no resistance because of Kadinsky's unconscious state."

"But why go to that trouble?"

"Well," said Friendly, his voice tightening slightly with unprofessional bafflement, "I don't know. But there is one conclusion I am certain about. The pattern of lacerations on the neck is so precise—three deep cuts on the right side, none on the left—that the person administering the strangulation must have had peculiarly elongated nails on the right hand but not on the other. You can't blame those lacerations on random struggle. They're too neat."

"What kind of weird bidness is that?" said Hudlow.

"It's almost as if it was done deliberately," said Friendly, "to highlight the lacerations on one side but not the other. Like a trademark."

The detectives bent close over Kadinsky's body and peered at the neck. In the flat light of the autopsy room, they saw three minuscule but distinct crescent-moon slits in the skin. Each stood open slightly, a dull maroon crevice, frozen in death.

Friendly returned the body to its original position and pulled the sheet over it. "Any questions?" he asked.

The three detectives stared at the sheet in silence. After a moment Magnus Johnson said, "Besides the fingernail pattern, John, is there anything else you can tell about what the person was like?"

"Not really. Except as you know, it would have to be a relatively strong person, probably taller than Kadinsky. It takes a lot of strength to strangle a male. It probably wasn't a woman. But this is speculation."

There was another silence. "Got a fingernail freak running loose in the Fruit Loop," said Hudlow. "Some kind of cult crap. I swear to God, this town got more goddamn migrant freaks than a brood sow got tits. Something about being the nation's capital. I'll take a straight boogiewump killing to this anytime."

"Who's to say it was a cult killing?" said Johnson, looking pointedly at Hudlow. "Just one boogiewump to another, Hud?"

Hudlow's eyes narrowed. "Neighbor," he said with a new but hostile intimacy, "you've run these streets as long as me. You know boogiewumps don't kill each other this way. No kinks. They do it reg'lar. That's all I'm saying."

"Well, if you gentlemen don't mind," said Dr. Friendly awkwardly, "I've got to close shop." He walked toward his office, pulling a mound of keys from his pocket. "The funeral home is picking up Kadinsky tonight for Chicago."

14

"Homicide. Toggliotto."

"Yes, is Detective Johnson there, please?"

"Hang on. Mag. Six-four."

A pause. "This Detective Johnson."

"Oh, I'm so glad you're there, Mr. Johnson. This is McHenry Goon at Seventeen sixteen L'Enfant Court. Remember me?"

"Yes, of course. You're in Three-B. The chess champ."

"How good of you to remember, but please don't gild the lily. I hesitated to call, especially on a Saturday night. I didn't think you would be there, but this may be important."

"Yes, I'm here and one of my partners, Detective Hudlow. If it's important, mind if I put him on the phone, too?"

"Please do." Johnson signaled to Hudlow to pick up an extension.

"Thank you," said McHenry Goon. "This all may be a mistake, but when I came into our building tonight just a minute ago, I passed Mr. Kadinsky's and Mr. Boldt's apartment on the ground floor and heard some noises inside. As you know, Mr. Boldt flew to Chicago early this morning to join Mr. Kadinsky's family. Mr. Boldt told me specifically he would be gone three days and that no one would be in the apartment. He left rather hurriedly and asked me to pick up his mail and newspapers while he was gone."

"What kind of noises?" asked Johnson.

"It's hard to tell. Sort of metallic clanking noises."

Johnson and Hudlow looked at each other and shrugged.

"Did you hear any voices?"

"No, only sort of random banging or clanking."

"Would you hold on a second," said Johnson, covering the speaker with his hand and turning to Hudlow. "Want to take a run at it?" Hudlow nodded.

Johnson removed his hand from the speaker. "Sir, we'll be right over. Give us ten minutes. And get Mr. Quaver, and both of you wait in the lobby."

"Of course," said McHenry Goon, a faint tension now in his voice.

The detectives put the telephones down and strode briskly from the office to the cruiser parked on Indiana Avenue. They got in and headed west.

"Hey, Mag, put the gum ball machine on," said Hudlow from the passenger seat. "We don't get to play cowboys and Indians very often."

"Sure," said Johnson, sliding the magnetized emergency light onto the roof. "But no siren." He pressed the accelerator gently.

"Guess we better call for backup." Johnson picked up the radio and asked for a uniform unit to meet them at L'Enfant Court. He felt a cool rush of anticipation in his stomach.

They rode in silence for a few minutes. Hudlow stared out the passenger window, his back turned partially to Johnson.

"I found something interesting at the library yesterday," said Johnson at length. He looked sideways at Hudlow, seeking his reaction.

"Library? What library?" said Hudlow.

"Remember Nestor and I went to Jeffrey Stanton's apartment and we saw his tongue hanging out like a side of bacon?"

"Yeah, circus act."

"Well, there's a little membrane of skin underneath the tongue called the frenum, or *fraenum linguae* in medical terminology. It holds the tongue like an anchor to the floor of the mouth. If you cut that membrane, the tongue no longer is restrained and can extend several inches outside the mouth."

"Ain't that wonderful. S'pose Stanton does parlor tricks with it?"

"Who knows. To be honest, maybe our eyes were fooling us when we saw him. The light was dim in the back hall there. Maybe there's nothing to it."

"So why'd you go to all the trouble to look it up?"

"Curiosity. The accidental cutting of the membrane is extremely unusual, but there are certain people, contemplative groups in the Far East, that cut the frenum ceremonially as part of their religion."

"Cut on theirselves?" Hudlow turned toward Johnson in disbelief. "What for?"

"To enhance their powers of thought and concentration. With the right exercises, a Hindu adept can learn to control the movement of the tongue and eventually extend it out far enough that it will touch the spot between the eyes where the eyebrows come together."

"Some people'll do anything to get in the Guinness Book of World Records."

"There's another interesting thing about Mr. Stanton's apartment. Remember the blue stone shaft on the table we told you about where he was getting his papers? It had little highlights of yellow scattered all in its surface. That kind of stone surface is unique. It is almost certainly a gemstone called lapis lazuli. It's usually dark blue or violet. The yellow flecks in it are iron pyrites."

"You losing me, Mag, real fast."

"Well, the interesting thing is that lapis lazuli is found in only a few places in the world. Like Chile and parts of the Soviet Union and California and Colorado in the United States. But it's also found in northern Burma."

"What's so special about northern Burma?"

"It's right on the border with India, the easternmost part of India called Assam. And eastern India is where some of these off-brand Hindu groups with the slit tongues used to live, especially in the eighteenth and nineteenth centuries. Some are still thought to be there today. Maybe the lapis lazuli thing we saw is some kind of idol or altar. Am I reaching, Hud?"

A glint of admiration shot across Hudlow's eyes. "Look here," he said after a pause, "that's a lot of homework. But even if it's right, what do we got? A fluky proofreader at the GPO that worships a blue rock and lets his tongue hang out? Where do we go from there, Mag?"

"Nowhere right now."

Johnson turned the cruiser down L'Enfant Court and double-parked in front of 1716. A marked Metropolitan Police scout car was already there. Two uniformed men waited on the building steps. The detectives got out and bounded up the stairs to the front doors, nodding a quick greeting to the officers.

"May be a burglary-in-progress," said Johnson. "It's in One-B. On the east side, first floor. Hud, you and one of these men go in the alley and cover the rear. We'll go to the front." Hudlow stood momentarily astonished, mouth agape, at Johnson's take-command manner.

Johnson motioned to the other uniformed officer to follow him into the building. Quaver admitted them. McHenry Goon held a forefinger to his lips and pointed to Kadinsky's apartment.

They approached the door and listened. For a moment they heard nothing. Then a faint rustling came from deep inside the apartment, followed by a muted thwack of metal striking the floor.

Johnson and the uniformed officer stared at each other. "Nobody's supposed to be in there," whispered Johnson. "Let's knock and see who we got." He gave a series of sharp raps on the door.

Silence. They waited, the uniformed officer and Johnson on either side of the door. Quaver and McHenry Goon stood at a distance. Johnson rapped on the door a second time. Still silence.

Johnson's brow furrowed. "This is not your routine house call."

"What you think?" asked the uniformed officer.

"We've knocked twice. Get the passkey from Quaver, the old guy over there. Knock one more time, announce, and then we go in."

Johnson's throat felt dry and a slight tremor came into his hands. The uniformed officer took the key from Quaver and gave it to Johnson. He motioned to the building engineer and McHenry Goon to stand back. The two policemen approached the door, the uniformed officer's hand resting on his holster. Johnson put the key into the lock and in the same instant shouted, "Police!" He turned the key and threw the door open.

The foyer was pitch dark. There was no movement or sound. Johnson reached around the doorjamb and felt for the light switch. He couldn't find it.

"Who's in here?" he shouted. No response. "Give me a flashlight," he snapped. The uniformed officer pulled a light from his hip pocket and flashed it into the foyer. Shadows of chairs and a small table danced in the light.

"All right," announced Johnson in a formal tone. "There are two of us out here and two more in the alley. Please step into the light immediately."

Silence came from the apartment. The only sounds were the two policemen breathing and the occasional hiss of a car passing on the street. Johnson fished under his suit jacket and found his service revolver. He stepped through the doorway and entered the foyer. The uniformed officer followed behind. Johnson found a light switch and turned it on. The shadows vanished, revealing a living room filled with furniture and rich warm rugs. The men advanced through the room and entered a hall leading to more rooms in the rear of the apartment. Johnson suddenly stopped and signaled silence. They heard a faint rustling again. It was coming from a room just ahead of them. Johnson swallowed quickly. Motioning to the uniformed officer to follow, he lunged toward the room in two quick strides, pivoted at the doorway and crouched with his revolver aimed into the darkness. "Hold it, police!" he shouted. The uniformed officer sprayed his light into the room. It was the kitchen. On the far side was a sink strewn with dishes and saucepans, and in the middle of the sink stood an enormous gray raccoon. Its masked eyes squinted in the light. Several large cooking pots lay overturned on the floor. Scraps of food were scattered on the counters to either side of the sink. Behind the sink a large casement window stood open. The rhythmic panting of the two policemen slowed as they stood at the edge of the kitchen. Johnson pulled a handkerchief from his pocket and wiped his face.

"Land o' Goshen," he muttered. "I didn't need this." He turned on the overhead light. The raccoon looked quizzically at the two men, licking its lips with quick precise swipes of its tongue. Then slowly it turned around and climbed up onto the sill and out the casement window to an adjacent tree and disappeared.

"Always knew there were coons in Rock Creek Park," said the uniformed officer, "but I never heard of one coming into Dupont Circle."

"They love the urban wilderness," said Johnson. "The more urban, the better."

"I'll go tell the others," said the officer. "Maybe they saw it coming out."

Johnson scratched his head. "Stohlbach's going to love this when he hears it."

15

"Well, where we at?" asked Captain Stohlbach as the detectives assembled. It was late Monday afternoon.

"Canvassed all the tenants," said Hudlow. "Still not picking up anything." He leaned forward in his chair and looked briefly at his notebook. "Cap, you got the tenants there in front of you. Let's take them one at a time, the easy ones first.

"First, you got Quaver and the Finger brothers, which they confirm and cancel each other. Then there's Shirley Diaz with the city Latino Affairs. Her supervisor confirms she got to work at eight-twenty last Thursday morning and was late for some kind of staff meeting, just like she said. Being as she had to leave for work around eight o'clock to get there by eight-twenty, that pretty much puts her outside the building when it happened.

"Then there's ol' McHenry Goon, the high school teacher. Same with him. He's the one said he was playing chess in Dupont Circle at seven forty-five A.M. with this Yugoslavian boy, Bek. I found Bek this morning. He confirms ever'thing. Whipped Goon. Sixteen moves. Just like Goon said. One of his bishops caught Goon's king with his peter hanging out.

"Next you got Ambrose Fairlyte, the health food geek, and this guy Stanton at the GPO. They're both problems. Fairlyte's my favorite granola bar. Remember? The one said he went to his health store at seven A.M. but can't produce no customers or other employees to put him there. And Stanton. He works nights at the GPO and said he come home and was in bed asleep by seven-thirty or seven forty-five. That would be a good half-hour before Kadinsky. His night supervisor confirms he worked that night till seven A.M."

Magnus Johnson turned in his seat toward Captain Stohlbach. "This Stanton interests me," he said. "Nothing specific to Kadinsky. It's just he's such a total misfit. Out of time, out of place."

"No such thing as a misfit in Dupont Circle," said Hudlow. "If you weird, you fit."

"One of the most interesting things about him," Johnson went on, "is he's the only tenant in the building in the daytime. Remember, he works nights."

"So what does that make him?" asked Hudlow.

"Daytime stalker."

"You stretching, Mag."

"No, just thinking. My mind keeps running back to that letter in Stanton's mailbox addressed to Jubal Symcox, whoever he is. The name just doesn't fit."

Hudlow turned back to his notebook. "And then there's the best one of all: ol' Rula Edwards, the buyer at Roper's store. Mag was right. She's a lying sack of shit. Said she had a doctor's appointment in Bethesda with this Dr. Egger Thursday morning. The receptionist there confirms she's a patient but said she hasn't been there in five months."

"More important than that," interjected Johnson, "she was in her apartment with somebody, and my guess is it was a man. Remember the cigar case?"

"Better pay the bitch a visit," said Hudlow. "Nestor here says she comes complete with large tits. Mind if I tag along?"

"There's one other tenant," said Captain Stohlbach. "Don't forget Florian Boldt, the roommate."

"Like I said before, I don't think he's a problem," said Johnson. "We've been over him several times. He knows we must be looking at him pretty close, but he hasn't spooked. If he did, he would have gotten a lawyer."

Stohlbach blew into his handkerchief. "What you make of the fingernails on Kadinsky's neck?" he asked.

There was an uncharacteristic silence. Finally, Johnson spoke. "Two things come to mind, Captain. One is we should resist thinking this is some kind of cult thing. There's probably an ordinary explanation for the fingernails, and it's not a bunch of hopped up druids from Stonehenge. The other thing is that whoever got to Frank Kadinsky could have cut the nails off and disposed of the evidence, so to speak." Johnson stopped a moment. "It would be nice to have a motive."

"Well, first things first," said Stohlbach. "It's getting late. Rula Edwards ought to be home 'bout now. Why don't you boys drop over for a cup of tea and a ladylike chitchat?"

"And check her fingernails," said Johnson.

"And her tits," reminded Hudlow.

"You two go ahead," said Skoda, pulling on his jacket. "I got practice. Fill me in tomorrow." He left the office.

"What's this practice he's rushing off to?" asked Johnson.

"For that hippie hoedown he goes to at church in Arlington ever' Sunday," said Hudlow. "Guitars and cowbells is what it is. He don't even play in it. Just likes to watch."

"Come on, Hud," said Johnson. "The Catholic folk Mass is okay. It's more than just cowbells."

"Thrill a minute," grunted Hudlow. "I tell you Nestor ain't been right since he bailed out of that seminary six years ago and came with the po-leece."

The two detectives walked out of the Homicide Branch together. In the corridor, a reporter for *The Washington Post* accosted them. "Anything new on Kadinsky, guys?" he asked.

"Ain't telling you jackshit," said Hudlow, brushing by the reporter.

"Ah, come on, Hud, you must know something new. It's been four days. Can't you at least tell me how you feel about how the case is going?"

"Yeah, I'm fucking pissed."

"You know I can't put that in the paper."

"Okay. Just say I'm pissed."

16

Quaver let the two detectives into the building, and they marched up the curved stairway to the third floor. They rang at apartment 3-C.

"Yes?" said Rula Edwards, her voice low and expectant.

"Po-leece, ma'am," said Hudlow.

The woman admitted them. They sat awkwardly on the edge of the flowered sofa while Rula Edwards watched them like a mongoose curled in a small leather rocker. Johnson introduced Hudlow to the woman. Hudlow examined her closely, his pale blue eyes filled with adolescent curiosity. Johnson noticed that the silver cigar case was no longer on the mantel.

"Ma'am," he began, "you have to understand sometimes we come back and reinterview witnesses and potential witnesses in cases when we need a clarification or something. It's routine, understand? That's why we're here this evening."

"Of course," she said.

"Now, do you recall that you told Detective Skoda and me the other night that you were not here early Thursday morning because you had a doctor's appointment in Bethesda and took the Metro out there?"

"I know what you're leading up to, Mr. Johnson," the woman said, her weak eyes flashing momentarily.

"What's that?"

"That you called my doctor and found out I didn't have an appointment. I should have realized it wouldn't work."

She remained coiled in her seat, arms folded across her chest.

"Yes, ma'am," continued Johnson. "Do you have an explanation?"

"Yes." She sighed heavily. "Yes, I do. But it's hard to tell. It's a very personal matter."

"We can appreciate that," said Johnson, "but in the same way we hope you can appreciate it's necessary for us to have the information."

The woman hesitated, looking at the floor.

"Go ahead," interjected Dewey Hudlow, speaking with an odd tenderness.

Rula Edwards looked up again. "There was a gentleman here that morning."

The two detectives glanced at each other. "Yes, ma'am," said Johnson. "We appreciate you being straightforward. That takes care of a good bit of the situation. But could we bother you to tell us who it was, ma'am?"

"I was afraid of that." Her voice was different now, almost meek, and her rigid posture had loosened. "Isn't there some way we could—" Her voice broke off. "I mean, if I have to say, can't it be kept confidential and not go in all your reports and things?"

"Absolutely," said Johnson. "Just between us. Except, of course, you understand we will have to verify it with the person himself."

"Oh, dear, I suppose you do have to do that, too, don't you? Well, he's ah—his name is Mr. Winter. Charles Winter."

"Yes, ma'am," said Johnson. He began writing in his notebook. "Can you tell us where we can contact him?"

"Yes, he's at Roper's. He's one of the vice presidents."

"Is he married?"

"Yes."

"Then we'll contact him at the department store."

"Yes, but could you please be discreet about it? You know, as though you're just checking on shoplifting or something."

"Of course, ma'am. That's easy enough to do."

"Thank you."

"So those were his footsteps that Shirley Diaz heard early Thursday morning in the hallway and not yours coming back in to get the subway ticket?"

"Yes," she murmured.

"One last thing, ma'am," said Johnson. "Does Mr. Winter smoke cigars?"

A brief look of puzzlement entered her face. "Why, yes, he does," she said. Then she glanced at the mantel, and the bafflement in her face dissolved into a small defeated smile.

17

"Gootch. Hey, Gootch, come over here." Dewey Hudlow beckoned from his seat behind the wheel of the Plymouth. A gangling man with enormous hands and feet broke away from the knot of other men in front of the liquor store and sauntered across the sidewalk to Hudlow's car. He leaned into the front passenger seat window, smiling briefly.

"Dolphus Gootch, I ain't seen you since your mamma's sister quit fucking white men. How you?"

"Making it, Hud. Making it."

"Ol' lady back from Alderson?"

"Yeah, been back a munt'. They didn't have her up there but ninety days."

"Tell her I said howdy. You still working the liquor store?"

"Same shit. Different day."

"It pays, don't it?"

"New owner in there. Want me to work evenings to nine o'clock."

"What's wrong with that?"

"Tory want me down at the tourist home by eight-thirty. Tricks coming in steady by then. Can't be both places."

"Tell Tory kiss my natural ass."

"Mu' fu' dance on my lips if I don't go along with the program."

"Tory selling you a bunch of woof tickets. Don't worry."

"Easy for you. You don't work for him."

"Just trying to help out."

"Try harder."

"Tell me, you seen Paganini Hart?"

"Say who?"

"Paganini Hart."

"Oh, you mean that buckwheat boy work a lot parties in Georgetown bartending?"

"Yeah, him."

"What you want with him?"

"Thought he might know more'n you."

"No, I ain't seen him. What you want to know?"

"Not your line."

"Try me."

"Dolphus, you know this white boy Kadinsky got killed the other night near Dupont Circle?"

"Yeah, I heard."

"You just heard? You ain't picked up nothing else?"

"That's right. Strictly gray boys. Couple sissies, I heard. You right, Hud. Ain't my line."

"That's why I want Paganini Hart. He picks up a lot at those Brownie fly-ups in Georgetown and Dupont Circle."

"Junior Tompkins might know where at Paganini Hart. He 'round on Seventh Street at Q right now. Just seen him few minutes ago."

"Thanks, Dolphus. I'll put a letter of commendation in your file."

"With a copy to Tory. 'Bye."

Hudlow pulled away from the curb and headed toward Seventh and Q. Glad to hear Gootch's ol' lady's back, he thought. Bitch got four kids under six. What in hell'd she do with them while she was in Alderson?

He spotted Junior Tompkins. A stout middle-aged man, he held a leash attached to a gaunt blue tick hound. Side by side, dog and man strode in meandering stateliness, oblivious to the children and adults milling around them on the pavement.

Hudlow tapped his horn but got no response. He tried a second time, and Tompkins turned and recognized him. He smiled and came over to the car window.

"Huddy, where you been, boy?" he asked, his voice thick with forced animation. His coarsened face seemed more swollen than ever, Hudlow thought. Cocaine. As he leaned into the window, the smell of hops and fermented fruit poured into the car.

"Hey, Junior," said Hudlow. "Where you get that sorry-ass dog?"

"Ain't mine. Just holding it for a frien'. He don't bite. You looking good, Huddy."

"All done with mirrors, Junior."

"Had me fooled."

"Listen, Junior. Ain't got much time. You seen Paganini Hart?"

"Yeah, he at the Grille on U Street. Just gone."

"Thanks, Junior. Next time I see you, I'll bring you a new hat. Says on the front: 'I May Be Fat. But You Ugly, And I Can Diet.'"

Junior Tompkins cackled and Hudlow spun away in a spray of dust. The blue tick hound strained feebly, trying to reach a fallen dome of ice cream on the pavement just beyond the compass of his leash.

In minutes, Hudlow was parked a half block east of the Grille on U Street. He watched the steady traffic of customers going in and out, young blacks talking and gesticulating easily, interspersed with an occasional white construction worker or telephone lineman looking vaguely lost.

He saw Paganini Hart emerge, his hands holding a canned drink and a large white bag. He started walking west. Hudlow moved the Plymouth slowly down U Street past the Grille and caught up with him.

"Want a lift, my man?" Hudlow asked, leaning toward the passenger window.

"Hey, Hud," answered Hart, his face brightening with recognition. He looked briefly in both directions along the sidewalk, then climbed into Hudlow's car. The car moved slowly westward along U Street.

"Wing?" Hart said, holding the steaming white bag toward Hudlow. The detective fished into the bag and pulled out a crisp brown thigh. "Mama Darcy still making good chicken?" he asked.

"Try it," said Hart. "What bring you this side of Chocolate City?"

"No big thing," said Hudlow. "Just poking."

"What you poking?" asked Hart, his light brown face ignited with curiosity.

"White folks stuff," said Hudlow.

"Oh, you mean that boy Kadinsky?"

"How'd you guess?"

"Only white boy killed in this city last six months."

"Well, I got him. You hearing anything?"

"Not around here. That's off-brand stuff, Hud. Cousin of the night clerk at the morgue told me that boy had strangle marks with fingernail cuts on one side the neck and not the other."

"That's about right. You picking up anything on the cocktail circuit?"

Hart thought for a moment. "Lot of chitchat," he said. "People wondering. But nothing solid."

"Where'd you work this last weekend?"

"Couple of embassies on Massachusetts Avenue. Lawn party in Georgetown. Oh, and yesterday, some kind of sissy feast up Kalorama."

"Hear anything there?"

"Lot of them knew Kadinsky. Ever'body trying to say they knew him better than ever'body else. I think some of them maybe worked with him on the Hill."

"Anything about a lovers' quarrel?"

"Not a word."

"Dope?"

"Same."

"What kind of talk you hear?"

"You know, Hud, such a sweet guy and he worked so hard and why was it him, and like that."

"I know. Ever notice when somebody dies, people always say nice things: poor Tommy Titsworth, always wrote his mother and helped Mrs. Numbnuts cross the street? Never he stole out of the poor box and picked his hemorrhoids."

"You on it, Hud."

"So, basically ever'body's drawing a blank?"

"That's right. No one know nothing. Too off-brand. Even for white people." Hart gave Hudlow a sidelong grin.

"That's what we're hitting all over town," said Hudlow. "Big zero. Five days after, we still sucking wind."

"Brass leaning on you, Hud?"

"Like tarnation."

"They don't do that when some nigger get killed, do they, Hud?" said Hart.

"'Less it's a city councilman or somebody," said Hudlow. "I tell you, give me a good cheap alley killing anytime to this shit. No brass on my back, and I can get down and lock the right sumbitch up in twenty-four hours."

"But why is that, Hud? The chief of the whole department is black. What's wrong with him?"

"Hell, half the assistant chiefs and deputies are black, too. Been that way for years. That don't make the difference. The difference is the real people that run this city, the merchants, the building owners and them candy-stripe jerkoffs on the Hill, including the black ones. They ain't going let some tinhorn Yassuh Boss in a blue uniform get in their way. In fact, they put him there in the first place, just to show how high-minded they are."

"How can they do that?"

"Anything they want is just a phone call away: *drinngg, drinngg:* Hello? Would you please put more patrols here and more men there and give that building special attention and arrest this man and stop that nuisance and crane those cars and fix that ticket. *Drinngg, drinngg:* Oh, you say Chief Whatshisface can't do that just now? Well, would you please call my good friend Senator Fugpuddle of South Dakota and ask him to have his staff review the budget of the Metropolitan Po-leece Department. And et cetera."

Hudlow's cruiser was nearing New Hampshire Avenue and Sixteenth Street. "Christ amighty," shouted Paganini Hart. "You taken me halfway to Chevy Chase. I got to get back home."

"Sorry 'bout that," said Hudlow. "Sometimes I get carried away." He executed a U-turn and headed back into the ghetto.

18

"Mag, this reminds me of a ol' hunting dog I had once," said Captain Stohlbach. "Send him out to fetch a bird, he'd come back with a rubber ball."

"I know, I know. Sorry we zipped on Rula Edwards' boyfriend," said Johnson.

"We got to start getting something solid here pretty soon. Studio A having fits."

"Well, let me tell you about Rula Edwards first. That lady knows how to go first class. Her boyfriend's the vice president of Roper's for operations. Charles W. Winter. Got a big farm in Potomac, horses and all. Also a wife and four children. Big good-looking Cary Grant kind of guy. Hud and I went to his office downtown this morning. I've never seen such a cool dude come unglued so fast when we told him why we were there. Here he is making millions, pillar of the community, big family man, just hitting his peak in the corporate world, and we catch him punching one of his employees."

"Did he acknowledge?"

"Oh, yeah, but he was so flabbergasted he seemed to think we were trying to make an adultery case instead of a homicide."

"Did he cool out?"

"Finally. We assured him it wouldn't get back to his family or the other ninety-seven vice presidents at Roper's. He was really worried about that. Said he would have to file some kind of formal report on our visit. Our presence in the corporate office was very visible. Winter's secretary almost soiled herself when we showed up at her desk, and I'm sure she was on the phone to her girlfriends as soon as we were with Winter. So we made up some cockamamie thing about how we had a tip that organized crime in New York was muscling in on the fur coat trade and had been trying to divert truck deliveries for Roper's from New York and could he help us out with the names of employees that might be involved. Store security comes under his jurisdiction, and he had to call in his security chief, and he was a little bent out of shape because we hadn't come to him first, and he recognized Hudlow and asked why a guy in Homicide was working interstate theft and we said it was a special detail, and the lie got bigger and bigger, but it seemed to put Winter at ease, and we finally left the place with a handshake. Isn't police work fun?"

"Okay, okay," said Stohlbach, "but still you're saying basically you and Hudlow don't have anything new. Right?"

"I cannot tell a lie, Chief," said Johnson.

"Just out of curiosity, did Vice President Winter happen to have long fingernails on one hand?" asked Stohlbach.

"I knew you'd ask that," said Johnson. "Yeah, dragging on the floor, but by the time we finished with him, he'd bitten them down to the nub. But you know what else he really did have, Chief? The silver cigar case we saw in Rula's apartment. That was our proof positive."

Nestor Skoda walked into Stohlbach's office and slumped into a chair. Stohlbach looked at him unhappily. "Mag here ain't got anything new for me," he said. "What about you, Nestor? What about your people over at Dupont Circle?"

"Same deal. Most of them have dried up on me, it's been so long since I worked the area. But this one guy, Jamie, remember him? Used to be a bartender at the Demeter Lounge?"

"Oh, yeah. The old Hung 'n' Bung on R Street."

"Right. Well, he's working around the corner on Connecticut

now. I saw him Saturday and asked him to take a few soundings. He called me yesterday and said the gays know nothing. Not just that. He said there's not even the usual buzz who was doing what to whom. Some people knew Kadinsky or had heard of him, he said, but there was no talk of a gay connection."

"Another dry well," said Stohlbach.

"Like I said."

"Wish it was like on TV where the cops solve it all in thirty minutes."

"Minus the commercials," said Magnus Johnson. "Dry wells, false trails, that's more our line. How can you have the thrill of the chase when the best you can do is plod?"

Stohlbach pushed his chair back. "I'm still catching extreme heat from upstairs. The longer you all stall the game, the more they blow the whistle at me. Evelyn Farnham from the L'Enfant Citizens called me direct this morning. Woman talk the rivets off a ship bottom. She wanted me to come and address her association and set their little palpitating hearts at ease. I said I had a conflicting engagement in New Zealand."

"Maybe Hudlow will have something for you when he comes in," said Johnson. "He's on the street working his snitches."

"I'm not asking for a miracle," said Stohlbach, "just divine intervention."

19

"Take foxes," said Hudlow, leaning back, his fingers laced behind his head. "Sumbitches canny. They know right off not to fool with a human. Ever see that fox I keep penned up behind my house, the one which I use her urine for trapping? It's a ol' gray she-fox me and Douglas MacArthur Cheek used to use. Still keep her in a pen, one of them hutch things sets up on stilts with a wire mesh bottom to let her piss through to a catch pan. Scatter it around on the ground when I'm setting the traps so I don't leave no human scent. See, them bastards'll come up to a trap to inquire, you know, and lot of times they know right off it's a trap and they smell the human smell, and they get down and dig the trap up, I mean actually dig it up and not step on the treadle and the damn thing not go off, and they'll turn it over and then back up to it and do their bidness right on it. I know you don't believe me, but it's the cold clabber truth. And that's after I've went to all the trouble making the fox lure and burying the traps and driving the pegs and spreading the urine and covering my own smell. I mean, hell, the pegs sixteen inches long, and you got to bang the sumbitches in all the way. Then you take the fox lure, which you need it for the bait. You know fox lure? They call it gland lure someplaces. What you do is you take a dead fox's genitals and mash them up and cook them real good over a fire. Then you let it cool and pour off the juice in a bottle. Looks like real heavy chocolate milk and smells like the back end of glory. Then you go and put your traps out, like maybe in a corn field when it's all stubble, November, December. The fox's fur is prime in December. Now a fox that gets caught, lemme tell you they can be mean. What I do is if I come up and find one, I hit him in the head with the trap shovel, just enough to knock him out, you know, and then I stomp on his back between his shoulders and mash his lungs and things. That's why you don't shoot a fox. It tears their skin up and ain't no good to sell. Me and ol' Douglas MacArthur Cheek, we used go trapping reg'lar. Course, that was before he lost his leg. You know Cheek? People call him Cheeks. Hangs around Ninth Street. Him and me had a right good bidness. We'd go out in them cold-ass fields, baiting traps, walking for hours, hooting and laughing. Cheeks would bring along a mickey or two and lay up in the ditch, happy as a dead hog in the sunshine. Next thing you know—"

"Hey, Hud," interrupted Captain Stohlbach, coming out of his office. "Snap to. We got unfinished business."

"I was just winding up," said Hudlow, looking injured.

"Well, you got to put your foxes away for now. Any of you guys looked at this inventory of stuff Mobile Crime found in Kadinsky's apartment?" Stohlbach scratched his head. "Is this weird or what?"

"Oh," said Johnson, "you mean the purple jockey shorts and the thousand dollars cash and the shoebox full of baseball cards and the bundle of horny letters?"

"Horny letters?" said Hudlow, his eyes narrowing.

"That's right," said Stohlbach, "and they're from a real live genu-wine female-type woman. Name's Genevieve Hall. Works for the World Bank. She's the one that Florian Boldt couldn't remember her name."

"You mean ol' Kadinsky wasn't—? He was a—? Damn!" Hudlow almost blushed.

"First time I seen your mouth out of gear in six months," said Stohlbach. He turned back to the file. "There's twenty-seven letters in all. Written over a two-year period. Lot of suggestive stuff about hot times at the beach and the mountains on weekends—"

"Where is this bitch?" said Hudlow.

"Down, Fido!" said Johnson. "We've already checked her out. She's in Suriname on bank business. Been out of the country for three weeks. Also, no other boyfriends in her life. No competitors."

"What's Suriname?" muttered Hudlow.

"What about the homosexual interface?" asked Stohlbach.

"Might still be one," said Johnson. "Maybe he was AC-DC. Maybe he was straight and turned some guy down. The important thing about those letters, though, is that they contain no threat-type language. There's no sign Kadinsky was having financial or personal problems. It's all negative evidence."

"The hell with the letters," said Hudlow. "Let's see the purple jockey shorts."

"You'll never go back to boxers."

"And the baseball cards and all that cash laying around. What kind of fruit pie was he?"

"Broaden your horizons, Hud," said Johnson. "Maybe he was saving the cards for a cousin or a nephew. Maybe he liked purple. Maybe he was absent-minded and didn't deposit his paychecks. It's all interesting but random junk."

"Not only that," said Captain Stohlbach, looking at the Mobile Crime Lab report, "the only fingerprints they found in the apartment was Kadinsky's and Boldt's. They even ran a silver nitrate on the walls and zipped."

There was a pause. Then Stohlbach spoke again. "I'm with Hud. There's nothing to work with here. Which brings me to the next thing. I hate to do this to you, and I know it's a little off the ceiling, but I'm running out of ideas. I'm going to ask you to put Kadinsky's building under surveillance. Just for a while, fellas. See what the traffic is. Give me some good running resumes so I can send them upstairs. They love paper up there."

20

The tree branches over L'Enfant Court moved in the gentle night breeze, throwing faint dancing shadows across the hood and windshield of the cruiser. Street lights stood like orderly sentries in diminishing ranks down each side of the street. Two large carriage lamps at the entrance to 1716 burned brightly, casting large circles of light onto the sidewalk.

"Wake up, Rip van Winkle," said Johnson to Hudlow sprawled on the seat next to him. "We only been here six hours."

"Six hours and nothing but two ants and a cockroach on crutches gone up them steps."

"You missed Shirley Diaz. She came out five minutes ago. Pulled up her dress and had Kadinsky's killer printed on her drawers."

"Who was it?"

"I don't know. It was in Spanish."

The two men sat in silence, their banter momentarily suspended, threatening the fragile alliance they had formed in recent days. Johnson closed his eyes, thinking, hoping. Hudlow stretched and pulled gently at his crotch. "Nuts near 'bout rolled up into my neck," he muttered. "S'pose we could get a hospital bed in here next time?"

The heavy glass doors at 1716 suddenly shimmered and opened. Hudlow and Johnson sat up. Two youthful figures emerged from the building, stood for a moment at the top of the stairs and then bounced down to the sidewalk. They walked toward the parked cruiser, talking quietly, passing the detectives without noticing them.

"The Finger boys," said Hudlow, disappointed. "Must be looking for a nighttime boodle."

"Bagel."

"Whatever."

The two men settled down into the car again. Silence enveloped the street. An hour passed.

The doors at 1716 shimmered again. A slender pale man stood at the entrance, looking out at the street. Johnson nudged Hudlow. "Hey, it's Stanton, the tenant in Two-B."

He came down the stairs and began walking rapidly, almost at a trot, in a westward direction away from the detectives.

Johnson looked at his watch. It was 10:05. "What's his rush, I wonder?"

"Pro'bly going to work," said Hudlow. "GPO. Night shift. Catching the subway over at the Fruit Loop. Didn't you say he doesn't have a car?"

"But his shift doesn't start till eleven. Only takes seven or eight minutes from Dupont to the GPO at Union Station. What's he running for?"

"You suspicioning too much, Mag."

"I say let's follow him. Nothing else to do."

Hudlow grunted unhappily but started the cruiser. "Damn near lost him already. You see him, Mag?"

"We'll catch up," said Johnson as the cruiser eased westward. Moments later at Dupont Circle, they spotted the man, slightly hunched, dressed in a light windbreaker, now heading south.

"He's going to the subway entrance," said Johnson. "Ditch the cruiser."

Hudlow parked, and the two men quickly got out. They scurried across the circle just in time to see the tenant vanish into the subway entrance, a vast escalator shaft slanting into the earth. As Hudlow and Johnson reached the entrance, they caught sight of him again. Now he was bounding down the escalator, two steps at a time. The detectives followed at a distance. They heard the distant rush of an approaching train beneath them. The man reached the bottom of the escalator. Without looking behind him, he crossed the mezzanine, slipped a fare card into the automatic gate and sped down a second escalator to the train platform. The train was roaring into the station. Hudlow and Johnson sprinted up to the kiosk at the fare gate, flashed their identification cases and were waved through the emergency swing gate by an attendant. They hurtled down the second escalator, their footsteps echoing against the coffered ceilings of the station. The train had stopped. They glimpsed the tenant stepping into a car and bounded onto the car immediately behind his. The doors closed, and the train began to move.

Gasping for breath, the detectives stumbled forward past the passengers in the car and peered cautiously through the glass emergency door into the car ahead of them. There he was, standing near one of the doors at the far end, looking expectantly around him, his thin gray hair hanging over his darkened eyes.

"Sumbitch see us?" panted Hudlow.

"No. He's not looking for us. I think he's looking for someone else." The train picked up speed, swaying noisily through the tunnel under the city. A minute later, it pulled into Farragut North station. The doors slid open. The man looked out momentarily, then examined his watch. The doors shut again. The train pulled away from the platform.

The detectives continued watching him, still catching their breath. "Hare and hounds," muttered Johnson, almost exuberantly.

"Beats real work, don't it?" said Hudlow. The detectives exchanged glances, shyly.

A minute and a half passed, and the train thundered into Metro Center, a busy station with scores of passengers waiting on the platform. The tenant scanned their faces as they poured into his car. He stood on his tiptoes, searching, his face filled with a new agitation now.

Suddenly, he darted out the door onto the platform, ran a few steps forward and dived into the next car ahead.

"Shitjimpiss," whispered Hudlow. "He's switched." Hudlow and Johnson leaped from their own car and moved up to the next just as the warning bell sounded for the doors to close.

"What kind of ants he got in his pants?" asked Hudlow as they worked their way forward in the car. The train was pulling out of the station.

"There's your answer," said Johnson, pointing into the car ahead. At the far end, they saw the tenant standing rigidly, speaking to another man, a short, swarthy figure with a glistening bald circle in the back of his head.

The two detectives watched. The train was slowing for Gallery Place. As it came into the station, the tenant pulled a small white envelope from his pocket and put it in the other man's hand. The doors flew open. The dark man stepped off the train and vanished. The tenant remained on the train.

"Quick," blurted Hudlow. "You stay with Stanton, I'll get the rag head." Hudlow jumped from the train as the doors slammed shut. He saw a blurred image of Johnson through the window of the departing train. Hudlow headed for the mezzanine escalator.

The dark man with the bald spot was not in sight. Hudlow pushed his way past several passengers on the narrow escalator leading up from the train platform and then ran toward the fare gate. A group of tourists wearing shorts and knapsacks was clustered at the information kiosk, asking an attendant for directions. They were blocking the emergency swing gate.

"'Scuse me, this a po-leece emergency," said Hudlow. "Mind letting me through?" The tourists gave him a baffled look. Like cattle in a storm, they bunched more tightly and refused to move, chattering among themselves, a language Hudlow did not know.

"May I see your identification, please," said the attendant.

"Fuck identification," shouted Hudlow. "You let me through, or I'll shuck your corn till your cob falls off." Hudlow ploughed into the tourists, knocking them to the side, and crashed through the swing gate. He raced toward the escalator leading to the street, the attendant's protests ringing in his ears. He glanced up and saw the small shining circle in the back of the ebony head at the top of the escalator now fading into the night.

Puffing heavily, Hudlow reached the top of the escalator and looked out into the darkness. He was at Ninth and G. The walls of the National Museum of American Art lowered at him under the street lights. To the north lay a broad empty parking lot, and across it Hudlow saw the dim figure of the man walking. He had a steady stride but appeared in no hurry. Good, thought Hudlow. Least he's not thinking about me. Keeping his distance, Hudlow followed. The man continued north to H Street, then turned east, his diminutive form now a silhouette against the lights of Chinatown.

The man made an abrupt turn into an alley and disappeared from Hudlow's sight. Moments later, Hudlow reached the alley and stared into its mouth. It had a familiar feel to it. He remembered now. It wound aimlessly through a maze of abandoned warehouses. He stepped into the alley, the ground soft under his shoes. In the dim light, he saw trash and broken auto parts scattered about. A faint odor of urine hung in the air. He turned a corner, and the sounds and lights of H Street behind him were cut off. He slowed his steps and fumbled under his jacket for his service revolver. He stopped and listened. Faint intermittent drops of water fell on the soft ground. He peered into the darkness. Christ, it was right here. *Blam! Blam!* The explosions echoed in his memory. Toby Shirtler, one of the young guys, down on the ground, the police flashlights zigzagging over the twitching body. Right here. He had no backup. A fool. A good fool. But a fool.

Hudlow stood paralyzed. He tried to step forward but could not. Sweat ran down his face onto his shirt. God amighty. Gimme a backup. Mag? Shit. His enormous frame shivered in the still air.

"Fuck that A-rab," Hudlow mumbled. He turned and walked out of the alley and back to H Street.

21

"And I says to Toggliotto, can't you smoke that damn thing outside? And he says it's raining and I'm staying here. And I says your cigar smells like a yak in heat. And we kept going back and forth and not paying much attention to the surveillance, and finally 'bout six o'clock we knocked off. Anyway, Cap, we logged it very official. Here's the paperwork to keep your girlfriends upstairs happy."

"Appreciate it, Hud," said Captain Stohlbach, placing the papers neatly in an empty wire basket on his desk. "So basically, you ain't seen nobody out there all that time?"

"Not a swinging dick, at least not when I wasn't fussing with Toggliotto."

"I sent him with you to keep you company, Hud. Nestor and Mag off."

"Chinese torture, Cap. You ever sat in a car for five hours in the rain with a man smoking a ten-inch cigar? Even when the fire's out, sumbitch stinks." Stohlbach braced himself for another lecture. "It's enough to break up a marriage in heaven. I been on this force seventeen years and had many a partner. Set with them seven, eight hours at a stretch, short ones and fat ones and white ones and black ones that all they do is talk about their model train. Guys that set there and don't say nothing, just sulk. It's all kinds, but the one I can't stand is the one that smokes a cigar. All these ACLU eggheads wearing Docksides hollering at us to integrate the cruisers, they don't know jack-shit. They ain't never been cooped up in a cruiser for eight hours straight with a human, black or white. You right up against their smells and sounds, two feet away from them for eight hours. Maybe they blink too much or pick their nose. When you living that close, that stuff can just swarm all over you. Black and white ain't what it is. I'd take Mag Johnson to Toggliotto, any time, even with all his chrome-plated palaver."

"Look," interrupted Stohlbach, "you're a big boy in CID now. You mostly drive solo. So stop moaning about one time with Toggliotto. You were solo working your snitches earlier this week, weren't you?"

"You got to work snitches private," said Hudlow. "Can't have a crowd setting ringside."

"You get anything?"

"Cap, you know I told you my snitches are no good for this one. No off-brand stuff. But I went up there anyway. I'll get up some more paperwork for you on it. Chief Flynn and them'll just love it: 'Informant Number One, Dolphus Gootch, black male subject, proved reliable in past, no information. Informant Number Two, Junior Tompkins, black male subject, proved reliable in past, no information. Informant Number Three, Paganini Hart, black male subject, proved reliable in past, no information.'"

"Well, what about this Stanton boy you and Mag chased out after the other night on the subway?"

Hudlow moved uncomfortably in his seat. "Like I told Mag, Cap, it was a . . . it was a dope connection. Just Stanton paying for his shit on the subway."

"On a subway?"

"That's why he was so jittery. He almost missed his man. Happens all over. I can't help it if I lost the surveillance."

"That ain't like you, Hud."

"Bunch of goddamn tourists from downtown Germany jammed me in the subway. How am I s'posed to help that?"

“You sure it was a dope connection?”

“What else, Cap? I mean, that’s all them sand niggers do. I say forget it. Let ol’ Stanton have his shit.”

“If you so sure, why didn’t you stop him?”

“No probable cause. You can’t stop a man for taking an envelope from another man on a subway. There was no prior pattern. A bad stop could fuck up the whole surveillance.”

“Mag says Stanton got off two stops after you at Union Station and went straight into the GPO, right on schedule.”

“Good little government grunt.”

The two men were silent a moment. Then Stohlbach said, “I can’t understand why we’re hitting such a blank.”

“Onliest thing I can say is at least I didn’t flush out a raccoon for you in Frank Kadinsky’s apartment,” said Hudlow with a giggle.

“Throw of the dice, Hud. How ’bout that other snitch of yours, Douglas MacArthur Cheek? You see him much these days?”

“Didn’t you hear he lost a leg? Can’t do a whole hell of a lot these days. Getting up in years, too.”

“That’s the boy you and him used to trap foxes?”

“The very same. Had to have his right leg cut off early this spring. Damn near bought it.”

“Good hospital?” asked Stohlbach.

“D.C. Central. But he’ll never be the same. When you been that close to the edge, you bound to be messed up. Like a brand-new car. You roll it in the ditch and get it repaired and have ever’ dent hammered out, but it will never be the same. The struts in it won’t ever run quite true again.”

“You sure ol’ Cheek was straight to start with?”

“Listen, Cap, it wasn’t nothing wrong with that boy. He hustled the onliest way he could. Sure he boosted. But you know what he done? He would go over to Union Station at Christmas time to the marshaling yards. Him and these other guys. They would break the seals on the freight cars and take out toys. Boxes and boxes of Sears, Roebuck roller skates and dolls and basketballs and Buck Rogers laser guns and give them out to the kids in Northeast."

"In this jurisdiction, that's stealing."

"Fuck jurisdiction. He didn't steal much for himself. It was mostly for other people. It's a difference. Some high-rolling lawyer up in Chevy Chase, he wouldn't do it that way, I know. He'd just charge three hundred dollars an hour to play word games for some scumbag merchant in court for skimming wage taxes. Your choice, Cap."

"You trying to make Douglas MacArthur Cheek a saint?"

"I don't know nothing 'bout no saint. But let me ask you this. Do you know how Cheeks came to lose his leg? I'll tell you how. He was out on the highway in Virginia down below Leesburg somewheres one evening near dusk, and this white boy had a flat tire and Cheeks drove by and seen him and stopped, and the white guy said he didn't have no tire iron, and Cheeks went back to his truck and got his own iron and was coming back toward the white guy with it. He had the iron raised up so the guy could see it, and some yo-yo on the road seen it was a nigger and thought he was going after the white boy, and run him off the road and knocked him down. Run clean over his leg. They flew him back to D.C., but they couldn't do nothing with the leg."

"He gets a free ride back in a chopper and the best surgeons in D.C. to save his life, and you complaining."

"I'm saying Douglas MacArthur Cheek ain't exactly had a run of good luck lately. Sure, they saved his life, but what kind of a life is it? Sumbitch in constant pain. Can't go but a few steps at a time. No more easy evenings on the front steps for him. No more nights laying up in the fields singing and waiting for Ol' Gray to come by."

"You call it luck. Some say God acts in strange ways."

"What you mean, strange ways?"

"Maybe Cheek comes out of it better. He ain't stealing anymore. Maybe the guy that run him over's received retribution. The Bible says it: If I sin, the Lord markest me and will not acquit me from mine iniquity. You don't know ever'thing, Hud."

"You damn right I don't know ever'thing. But there's a few things I am acquainted with. Just because I growed up in a cow pasture don't mean I'm a complete ignoramus. We had preachers and the Bible out there. We was loaded up with them. I remember this one rascal when I was a kid, told us always to follow the commandments and we'd be okay. Said it over and over. He would read from the same place in the Old Testament. I can remember it to this day. Deuteronomy six: Keep the commandments and statutes that it may be well with thee in the land that floweth with milk and honey. Well, damnit, in his own way, Douglas MacArthur Cheek kept the commandments. You could trust him. He never hurt nor harmed nobody. I never heard him speak down on a person. Maybe he took a few gross of roller skates, but it didn't harm Sears, Roebuck. Just a wiggle on their goddamn flow chart. But where's the milk and honey for Douglas MacArthur Cheek?"

Hudlow stopped abruptly. Delicate beads of sweat had formed on his forehead. "Basically," he said, "God sucks."

22

The tones, like minuscule prints across an imaginary snowfield, ascended to the ceiling of the church, as the lutenist bent in concentration over his instrument. His fingers worked and kneaded the strings, drawing the notes in alternating arpeggios and throaty chords. The sounds from an ancient pavan floated over the congregation, then slowly rose to the narrow clerestory and expired in the vault. The music filled Nestor Skoda with an immense sadness and yearning, though he did not know why. Tears rose to his eyes. They always did when he heard the lute. Its melancholy sounds intimated something lost or perhaps never won, a terrible emptiness now filled, only partially, by the brief beauty of the music. Yet he looked forward to it every Sunday, always taking a place near the folk Mass ensemble where its members gathered below the pulpit. The tambourine, the flutes and the recorders were silent now as the lutenist, an earnest, bespectacled man in a shaggy sweater, played the post-Communion meditation. He cradled the pear-shaped instrument in his lap, as his right hand struck the strings and his left hand darted spiderlike in intricate patterns across the fretboard.

Sokda was mesmerized, but with considerable effort he broke his attention. He looked about the congregation. He saw the Vietnamese family in its accustomed place, as were the spinster in the blue flowered dress and her sad-faced niece, the man with the crutches and the fop with the drooping bow tie. He drew comfort from their unerring presence every Sunday, a warmth that was as much a part of the church as its canticles and spires. Today, he noticed dreamily, there was a new face, a woman's, broad and commanding. She wore a chalk-white blouse buttoned closely at the throat, her lips set in a faint incandescent smile. He stared at her, wondering vaguely if she was returning his look. At that moment, the priest, having completed Communion, lifted the chalice from the altar cloth and raised it to his lips, draining the final drops of consecrated blood. The chalice glinted in the warm light, casting a sudden nimbus over the woman's head. A carnal halo, wondered Skoda, a fantastic imprimatur emblazoned above the altar of God? It danced lightly about her head while the priest held the chalice aloft, then shattered into a thousand dying embers as he brought the chalice down. Skoda felt a warm stirring. The intimation of something lost or never won?

He turned away, reflecting on the music again. The lutenist had moved into a more sprightly galliard now, his hands whirring over the strings like the wings of a hummingbird, as the piece gathered momentum. The notes built to a fragile crescendo, lingering at its peak, then crashed to a final triumphant major chord. Silence followed. Skoda watched as the lutenist leaned back and rested his hands on the instrument. The man looked indifferently toward the priest, waiting for the next cue in the theater of the Mass. Skoda, sitting only a few feet away, studied the lutenist's delicate, powerful hands, now that they were at rest. The fingers of his left hand still clung to the fretboard of the instrument. His right hand was draped over the soundbox, the fingers tapering down to elongated curved nails. At first, Skoda's stare was unfocused. Yet he felt a vague tugging at his senses, a remote urgency. Then sudden recognition erupted. His eyes zoomed in on the musician's hands. Yes, the fingernails. On the right hand. They were long, grotesquely long. The curved gouges on Frank Kadinsky's throat flashed before him. Skoda glanced quickly at the lutenist's other hand. The nails were short, cut back almost to the quick.

"My God," Skoda muttered under his breath. He rose from his seat before the recessional hymn and fled from the church.

23

"Mag, Mag!" It was Skoda's voice on the telephone, tight with joyous alarm. "You're not going to believe this. You won't believe what I just saw."

"Slow down, Nestor," said Magnus Johnson.

"I tried calling Hudlow. He's not at home. We got to get together. I got a terrific new lead. Maybe a break."

"Well, go on."

"I was just at Mass over here in Arlington. You know, the folk Mass I go to? There's this guy that plays a lute in the group. You've seen a lute?"

"Yeah, sort of a second cousin of the guitar?"

"Right. Well, this guy plays it almost every Sunday. I was sitting there very close to him today. When he finished playing, his hands stopped moving, and I noticed he had these incredible fingernails on his right hand and hardly any on his left. Like on Kadinsky's neck. Got it?"

There was a pause. "Nestor, you saying the way this guy's nails were cut might have something to do with playing the lute?"

"Well, I don't know," said Skoda. "I'm just saying it's the same configuration the M.E. found on Kadinsky."

"Didn't you talk to the guy when you were there?"

"Never crossed my mind. I ran out of the place, I was so jacked up."

"Cool-headed Nestor. We'll probably never find him on a Sunday afternoon." Johnson paused. "So, you're thinking maybe Kadinsky's man is some kind of lute or guitar player," he said slowly. "Do you have any idea how many lute and guitar players there are in Washington?"

"Hundreds? Thousands? I don't know, Mag. That's beside the point. You yourself said the guy is probably one of the other tenants right there in the building. We're not talking about hundreds or thousands. We're talking about eight people."

"We've got to go back and see those people again."

"Sooner than later."

"Well, wait a minute. What's the rush? The situation's the same, whether you know about lute players or not. The people at Seventeen sixteen don't know you went to Mass and had this sudden revelation. Today's Sunday. Everything's shut down. But tomorrow first thing, we should go to a stringed instrument dealer or teacher and test your theory. See if what you saw is what you think."

"You're too thorough, Mag. I say lock 'em all up now and swallow the key."

"And the second thing is let's get the benefit of Hudlow's expertise. Didn't you know he's an authority on geekey lute players with lopsided fingernails?"

"All right, I'll wait. But if any of those tenants skip tonight, just remember, Mag, it happened while you were asleep."

"I'll live with it." Johnson hung up. He leaned back and looked out through his kitchen to the garden. The drooping columbines shimmered in the growing heat. Slowly, he walked through the kitchen and onto the back porch where he sat down. That was a snotty thing to say to Nestor just now about Hudlow, he thought. Would it ever change? Johnson did not know. Yes, there had been a few feeble moments these last days, like a winter sun struggling through an ashen sky. But he had seen the face of Dewey Hudlow on too many people in his life, the pale unfinished lines of jaw and eye, the curl of the lip lingering tentatively between suspicion and contempt. It came to him again, faint and illusory: Driving with his father, heading home at night after a day in Orangeburg, when the pickup ran out of gasoline. They were ten miles from home. Get the gas can, said his father. He fetched it from the back of the truck, and the two of them walked down the darkened road. They saw a light in a house. As they drew near, the two stopped for a moment, and the boy saw his father take a deep breath. Then they walked up the wooden steps of the front porch and knocked gently on the door in the darkness. There was the heavy shuffling of boots and the door opened. The dim light from within showed the lean freckled face of a man in overalls. Yessir, he said, what's the trouble? Out of gas, his father said. Could we siphon a gallon or two to get us home? The man looked at the two for a moment. Step around to the back, he said, and he disappeared into the house. The boy and the father stepped off the porch and felt their way through the tall grass. The evening dew wet the boy's legs through his trousers. Always go to the back door, remember that, his grandmother had scolded him many a time. They reached the rear of the house. The freckled-face man was already there and began leading them to a nearby barn. There, a hand-crank gasoline pump stood like an ancient sentinel in the gloom. The man raised its handle and slowly began pumping. The boy's father pointed the nozzle into the fuel can. The boy could hear the gentle splash of the fuel falling into the can. Its fragrance surrounded him. You folks from nearby? the man asked. Yessir, said the father, other side of Aimesbury, about ten miles. Well, said the man, this should get you there. He stopped pumping and the three of them walked back toward the road. The man turned to the father. My wife's sick inside, he said. Otherwise you could've come through the house. Grass around here ain't been cut in a while. Sorry, hope you didn't get too wet. Can I pay you? the father asked. No indeedy, said the man. Next time I'm in Aimesbury, I'm sure to run out of gas. He laughed lightly. Maybe I'll come calling on you. Good night. He disappeared into the darkness.

Johnson leaned back against the porch and looked at the elm trees fringing his garden and beyond them the massive sycamores. A thousand times he had thought of the freckled-faced man on the dark South Carolina road. A decent man with the trust of a child about him. There had been no exception, no hesitancy in his charity. All of Magnus Johnson's assumptions had been shattered in that one brief encounter. Yet he knew it could never wipe away the stain, the stain of a hundred years soaked in the dark evening memories of his grandmother and his father and now himself. Even if the encounter were to recur again and again, he knew in his heart that he would always take a breath first, like his father, before climbing the wooden steps and hold the gas can trembling in his uncertain hand. He would always wonder why he was asked to walk through the tall wet grass.

24

The Reverend Quovadis Logan brought the brush down in a neat curving stroke, completing the final parenthesis on the sign. If ever I have it to do again, she thought, it'll be shorter. Fifth Rising New Day in the Morning Church (Independent). Not very practical, but sort of . . . toney? Yeah. She was not unhappy.

The woman retreated into the church, her brown and white robes grazing the oaken pews, and looked back through the narrow entrance onto Ninth Street. Its absurd Romanesque arch framed the hot sunny street. An occasional car or pedestrian broke the symmetry of the archway, a quick dark intrusion in the brilliant light. Her parishioners had gone for the day, and she could relax now, exhausted from the exhortations to faith and giving. The faith was strong, but the giving small: $47.34.

A boy of eight or nine sauntered into the church from the street. "Mama," he said softly and came to her side. His eyes, set in his broad dun-colored face, looked to his mother. "What can I do, Mama? Teepo and them went down Southeast."

"Honey, it's plenty other boys on the street. Go on out."

His cheeks and nostrils were suffused with the same faint ruddy glow as his mother's. She ran her fingers through his matted hair. "Go on, now, Thomas. Give Mama a rest."

He lingered, and she did not push him away. He looked abstractedly at the pulpit and the plain wooden walls of the church. She sank into a pew, the boy resting against her side.

She dozed. The sounds of the street receded, and the warm afternoon embraced her. A faint redolence of chicory and late wisteria hung in the air, and she saw a wide dusty road, two ruts with a ridge of pale green down the middle. Three girls dressed in white Sunday pinafores teetered along the ruts, holding hands. Bright red ribbons in their hair danced in the sun. Then she saw her father, dressed in his thick black wool suit, beckoning sternly to the three of them. They ran to him. Rivulets of sweat ran down his heavy face and neck, soaking into his starchy white collar. He picked up the girls one at a time and placed them in the back of the truck. His hands under her arms made her feel safe. As he picked her up, her face brushed his, and his skin smelled of pitch and wood fire. He had split a rack of pine slabs that morning, his big hands wrapped round the ax, coming down in steady blows to the ground. The engine of the truck coughed to life. It sputtered momentarily, then settled down into a smooth purr. Her father was good with trucks. Could take a pickup left in the ditch and with parts borrowed here and there put new life into it. Once he built his own sawmill. Bought a huge circular blade with teeth an inch long down Shreveport, carried it home and hooked it up to the engine and the long leather belts of the mill. Worked just fine, and he was making a pretty good go of it, till one day Mr. Hebert came around in his shiny gray car and rolled the window down with the automatic push button and said her father couldn't cut on his land anymore and canceled the lease. And just before they moved away, Mr. Hebert's boy Joe came to the house and called her down to the sawmill where they walked out past the new grove of pine saplings and he made her pull her panties down.

Quovadis Logan awoke with a start. The boy had gone, and she sat in the church alone. She shook her head and turned toward the front entrance. In the archway stood Dewey Hudlow, his square silhouette blocking much of the sunlight.

"Should I have knocked first?" he asked.

An initial wave of revulsion swept over the woman, but it receded, and she found, oddly, she was almost glad to see the man. "No, Hud, come on in."

Hudlow entered the church. The boards of the old building creaked under his weight. He came up to her pew and sat down.

"Been a week," he said.

"Yeah, you run off a whole week this time."

"Busy."

"Don't worry, Hud. I ain't going get on you about Fronie this time. That's already done."

"Seen Thomas outside on the street."

"Ain't he growing?"

"Like a alligator in a bathtub. How's he doing in school?"

"School out, Hud. But his report card this spring was good."

"He had a tear in his britches. Need some clothes for the summer?"

"It would help."

Hudlow pulled a wallet from his hip pocket. He looked through it carefully and pulled out two $20 bills. "Thanks, Hud," she said.

Hudlow stretched his arms out along the back of the pew and surveyed the dim ceiling of the church.

"How'd you do today?" he asked.

"Less than fifty dollars."

"Pays the rent, don't it?"

"Rent's easy. It's the preaching I'm running out of."

"Just do retreads."

"I'm already doing retreads on retreads."

"Bet you good at it."

She nodded. "You working that Dupont Circle thing, the one with the white boy?"

"Yessir, ma'am."

"I seen it on TV. He was a politician, wasn't he?"

"I don't know if he was a politician. He worked for Congress."

"That's a politician."

"You ain't heard nothing, Vadis?"

"What, about that case?"

"Yeah. Dope connection or maybe queers?"

"Come on, Hud, you on the wrong side of town."

"I know, I know." Hudlow paused. "But what about that cousin of yours, Sardrita? Don't she clean a lot of them houses up around the Fruit Loop and Kalorama? Maybe she heard something."

"What would they say around her?"

"Most anything, Vadis. Them people, they set around and talk like the cleaning lady wasn't even there half the time. I just thought she might've heard something."

"She hasn't told me if she heard anything, and if she did, she would have told me. Her mouth don't ever stop."

"Just thought I would try."

"Why you asking about niggers waiting on white people?"

"They see and hear a lot. They might steal the silver and the missus' fur coat, but they see the stains on the sheets. They see the letters laying on the dresser and the checkbook in the hall. They like ghosts floating through the house."

"What's pushing you? I never seen you bark so much up such a wrong tree."

"Boss man wants an arrest, Vadis."

"They always want that."

"Homicide chief getting pressure from the CID chief, which he's getting it from one of the assistant chiefs of the whole damn department, and he's getting it from this bitch that runs the citizens association up there. And me, I'm at the bottom of the heap. Me and ol' Mag Johnson."

"Ain't they always pushing you?"

"This one's different. We ain't hardly moved from square one since the thing opened a week and a half ago. It's making the Homicide chief look bad, and he's peeing in his britches. Wants a promotion or retire or something."

"So let him pee."

"It's a Triple A case, Vadis. Congress and maybe queers and all. The media's took out after it and won't turn loose. It's the kind of situation where we could rush into a bad arrest. Putting the pressure on, see, and the chief he's got me and Mag on the same case. You know Mag. Whenever we together, it's demolition derby time."

"Mag still got his head in the clouds?"

"Including his ass."

Hudlow tapped the back of the pew idly with his fingers. The preacher turned toward him. She touched his sleeve and said with unusual softness, "Take the afternoon off, Hud. With me. It's the sabbath."

Hudlow ignored her and looked up at the ceiling. Her hand slipped down his side and into his crotch. He stirred for a moment and turned to embrace her, then stopped abruptly and shook his head.

"Muddy waters?" she said.

"Got to run," said Hudlow.

25

"Dadlem," proclaimed Captain Stohlbach. "A real live guitar-picking asphyxiator. What's the other thing called, Mag?"

"A lute, Chief. L-U-T-E. Looks like a guitar, except its neck is kind of bent."

"Lucky thing one of us goes to church once in a while," said Dewey Hudlow, bowing toward Skoda and crossing himself clumsily.

There was an air of muted triumph in the office. Skoda paced the floor like an expectant father. Johnson was busily thumbing through the yellow pages of the telephone directory.

"This is all very good," he said, "but we've got to test the theory." His hand stopped at mid-page in the telephone book. "Here's one. Michaelson's Guitar Shop, 'specializing in repairing and restoring classical guitars and ancient stringed instruments.' It's on Nineteenth Street between L and M."

The three detectives left the office and piled into the Plymouth. Minutes later, they reached Nineteenth Street and parked. They approached the guitar shop, its display window hung with dusty instruments. Inside, an elderly man wearing a velvet waistcoat with no jacket looked up from his work and eyed the three visitors. He was alone.

"Morning," said Magnus Johnson. "I'm Detective Johnson from the Metropolitan Police. This is Detective Hudlow and

Detective Skoda." Johnson displayed his ID case. "You Mr. Michaelson?"

"Yes," said the man guardedly.

"Good," said Johnson. "We thought you might be able to help us with a couple of technical questions."

The man's graying face took on a look of formal alarm. "What is it?" he asked with a faint accent.

"Well," said Johnson, "what we wanted to know is when somebody plays the guitar or one of these other stringed instruments, do they have to cut their fingernails in any particular way to help them play?"

A silence followed that seemed to last for minutes. The alarm on the man's face changed to mystification. He stared down at the counter in front of him, avoiding their glances. They waited. Finally, the man raised his head. He said:

"Yes. You are right. Most players trim their nails, the right hand one way, the left another."

The detectives looked with relief at each other.

"Good," said Johnson, "but could we bother you to tell us exactly how they do it."

The man relaxed his rigid stance. "Yes. In general, players of the classical guitar and the lute keep the nails of the left hand as short as possible. That is the hand that plays the fretboard. A nail extending beyond the end of the finger tends to dig into the fretboard and interferes with placement of the finger pad on the string. In contrast, the fingernails of the right hand, especially on the first three fingers, are kept long, extending beyond the ends of the fingers. The right hand is the hand that plucks the strings over the soundbox. The long fingernails allow the player to pluck the strings in a variety of ways, to obtain a range of tone qualities."

Another silence followed. "Is this true for both the guitar and the lute?" Johnson asked.

"Yes, generally," said the man. "Many performers play both instruments."

"Do you play either of them?" Johnson asked.

“Yes,” said the man, a faint breath of pride in his voice. He relaxed a little more. “I play the guitar.”

Johnson hesitated a moment. Then he asked: “Do you mind if we look at your fingers?”

A tremor of surprise crossed the man’s face. He placed his hands on the counter, palms down. The detectives bent over. His fingers were surprisingly short and swollen at the knuckles. Like sausages, thought Johnson. But there they were: the nails of the left hand cut short, the nails of the right extended beyond the fingertips. The detectives stared at the hands as if hypnotized.

“Is this true only of classical performers?” asked Johnson at length. “What about people who play other stuff, you know, blue grass, rock ’n’ roll?”

The man stiffened again slightly. “I cannot speak for them,” he said, “although I suspect that the nuances of the plucked string are largely lost on those particular forms of music.”

“Are any other instruments played with long fingernails on the right hand,” asked Johnson, “like the violin or harp?”

“No,” said the man. “Basically, the only categories are guitars and lutes.”

The detectives looked at each other again. The interview was finished.

“Hot damn,” whooped Nestor Skoda moments later, skipping down the sidewalk like a schoolboy. “We’re going to lock us up a lute player tonight.”

26

The evening air was just beginning to cool when the Plymouth stopped at L'Enfant Court. The three men tumbled out of the car and walked toward 1716.

"All these bozos ought to be home now," said Hudlow. "Even Stanton, the GPO guy. He don't go to work till eleven."

Johnson rang the bell. Quaver emerged from the back of the lobby and tottered toward the detectives. He gave an imbecilic wave and opened the door.

As they entered, they stood awkwardly for a moment around the little man. "We're not actually going to ask him if he plays the lute or something, are we?" muttered Johnson.

"Hell, he don't know Varsol from mother's milk," said Hudlow, "let alone a lute from a fingernail." They brushed by Quaver and headed down the long hallway. Hudlow and Skoda began climbing the curved stairway to the upper floors, and Johnson knocked at 1-B, the apartment of Florian Boldt and the late Frank Kadinsky.

"Yes?" came the clear voice of Florian Boldt.

"Detective Johnson from the Metropolitan Police, Mr. Boldt," said Johnson.

He heard the security chain slide back. The door opened. Boldt stood in the entrance, shoeless and in his shirtsleeves, holding a newspaper.

"Sorry to bother you again," said Johnson.

"That's quite all right. What can I help you with?"

"How was Chicago? The family all right there?"

"Bearing up as best they can. Mrs. Kadinsky is still barely able to speak. They lost another son, you know, Frank's only brother, about ten years ago."

"Yeah, the father told us. An accident or something?"

"I don't really know. Frank never talked much about it. His family life was very private."

The detective gave Boldt a quizzical look. He was about to press further but realized from Boldt's expressionless face that he was at an impasse. Something to pursue later, he thought.

"Sorry about the raccoon business last week." Johnson grinned.

"Oh, that. Don't apologize," said Boldt, brightening. "That was really my fault. I left the kitchen window open. I was in a rush to catch the plane to Chicago. The sink was full of dishes. We do have raccoons, you know, even in this part of the city. The building management has warned us about them."

"I hope we didn't break anything when we came in."

"Heavens no. Everything was perfectly in place when I got back. Including the dirty dishes." Boldt smiled modestly at his small humor.

There was a pause. "Mr. Boldt, as I said, I'm sorry to have to bother you again. Something new has come up and that's why I'm here."

"What is it?"

"Well, this may seem a little silly. But actually it isn't. So please bear with me. Do you happen to play any musical instruments?"

"Like what?"

"I'm asking you."

Boldt stiffened slightly. "No," he said.

"Are you familiar with the classical guitar or lute?" Johnson asked. He watched Boldt for reaction. A flash of uncertainty across the man's face quickly dissipated.

"Guitar or, what was the other thing?" Boldt asked at length.

"Lute, sir. It's kind of like a guitar."

"No," Boldt said slowly. "I don't really play any kind of instrument. I'm terribly unmusical. Although as a child I was pretty good on the comb and paper." He smiled again modestly.

"Do you know anyone who plays the guitar or lute?"

"No, not really."

"Did Mr. Kadinsky have any friends who owned or played these instruments?"

"Not to my knowledge."

"Anyone possibly in this building?"

"No, I don't think so." Boldt's eyes filled with puzzlement. They reminded Johnson of the old man at the guitar shop.

"Ever heard such an instrument being played around here or seen one in one of the apartments?"

"No. We seldom go into each other's apartments."

"Yes, but you've attended some of the building security meetings in other apartments, haven't you?"

"Yes, you're quite right. But only two or three."

"Which ones?"

"Well, I know I was in Mr. Goon's apartment once on the third floor. I remember it well. He served us all some kind of frightful goat's curd."

"See any stringed instruments there?"

"No."

"Any other apartments?"

"Yes, one other that I remember. The Fingers. The twin brothers in Two-A. We met there once. But there was nothing there. At least not in my sight."

"Have you been in any other apartment for any other reason?"

Boldt gave the detective an odd look. "Well, not really. You mean to borrow a cup of sugar or something like that?"

"Any reason."

"No, not that I recall."

Johnson sighed heavily. "Do you mind if I ask you one more question?"

"Please go ahead. I'm fascinated."

"Would you hold out your hands, palms down, so I can see your fingers?"

New furrows formed on Boldt's forehead. "Of course," he murmured, holding his hands out and looking at the detective. Johnson peered at the fingers. They were slender tapers radiating from pale veinless hands. The knuckles were barely discernible on the smooth surface of the fingers. At the ends, faint pink nails had been rounded with care, manicured in neatly curved lines well back from the fingertips on both hands.

Johnson's face fell slightly. "Thank you," he said, as he prepared to leave.

"Well," said Boldt, "I certainly would like to know what this is all about someday. Do you suppose you could tell me?"

"Someday, I hope," said Johnson. "I know it's a little off the wall right now. Please bear with us."

Boldt closed the door. Johnson heard the security chain sliding back into place as he headed across the hall to apartment 1-A. The name Ambrose Fairlyte appeared in neat block letters on the door. Johnson rang the bell.

"Who is it?" came an immediate response.

"Metropolitan Police," said Johnson, trying to sound as official as possible. Again he heard the scraping of a security chain, and the door opened. A large man with a tangle of light brown hair stood at the entrance. His frame, though large, sloped to narrow shoulders from his waist. His face was smooth and had an almost adolescent softness about it. Johnson remembered now: the health food store owner that Hudlow had tangled with more than a week ago. Hud was right: soft and squishy.

"Evening. I'm Detective Johnson, Metropolitan Police. You Ambrose Fairlyte?"

"Yes, I am."

"I believe you met one of my partners, Detective Hudlow, last week in regard to Franklin Kadinsky."

"There was another detective here last week. I don't remember his name," said Fairlyte.

"Sort of big fellow," said Johnson, "with a barnyard accent?"

"That's him," said Fairlyte. "We didn't exactly hit it off."

"Oh, that's just old Hud," said Johnson lightly. "He's mostly wind and bluster. Don't mind him."

"It's kind of hard to ignore a noisy ignoramus at your doorstep. Sorry, he's probably one of your best friends."

"Don't worry. You ought to hear the names we call him in the office."

"What can I do for you this time?"

"I apologize for having to bother you again," said Johnson, reconstructing his preamble, "but I'm here about a new thing that came up."

"New thing?"

"Yes, sir. It may seem a little silly. But actually it isn't. So I ask you to bear with me."

"Please go ahead."

"I know you're in the natural food business. But I was wondering if by any chance you might also do music, you know, play any musical instruments?"

"Why, yes, I do," said Fairlyte. "Play and teach, on the side. What did you have in mind?"

"Tell me what you do."

Fairlyte's voice tightened slightly. "Well, I specialize in ancient instruments. Rebec, psaltery, other stringed instruments, bowed or plucked."

"How about the lute or classical guitar?"

"As a matter of fact, I do," said Fairlyte again, a look of amazement on his face. "How did you know that? I play baroque period lute and guitar transcriptions."

A sudden chill shot through Johnson's stomach. My God, a hit. He looked in stunned disbelief at Fairlyte. The man with the tangled brown hair peered back at him, equally stunned.

Pulling himself together, Johnson said, "Well, tell me about it a little. Do you play professionally or what?" He studied Fairlyte's smooth round face.

"I play with small groups," said Fairlyte. "You know, trios, and quartets, chamber stuff. Sometimes with original instruments. That's when I play the lute. It's a much older instrument than the guitar. Do you know the baroque period?"

"No, I, uh, no, I don't. What else do you do?"

"Teach. I have several students. I teach in the afternoon when I've finished at the food store."

"Here in the apartment?"

"No, in a studio. Would you like to see one of my instruments?"

"Oh, do you mind?" said Johnson, his head spinning.

Fairlyte led the detective into the apartment. The living room was sparsely furnished and strewn with books and sheet music. He kneeled down and pulled a large oblong case from under a sofa.

"I have several guitars," he said, "but this is my favorite." He opened the case and from it took the instrument. He held its hourglass soundbox in his hands. Its waxed top glistened in the light.

"Play something," said Johnson.

Fairlyte sat down. He placed the narrow waist of the soundbox across his left thigh and leaned over the instrument. His left hand moved to the fretted neck, while the fingers of his right hand struck a few random strings over the soundbox. He tuned one of the strings briefly, then positioned himself more securely on the sofa and began playing a series of arpeggios. Delicate notes filled the room. His hands moved confidently over the instrument. The arpeggios increased in speed and shifted into new keys, repeating the sequence but at an ever ascending pitch. Then the pace slowed; the notes descended and came to a halt. Fairlyte rested his hands across the instrument and looked up expectantly at Johnson, like a dog waiting for a biscuit. Johnson's eyes leaped to the hands. Just like Michaelson's at the music shop: the nails of the left hand were short, those of the right hand long.

Johnson, despite his years of experience, barely suppressed a yelp. He half expected Fairlyte to bolt from the room. The musician appeared mystified, a look of dumb innocence on his face. After all, he had just been asked, out of the clear blue, by a police officer, to perform on a musical instrument. Not your everyday occurrence. On the other hand, thought Johnson, perhaps he was engaging in a much tougher game than his soft exterior suggested, an intricate gambit of high theater, of endurance and nerve with a heavy wager on Johnson's naïveté. Johnson pictured the three crescent-moon cuts on Frank Kadinsky's frozen neck at the morgue. Then he looked at Fairlyte's right hand again dangling just inches away in front of him. It was too much to assign to coincidence.

He turned to Fairlyte. "Would you excuse me a moment? I think my partners may be waiting out in the lobby."

"Certainly," said Fairlyte. He accompanied Johnson to the apartment entrance and closed the door gently behind him as Johnson stepped into the hallway.

The detective felt helplessly exhilarated, a rush he had not known in years: the quarry at bay. Fairlyte was, in effect, trapped in his apartment, but Hudlow and Skoda were still upstairs interviewing. Johnson hesitated to leave Fairlyte's apartment untended, yet he needed his partners desperately. Should he go upstairs and call them? He decided to wait. After some minutes, he heard the tread of Hudlow coming down the wooden staircase.

"Hud, Hud, come here!" Johnson called in a hoarse whisper. The two men met in the hall. "You're not going to believe this. I think I got a hit. Your buddy, Ambrose Fairlyte, in One-A. He's a music teacher, lute and guitar. Got the long nails on the right hand and everything. Textbook."

"You sure?" asked Hudlow. "He's the health food freak."

"Yeah, but he teaches on the side. He showed me one of his instruments. Played it for me."

"Well, he don't seem too upset about you blowing in on him," said Hudlow, glancing at Fairlyte's apartment door.

“I know, I know. But maybe he’s just trying to cool the situation out. You find anything upstairs?”

“No. A complete blank.”

The two men turned and saw Skoda descending the curved stairs. As he approached, Skoda shrugged and turned his hands up in failure. “Zip,” he said.

“Nothing for me, either,” said Hudlow. “But listen to what Mag got.”

Johnson pointed toward apartment 1-A and whispered, “Fairlyte. Ambrose Fairlyte. He’s in there now. Not only that. He’s got a guitar and a bunch of fingernails on his right hand that won’t quit. So help me God.”

Skoda’s eyes widened. “You kidding. Fairlyte, the health food guy?”

“Scout’s honor,” whispered Johnson. “He showed me the instrument. I can’t figure out if he knows we’re onto him or not.”

“Big bad lute fruit,” mused Hudlow. There was a prolonged pause. Then Hudlow spoke again. “Well, do we question him here or downtown?”

“I say here.” It was Magnus Johnson.

“Downtown might be better,” said Hudlow. “Home field advantage.”

“What’s wrong with right here, right now?”

“Sucker might break bad.”

“You can’t force him downtown. It’s not an arrest.”

“Muscle him a little.”

“What kind of talk is that?”

“We need that boy, bad.”

“Why are you so hot for him now?” said Johnson, looking pointedly at Hudlow. “I thought he was the guy you said didn’t know anything about Kadinsky.”

“Bitch in heat got a right to change her mind.”

“We don’t even have a motive in this thing, Hud. What kind of questions you going to ask him?”

“Leave it to Beaver,” said Hudlow, jabbing a finger at his own chest. “Ask him downtown. Real polite. But let me work him first when we get there. He'll pop off. I know these guys. He'll call in the Pope and Amnesty International and have us in contempt of Congress in five minutes for messing up his evening."

"Then what?" asked Johnson.

"Then you come in. Game-play him. You know: the nice daddy after I knock over his tricycle. He'll tumble. I've seen it happen a hundred times."

"Awful risky." Johnson stared at Hudlow. "Kind of close work. You and I haven't exactly—"

"I'll take a flier on it."

"Well," said Johnson, "keep it short. And easy with the matches under the fingernails."

"I'm a peaceable man."

Johnson took a deep breath and stepped toward Ambrose Fairlyte's apartment.

27

Fairlyte walked blinking into Homicide. It was a world of vivid gray fluorescence. A faint hissing sound filled the air. A handful of men in shirtsleeves sat at desks.

"Got a cash customer," announced Hudlow. "Come on back this way, Mr. Fairlyte." Hudlow led Fairlyte past several desks to a small windowless room, one of several interrogation cubicles in the rear of the office. Fairlyte stepped into the room. Hudlow followed, closing the door behind him. Johnson and Skoda stationed themselves outside. The room contained two metal frame chairs and a large metal desk. On its top sat a battered typewriter, a yellow legal pad and a small stack of police department forms. A length of chain with a single handcuff dangled from one side of the desk. The walls of the cubicle were decorated in faded green acoustical tile.

Hudlow sat down heavily in one of the chairs and motioned Fairlyte to the other.

"Okay, Ambrose," said Hudlow cheerily, "the way this is going to work is we want you to help us out a little with ol' Frank Kadinsky."

"How can I possibly do that?"

"Like tell us how much you knew him."

"I've told you several times already I never knew him at all, at least not personally."

"But you knew him a little."

"Of course, a little."

"How much is a little?"

"Damned little."

"Come on, Ambrose, you can let on with me."

"There's nothing to let on."

"You mean all these years snuggled up there at the Fruit Loop—"

"Beg pardon?"

"Dupont Circle, home of the eastern fruit fly."

"Oh, for God's sake, don't start that business again. I'm no . . . fruit."

"Take it easy; we're not asking for a confession."

"I'm not going to take it easy. And you *are* asking for a confession. You're outrageous."

"Sure you didn't get a little fired up the other morning when Frank wouldn't let you cuddle up with him?"

"You're crazy. You're trying to set me up. You're trying to put words in my mouth. You're trying—"

"Nice boy like you don't like a little pushing and shoving? 'Fraid your sailor suit might get messed up?"

"Look here," said Fairlyte, turning around to the closed door. "Do I have to put up with this insulting business?" He stood up and threw the door open. Johnson and Skoda, standing just outside, stared at him passively.

"I can't believe this is actually happening," Fairlyte sputtered. "Right here in the capital of the United States."

Johnson and Skoda continued to look at him in silence.

Fairlyte was fuming. "I'm sorry. I refuse to cooperate. Why should I put up with this . . . this creature and his insults and warped presumptions about other people's sex lives?"

"Okay, okay," said Johnson finally, stepping into the room. "That will do." He turned to Hudlow. "Would you mind stepping outside a moment?" Hudlow lumbered from the cubicle, leaving the door open. Johnson took his place behind the metal desk.

"Kafkaesque," muttered Fairlyte, "absolutely Kafkaesque."

"Whatever it is," said Johnson, "maybe we can smooth things down a bit now. Perhaps Detective Hudlow is a little heavy-handed. We apologize."

"He's got the mentality of a wrecking ball," said Fairlyte. Anger still filled his face.

"Okay, okay, I know how you feel. Look, how 'bout a cup of coffee? On the house."

"No, thank you."

"Smoke?"

"No."

"Soothed down a little now?"

Fairlyte shrugged.

"Now," said Johnson, signaling Hudlow and Johnson to re-enter the room, "I think I should tell you first, Mr. Fairlyte, that we are going to ask you some specific questions in regard to Franklin Kadinsky. But before we do that, this is probably a good point to tell you that we would like to give you a formal warning, which we will give to you in writing as well as orally, advising you—"

"I don't need your warning," blurted Fairlyte, "your silly Miranda warning. I know all about that. I've got nothing to hide."

"Even so, Mr. Fairlyte," Johnson continued, "we would like you to review the language—"

"The Miranda warning," Fairlyte snapped, "was designed to protect the poor and ignorant from underhanded police tactics. I am neither poor nor ignorant."

"Will you at least sign the form saying you have reviewed the warning language, Mr. Fairlyte?"

"Oh, all right." He scribbled his signature on the paper Johnson had placed in front of him.

"Now I think we can get down to basics," said Johnson. "We have in this office a copy of the D.C. Medical Examiner's report and supplementary toxicology and addendum, which give the findings in the death by manual strangulation of Mr. Kadinsky. In the addendum, the medical examiner notes three small curved lacerations in the skin on Mr. Kadinsky's right neck adjacent to contusions created by the pressure points of the fingertips of the hand that administered the strangulation. But there are no corresponding lacerations adjacent to the contusions on the left side of the neck, only the dull round impressions of the fingertips. Do you follow me?"

"Yes, go ahead."

"The medical examiner says this evidence is consistent with a person who has elongated nails on the fingers of the right hand and close-cut nails on the fingers of the left hand. Do you still follow me?"

"Why, yes," said Fairlyte, the earlier anger in his face now waning. In its place, lines of disbelief were beginning to form.

"In our inquiry," continued Johnson, "we have determined that this particular pattern of fingernails is unique to people who play classical stringed instruments, such as the lute or guitar. Further, when we canvassed your apartment building tonight, we determined that you are the only tenant who fits that category. Do you have anything to say about that, Mr. Fairlyte?"

An immense silence followed. The three detectives leaned forward. Fairlyte looked down at the floor, his hands dangling helplessly between his knees. His mouth began to move, as though he were trying to speak, but no words issued. He glanced up at the three detectives, then dropped his head again. "Oh, Jesus," he muttered under his breath.

Johnson stood up. "That's all right, Mr. Fairlyte," he said. "Everything's okay. Can we get you that cup of coffee now?"

Fairlyte shook his head.

"Perhaps you'd like to make a formal statement now. Nestor, get the man some coffee. Hud, have Mr. Fairlyte step next door where we can videotape—"

"No!" shouted Fairlyte suddenly. "No, no, no, goddamn it!" He stood up, a raging clumsy bull. Hudlow grabbed his arms and shoved him back down into his seat. "Sit down, Yogurt Breath."

"Let go of me, you fat ignoramus," Fairlyte bellowed at Hudlow.

The detective's eyes narrowed. "What'd you call me, neighbor?" He leaned toward Fairlyte. Johnson quickly interceded, placing a hand on Hudlow's huge arm.

"I don't get paid for being called no ignoramus," Hudlow snorted.

"And I don't get paid for being called a fruit and a fire fly and all these other reverse macho names you and your circle of pathetic friends have committed to memory," said Fairlyte. He spat angrily on the floor.

"Get hold of yourself, Fairlyte," snapped Johnson.

"Ooh, Lordy," said Hudlow with a short whistle. "Captain Stohlbach going to be pissed in the morning. He don't like faggot spit on his office floor—"

Fairlyte lunged at Hudlow and struck him hard across the face. Hudlow was momentarily stunned. Then with a primitive growl he rammed back, his head down, grabbing Fairlyte by his narrow shoulders and throwing him against the metal desk. Johnson and Skoda leaped toward the two men, trying to pull them apart. Other detectives rushed from their desks and crammed into the tiny room.

"Stop it, stop it!" shouted Skoda. The two men crashed to the floor. Hudlow's service revolver slipped from his waist band and clattered onto the floor. Blood was pouring from his ear. A detective kicked the revolver away as the two men rolled and thrashed. They embraced on the floor, making short brutish grunts, while the other detectives looked on helplessly. With a gargantuan heave, Hudlow suddenly turned Fairlyte over and slammed him to the floor. He raised his fist, a massive bloodied maul, and held it over Fairlyte's shuddering face. In the next instant Magnus Johnson vaulted to Hudlow's side and grabbed his upheld wrist.

"Hud!" called Johnson with low guttural certitude. "Don't! You've already pulled him down. He's in the sewer. He's down here with us now. He doesn't need any more." Johnson's arm was shaking as it held Hudlow's defiant fist. Hudlow stared into Johnson's eyes. In the depths a faint light flickered, signaling gently. It held Hudlow motionless. He broke the gaze and looked down at Fairlyte's frozen face, then turned back to Magnus Johnson. The moment of decision had passed. The rigidity began to recede from Hudlow's upraised arm. The fingers of his clenched fist slowly opened, and he lowered his arm.

Johnson helped the two men up, pushing them away from each other. They gasped for breath.

"You all right, Hud?" said Johnson, examining his ear.

"Nothing a Purple Heart won't take care of."

"How about you, sir?" said Johnson to Fairlyte.

"I'm all right, I guess," he answered, his face crimson and smeared with sweat.

"You know that was assault on a po-leece officer," blurted Hudlow. "Goddamn APO. That could get you fifteen years, mister."

Fairlyte glared at Hudlow but did not answer.

"Enough!" snapped Johnson. He turned to Skoda. "Could you take Mr. Fairlyte out to the men's room, please, and let him clean up. Hud, you could do with a little cleaning up yourself. Use the john upstairs. Then maybe we can get back on the track."

Skoda escorted Fairlyte from the office. Johnson turned to Hudlow. "Jesus Christ, didn't you overdo it a bit, Hud? You weren't softening him up. You were provoking him."

"Done it before and never had one buck on me."

"I had a feeling it was going to go sour. Fairlyte's tougher than you think."

"Taking up for the fucker again, aren't you, Mag?" Hudlow dabbed at his bloodied ear.

Johnson straightened his tie and started brushing several smears of dirt on his sleeve. "Better clean this joint up a little," he said. He glanced at Hudlow. "Good thing the night commander wasn't here just now."

"Hell with the night commander."

"Your gun. You forgot to lock it up when we came in. You mind sitting out the rest of this thing? We've had enough fireworks."

o

Fairlyte returned minutes later with Skoda. Fresh water was still on his face and a shred of paper towel was caught in his hair. He walked back into the cubicle with Johnson.

"Now," said Johnson, ordering his thoughts, "see that chain with the cuff on the desk there? I'm going to put that on you if there're any more disturbances. Understand, Mr. Fairlyte?"

"Perfectly clear."

"We were talking about whether you might want to make a formal statement."

"Yes, and I was about to say I have no formal statement to make, when we were rudely interrupted by your resident Neanderthal. Look, all I want to do is stop this nightmare, to bring this madness to an end and go home."

"Well, you're not going to stop it that easily."

"How do you suggest I stop it?"

"There's one simple way. Explain away the coincidence of your fingernails and the lacerations on the neck of a man who lived one door away from you."

"That's exactly what it is," said Fairlyte. "An incredible, grotesque coincidence. I can't explain it any other way. And I've told you a thousand times I wasn't even there that morning. I was at my store."

"But you haven't produced any employees or customers who put you there. Isn't that a little too convenient?"

"I can't help it if I can't remember the customers. There are so many, and the different days all sort of run together."

"You know that's not going to work," said Johnson. "Now tell us: didn't you know Frank Kadinsky a little better than you've said?"

"Oh, God, please don't get on that again. Is there some kind of sexuality litmus test I can take to make you happy?"

"This is not a laughing matter," said Johnson. "I asked if you knew Kadinsky better than you've let on. I didn't ask if you were gay. There are other ways to know Frank Kadinsky."

"Like what in your narrow little minds?"

"Like knowing him as a straight. Like fighting over a woman. Like knowing him as a partner in a business that went sour. Like knowing him as a source for political information on Capitol Hill and he crossed you. Like knowing him as a client for dope and he didn't pay you."

"Dope, sex, politics? You guys have been watching too much television."

"Frank Kadinsky was a well-connected individual. Things can get very volatile in the privileged world of Capitol Hill. Maybe it would help for you to keep in mind that if you cooperate, Detective Hudlow might consider dropping the assault charges against you."

"Assault charges? That is outrageous blackmail. It simply will not work with me."

"And of course there is always the press. The reporters have been in here every day asking about Kadinsky. They want details. We can control the press to a certain extent, but a lot depends on—"

"The *press*!" ejaculated Fairlyte. His face suddenly burst with joy. "I just remembered. Gutenberg. Oh, my God, yes. It was Gutenberg that morning."

"What in hell are you talking about?" asked Johnson.

"There was a guy named Gutenberg, Robert Gutenberg, at the store. We went to high school together in New York. It was just happenstance he was in town and came into my store. I'd forgotten it was that day."

"How sure are you?"

"He was at the store early. About eight o'clock. I remember he said he was in a hurry and had to catch a plane out of National by nine or nine-thirty to St. Louis. Hallelujah! Bob Gutenberg, you're my ticket out of here."

o

"Not so fast," said Johnson. "What's the guy's full name?" He pulled out his notebook.

"Robert Gutenberg. G-U-T-E-N-B-E-R-G. Just like the guy that invented movable type."

"Where does he live?"

"He told me he had moved to a small town in southern Illinois. Across the river from St. Louis. What was it? Carterville? No. Carteret. That's it. Carteret. He's a graphics artist and got a job at a school there."

Johnson wrote down the name. "You got his phone number or address?"

"No. But he told me he was the only Gutenberg in the town."

"Did he buy something at your store?"

"As a matter of fact, he did. He bought two tins of brewer's yeast. I remember because he joked about how when we were in high school, he wouldn't have touched the stuff."

"Do you have your own labels on the products you sell at the store?"

"Yes, we do. I can assure you of that."

"Very well," said Johnson. "We'll call this Mr. Gutenberg right now and see what he has to say."

"I just pray he's home," said Fairlyte.

"You stay here with Detective Skoda," Johnson said. "What's the area code out there?"

"God, I don't know," said Fairlyte. "It's the southern end of Illinois."

o

The minutes passed slowly as Fairlyte and Skoda sat in silence. They could hear Johnson's voice at a distance, a low intermittent murmur. A fly swooped over Fairlyte's head. He pawed at it absently, then ignored it. He paged through a Metropolitan Police newsletter Skoda had passed to him. With stilted paramilitary dignity, it announced promotions, transfers and new scout car sector boundaries. An improved communications center was still under construction at headquarters, and Assistant Chief Flynn had just become a grandfather.

The drone of Johnson's voice stopped. He came into the cubicle. Dewey Hudlow was with him.

"Would you mind stepping out, Mr. Fairlyte?" Johnson asked. "Go over to Detective Brown's desk over there, where the detective is in the blue striped shirt. He'll keep you company."

Fairlyte left the room, and Johnson closed the door. "The guy in Illinois checks out. Says he remembers going to the food store. Pretty much the same story as Fairlyte. He's still got the carbon of his air ticket from D.C. to St. Louis, Ozark Airlines, nine-twenty A.M., Thursday, June ninth. He's sending it to me tomorrow, registered mail, along with a notarized statement summarizing our conversation on the phone and one of the labels off the brewer's yeast he bought at Fairlyte's store. He was pretty persuasive."

The three detectives stared at one another. "Shitjimpis," mumbled Hudlow.

"Can't hold him anymore tonight," said Skoda. He turned to Johnson. "What do you think?"

"The plot thins."

28

"Take niggers," said Dewey Hudlow. He belched softly behind his hand, as his eyes roved across the Homicide office. A wad of cotton protruded from one ear. "I been running with them for seventeen years, and I swear I have to laugh sometimes. I have to laugh at these sociologists that come around to the academy and give us the lecture on—what do they call it, Nestor?—'cultural deprivation'—and all this sensitivity shit about working in the ghetto. I call it the jitterbug-handling lecture. That's what it is. These Professor Jerkoffs with their three-piece suits and traveling slide shows telling us ever'body east of Fourteenth Street is culturally disadvantaged, that they suffer from this stuff they call 'deficit models' or something, and the sumbitches hadn't ever seen a real jitterbug up close in their life. I know, they might invite a few in for tea and cookies and maybe drive down U Street on a Saturday night to 'observe' all the deprived folk boogiewumping on the sidewalk, but they ain't never really got down in among them and dealt with them face to face. They ain't never slept with them or shit with them or sat down and drank a little Thunderbird with them. They talk about all these minorities—that's what they call them, isn't it, Nestor?—how they all deprived, and that's why they stand on the corner ten deep with their hands in their pocket, ain't nothing to do. Shit, you name me any corner in this city and I'll show you ever' swinging dick there's doing something, I mean something specific, not just standing around whistling Dixie. Well, maybe not Dixie, maybe Tina Turner. But it'll be a hundred of them at Ninth and U or Fourteenth and Florida at ten o'clock at night. I can see them. There's ol' Jeeter Lawson, just got off from Metro cleaning rail cars, waiting for his ol' lady to take him home; there's Money Smith, with his raggedy ass three-legged dog, telling ever'body it's a genuine freak bitch, trying to sell her to the first sucker; there's Lester Veeney, sixty-five years old, walking down the sidewalk, doctor's orders, for a light stroke he had six months ago; there's Johnny Jimson, standing next to his Olds Cutlass with the trunk open, selling topcoats he boosted from Roper's; there's White Top Jefferson, just had a fight with his ol' lady and taking a breather. They all there, Nestor, doing one thing or another. And they call them culturally deprived, say they ain't got nothing to do but stand on the corner. You tell me how what they doing's any different than what's going on in Chevy Chase or Cleveland Park? It's people up there in four-hundred-thousand-dollar houses that get off work late and walk nights and fight with their ol' lady and try to sell each other bad shit. Maybe not a three-legged dog, more likely a short-sheeted life insurance policy. But it's the same thing. Only they don't call it culturally deprived. Goddamn sociologists say because it's jitterbugs, they deprived as far as money and education, and their society is broke down and social disorganization and ever'body running in the street. But it seem to me near 'bout the opposite. Seem to me they working the system to the max. They out there trying to make it at least three different ways—reg'lar work, welfare and stealing. I mean when you getting three-thirty-five a hour washing dishes, you can't make it. You got to do something else. You got to hustle. That's why you see so many of them on the street at night. They on their second shift. White folks gone to bed. Next time you go by Fourteenth and Florida and it's a hundred people standing there, just remember it ain't no bunch of social disorganization, neighbor. That's folks at work. Just the other day, I seen—"

"Hud, if you don't mind," interrupted Captain Stohlbach, poking his head out of his office. "We got stuff to do now."

"Sorry," grumbled Hudlow. He probed gently at his ear with a forefinger.

"Nestor, you and Hud come in here, please, so we can go over this thing again," said Stohlbach. The two detectives marched into the chief's office.

"Where's Mag?" asked Stohlbach.

"Supposed to be on his way," said Skoda. "Maybe he stopped at the cemetery."

"He still ain't got the airline ticket from that Gutenberg boy in Illinois?"

"It's only been a couple days."

"Fairlyte's still around? He hasn't tried to take off?"

"He showed up for work yesterday and this morning."

"Well, then will you tell me how in tarnation we got in this mess? Here we got a dead man with fingernail marks all over him from some lute player, and the only one we can scare up for five hundred miles's got a alibi tighter'n a nun's pantyhose."

"There are others out there," said Skoda. "We just got to get the right one."

"Listen," said Stohlbach wearily, "Chief Freeman in CID really don't go too much for all this razzle-dazzle about fingernails and class-type music. He's beginning to think this is Disneyland East. We got to start putting some meat and potatoes on the table, some informant reports, some motives. Lord, we don't have any idea what's going on. What kind of case is this?"

"You tell me," grunted Hudlow. "Maybe it ain't got nothing to do with guitars and fingernails. Maybe the marks on Kadinsky's neck's from something else."

"Any bright ideas what else?" asked Skoda.

"No bright ideas, except maybe we been zeroing in on the tenants too much. It's got to be somebody out there we missed. Maybe somebody on the Hill. I heard ol' Mag Johnson the other night talking to that Fairlyte boy 'bout the dope and pussy on the Hill. Much as I hate to say it, he's right. It's all kinds of opportunities to get crossed up there."

"Sodom and Gomorrah," said Stohlbach.

"But all Kadinsky's coworkers say he was Mr. Johnny Straight Arrow," said Skoda.

"They always do."

Magnus Johnson entered the office, carrying an envelope. "Any surprises?" Stohlbach asked.

"Afraid not. Everything's exactly like Gutenberg told us on the phone." Johnson held up the envelope. "The Ozark Airline ticket from Thursday, June ninth; the brewer's yeast label from Fairlyte's store; and his notarized statement. It's all here. Even a dated receipt from the store." Johnson passed the envelope to Stohlbach, who began scanning its contents.

"About all you can say is it absolutely eliminates Ambrose Fairlyte from the picture," said Skoda. "Now we only got four-point-two billion more people in the world to go."

"Can't we cut it down to just the three million that play the guitar?" said Stohlbach.

"Don't count on it being one of them," said Hudlow. "I think we got to look further than that."

Magnus Johnson glanced at Hudlow and spoke slowly. "You know, Hud, I am tempted to agree with you."

"Well, glory hallelujah," said Hudlow.

"But let me tell you why. At first glance, the M.E.'s evidence and the guitar-lute theory seem so close that it could only happen that way. But there's another possibility. It's just a theory."

"Not another theory," groaned Stohlbach. "Give me some live meat."

"I'm suggesting that the homicide was set up. It was a simulation job to make it appear that it was done by a guitar player or a lute player. Whoever it was mimicked being a musician. He grew his nails long, did the homicide and then cut the nails off."

"Somebody setting up Ambrose Fairlyte?"

"Possibly, or at least throwing the trail off himself."

Hudlow looked incredulous. "You saying this whoever-it-was set it all up knowing in advance that the medical examiner would pick up on the nail cuts and a week later ol' Nestor here would get a pain in his soul and decide to go to church and out of the clear blue see some Yippie banging a ukelele in Arlington, Virginia, and, slam-bang, make the connection? Is that what you saying, Mag?"

"In its simplest terms, yes," said Johnson.

"Well, I don't need to tell you that's ten pounds of shit in a five-pound bag."

"Paraleipsis," muttered Johnson.

"It does stretch belief," said Skoda.

"Maybe," said Johnson. "But the scenario is not as simple as Hud has it. Of course the killer didn't think in specific terms of a detective seeing a lutenist at Mass a week after the homicide. But it's not unreasonable for him to assume that a skillful medical examiner would bring the nail cuts to our attention and we would research it and eventually make the connection. And if we turned out to be dumb and weren't getting anywhere, he would help us."

"How would he do that?" asked Hudlow.

"I don't know. Maybe drop a hint during an interview. Maybe an anonymous letter or phone call giving us a nudge. I don't know. But it would point us to Ambrose Fairlyte and take us off the real guy."

"So he would have to know that Fairlyte was a guitar player, wouldn't he?" said Skoda.

"Of course."

"Well, goody, goody," said Hudlow. "That narrows the field down to Fairlyte's friends and relations. Only five thousand people."

"No, now I'm beginning to think it could only be one of the other eight tenants in L'Enfant Court. They all know Fairlyte, at least casually, from the building security meetings. Maybe he told some of them about his musical talents."

“We already worked the guitar routine on the tenants. They all drew a blank, except Fairlyte. Remember?”

“Work it again. Jog their memories.”

The door of Stohlbach’s office opened. It was J. T. Greene, the secretary.

“John Hero Smith just called. Remember him? The guy at the House Public Works Committee that worked with Kadinsky?”

“Yeah, Wally Wheelchair,” said Hudlow.

“Says he was going through Kadinsky’s papers and came across something. He wants you over there at two o’clock. Something about a brother of Kadinsky being killed in a cave.”

29

Magnus Johnson sat alone in the Jade Sea Restaurant. O regarded him from a distance, his jaundiced skin pressed against his cheekbones. He waited for Johnson to make his inevitable selection. The detective moved in slow and immutable rhythms dictated by a need for reflection and considerable ceremony, no matter how foreordained the outcome. Johnson's weekly journey to the Jade Sea in the heart of what purports to be Chinatown in Washington was an occasion to which O looked forward with, at best, mixed feelings. Johnson always came alone but insisted on a table for four, the same table each time, on which he spread sheaves of papers, poring over them intently, his spectacles suspended over his basalt nose. He often ignored his food until it was cold and then demanded testily that it be reheated. Today, O observed with relief, Johnson brought no papers and seemed intent instead on eating. He took a brief sip of his Tsingtao and then pushed away the glass, as he always did, three-quarters full, not to be touched again until after the meal.

"O." The detective beckoned the waiter, who glided toward him. "Yes, I'll have Number Four, with spring onions; easy on the ginger. Bring the marrow on the side. No chopsticks."

O elaborately traced over the markings he had already made on the order slip. "Yes, sir," he said, bowing slightly, and disappeared into the kitchen. Minutes later, he returned, presenting Johnson a covered stainless steel dish steaming with Szechwan frogs' legs. With a small flourish, Johnson unfurled his napkin and tucked a corner of it in his shirt below the collar. He removed the cover from the dish and bent over the curling steam. He gave O an approving nod and then began transferring a large portion of the contents to the plate in front of him. Next he turned to a small vial that O had placed at his right. He held it to the light and examined it. Then he cradled it in his hands, warming the rounded glass, and poured its contents onto his plate, a thin sebaceous gruel attested to on the menu as bat's marrow. Johnson viewed that claim with some skepticism but nevertheless looked forward to its taste with relish.

Dewey Hudlow and Nestor Skoda entered the restaurant. They spotted Johnson and approached his table.

"Slipped out on us for awhile, didn't you?" said Skoda. "This your regular day at the Jade?"

"Just getting a bite before our two o'clock with Smith," said Johnson, motioning to the two men to sit down.

Dewey Hudlow looked with aversion at Johnson's steaming plate. "That your usual tadpoles and sheep's eyes?" he asked.

"You forgot the human testicles," said Johnson without looking up. "Have some. You could use a couple."

Johnson ate in silence. After several mouthfuls, he said, "This cave thing Smith called about. This is the first time I've heard anything about a cave. Nestor, didn't you talk to the old man about that when you first called out to Chicago to notify him of Frank's death?"

"He just mentioned an 'accident,' like it was maybe a car or something. He was kind of vague. The old lady couldn't talk at all."

"Why didn't you press?"

"Didn't seem important at the time," said Skoda. "It happened ten years ago. Ancient history. What's in it for us?"

Johnson was silent again. Then: "Something else's been nagging me."

"Your frog legs getting cold," said Skoda.

"This guy Jeffrey Stanton in apartment Two-B," Johnson continued. "Something about that letter to him we saw just isn't right. How was it addressed, Nestor?"

"Said 'Jubal Symcox, care of Jeffrey Stanton.' What's the big deal?"

"Jubal Symcox. Jeffrey Stanton. Same initials."

"And you figure, same person. How many millions of different people in this world have the same initials?"

"And the envelope. It had metered postage and an address window, but no return address."

"Official, but private."

"Very. Like maybe a bank payment, except this one doesn't sit right somehow. Jubal Symcox. That name's been ringing in my head for days. Like a bell that won't stop."

"Hearing things again, Mag? Look, we can check it out, but we're late for Smith on the Hill."

o

At the House Public Works and Transportation Committee, the men threaded their way through a winding corridor to the windowless room.

"Good afternoon," said John Hero Smith in his thin dry voice. "I gather you have progressed little since I last saw you."

"Basically, that's right," said Johnson. "We've had some leads but a lot of dead ends, too."

"Well, as I told you before, it doesn't surprise me," said Smith. "In the meantime, I've had a chance to go through Franklin's papers and other effects here. I came across something completely out of the ordinary."

"The cave with the brother?" asked Johnson.

"Yes. But far more than that. It involves a curious letter I found in Franklin's papers. It is all utterly new to me. I never knew until now the brother's death occurred during an exploration of some caves in Alabama. It involved a task force of federal highway experts who disappeared and apparently died. The bodies were never recovered. It all happened more than ten years ago. Before my time here, before I knew Franklin. He never told me."

"What was a bunch of highway people doing in a cave?" asked Hudlow.

"The caves," said Smith, "are in a remote section of northeast Alabama near the Georgia-Tennessee line where Interstate 59 was built some years ago. Very mountainous. I don't know the area myself, but apparently it is honeycombed with underground formations called vertical pit caves, narrow chimneylike shafts that penetrate into the ground several hundred feet and open out into huge domed rooms. The ceilings of these rooms often can be very high—more than a hundred feet from the floor of the cave—and can come deceptively close to the surface of the earth above. The task force was concerned that the crust of earth in some places might be so thin that the weight of the I-59 roadbed and volume of traffic could cause a collapse into the cave below. As I say, the area was remote and not well known. It's in Buncombe County, if you look on the map here. Few of the caves have ever been entered or explored, and no one knew how extensive they might be. In most cases, entering them required descending a narrow vertical pit several hundred feet by cable ladder or ropes—"

"So what happened?" prompted Johnson.

"As I said, sometime after I-59 was completed, this task force was dispatched to Buncombe County from Washington. There were seven people in the group altogether, some contract engineers and geologists and a couple of people from the Federal Highway Administration. One of them was Monroe Kadinsky, Franklin's only brother. He was maybe two years younger than Franklin. Remember this was ten years ago. Both Monroe and Franklin had just come to Washington. Monroe was working for the Highway Administration at the time and apparently wangled a place on the crew going to Alabama. I say 'wangled,' because he was neither an engineer nor a geologist. He was some kind of administrator. That puzzled me at first. But he apparently had became aware of the agency's concern about the caves from paperwork crossing his desk and started looking for an opportunity to go. In any event, according to local news clippings and Franklin's notes as best as I can piece them together, the federal contingent flew to Atlanta and drove to Goshen Shoals, the county seat of Buncombe County, where they teamed up with two engineers from the Alabama highway administration and two professional speleologists as guides. They were apparently prepared to stay down below for several days, surveying and measuring the height of the large domed rooms they expected to find there. Well, they drove off from Goshen Shoals in a rented truck one April morning, and were never seen again."

"Just like that? No trace?" asked Johnson.

"Yes. After a week with no word from them, the feds notified Alabama authorities, and a search was started. It was not easy. They had disappeared in a sparsely populated area of rough terrain high up in the Appalachian foothills. A couple of county deputy sheriffs eventually found the rented truck on a timber road miles from anything. It was empty but locked and appeared to be just as the crew had left it when they went off in search of an entrance to one of the caves. The entrances are often small and covered by underbrush and difficult to find. State police eventually found one a good distance from the truck and sent a rescue team down into it, but without luck. There was not a trace of them, not a rope, not a piece of clothing, not a scrap of food."

"This is all very interesting," said Johnson, "but it happened ten years ago. What does it have to do with today?"

"You're getting ahead of me," said Smith. "The search was called off, and the members of the group were declared officially dead. About two years later, another engineering team went to the area and determined that the caves did not pose a threat to the interstate roadbed. They also determined that the original engineering group probably had been way off the mark and entered a cave system some distance east of the Interstate. In any event, the second team found no trace of the first team."

Magnus Johnson was about to speak again, but Smith signaled silence.

"Now," he continued, "of primary interest to you should be this letter I found in Franklin's file yesterday." Smith handed Johnson a single gray folded sheet of paper. Undated, it read:

> Dear Frank,
>
> Against your urgings and my better judgment, I am going to Buncombe County. I can no longer tolerate not knowing. It is too monstrous to be true. Please don't tell Mother, at least not now. The I-59 field trip provides a perfect pretext. All the paperwork is done. In case there is an encounter, I will bring the family ring from Mother.
>
> Monroe

The detectives passed the letter among themselves, staring blankly at its words.

"What do you make of it, sir?" asked Johnson.

"Well, one or two things. First, it explains why Monroe 'wangled' a spot on that field trip. He had an ulterior reason for going. Second, that reason involved some kind of very private family matter. As for the 'monstrous' thing or the 'encounter' he expected, I don't know."

"And the ring, the family ring," mused Johnson. "What's that all about?"

"Impossible to say."

Johnson examined the letter. "It's all in the context of the mother," he said. "No mention of the father. That's strange. Remember the mother? Alba. Alba Kadinsky."

"We got to get to her," said Hudlow. "She still in bad shape?"

"Boldt just got back from in Chicago," said Johnson. "He says she's a mess."

"Mess or no mess, she's got the answers."

"Next," continued Smith, sorting through a manila folder, "there are copies of some correspondence here showing that Franklin, in much more recent times, wrote to the Buncombe

County authorities, asking for a survey or tax map of the property just east of I-59 where the original engineering team's rented truck had been found. His interest in the matter had somehow been rekindled about two years ago, going by the dates on the correspondence."

"What about the more recent stuff you mentioned," said Johnson, "the handwritten notes?"

"Well, now those," said Smith, "are just little scribbles, mostly in Franklin's own indecipherable shorthand. But true to form, each slip of paper is dated in the upper right corner—some in recent weeks—just the way Franklin always did in committee work."

"And you think all this renewed activity is what set off his agitation and nervousness?" asked Johnson.

"I do," said Smith, "although I find it strange he never took me into his confidence. Perhaps he thought I would pooh-pooh things. I mean, it sounds to me as if he thought Monroe may have met with foul play and he wanted to satisfy himself about it."

"What makes you say foul play?" asked Johnson.

"Nothing in particular. But I just remember Franklin saying years ago that Monroe was an extremely cautious person who left nothing to chance and would never go off on such an excursion without planning every detail."

The three detectives stared at one another. Hudlow shrugged noncommittally. Johnson turned to Smith. "Tell me, sir," he said, "that property near the interstate in Buncombe County that Kadinsky asked for. What is the name of the owner?"

"Let's see," said Smith, thumbing through the file. "I've got it here somewhere. Yes, here it is on the property record card. The name is Symcox."

30

Their heads were thrown back against the seats, eyes narrowed, as they watched the heavy glass doors at 1716 L'Enfant Court. Darkness enveloped the cruiser crouched well away from the street lights.

"Don't doze," Skoda said to Magnus Johnson. "We're coming up on seven hours."

"What, me?" answered Johnson. "I never could sleep in a car. Too much like a cell block."

"Except in a cell, at least you got running water."

Johnson grunted.

"And three squares a day," said Skoda. "Sometimes the security of a jail can be very appealing. Steady food, sleep, light, no bills, no taxes."

Johnson said nothing, his eyes wandering.

"Reminds me of when I used to play Monopoly with my big brothers and sisters," Skoda went on. "They'd get hotels on that whole strip from Marvin Gardens to Boardwalk, and I just prayed before I got there I'd go to jail. No rent for three turns."

Skoda fell silent, abandoning the small talk. Johnson squirmed uneasily. Prolonged surveillances were never simple for him. The confinement was more than just oppressive; it filled him with a faint unease. He felt the sides and roof of the cruiser pressing in. A fleeting image like a shadow crossed his memory—his frail adolescent fists beating frenziedly in the blackness against the inside of the abandoned car trunk where the gray boys from Orangeburg, their eyes tight with harsh merriment, had stuffed him. He struggled against—

"Look," said Skoda abruptly, "if Jeffrey Stanton doesn't come out in the next fifteen minutes, I'm for going in there and tapping his tepee."

Johnson shook off his reverie, vaguely embarrassed. He looked at his watch. "It's only ten-thirty," he said. "If he's working the eleven o'clock shift, he still has time to make it."

"What I'm thinking is maybe he's split," said Skoda.

"Don't be thinking bad thoughts, Nestor. We got problems enough."

"Including Captain Stohlbach. Did you see his face when we told him about Monroe Kadinsky and the Alabama cave? He couldn't handle it. You'd think we were talking about an astronaut on Jupiter. First thing he said was, 'That's out of our jurisdiction.'"

"Bureaucrat to the core."

"Yeah, he shits in triplicate," said Skoda, settling back into the driver's seat. "But at least when we showed him the name on those Symcox property records, he sat up straight."

"It is an incredible coincidence, if that's what it is," said Johnson.

"It isn't a coincidence. You know that down in your bones, don't you, Mag? Otherwise, why would we be sitting out here waiting to see what he does?"

"And the Kadinsky connection. Is it personal, business, what?"

"Maybe family. Remember the ring?"

"My mind keeps going back to Kadinsky's mother," said Johnson. "Alba Kadinsky. Alba. Something about that name that makes me feel uncomfortable."

"Aren't we being extra color conscious tonight?"

"No, just uncomfortable."

"Did you tell me earlier today that Hudlow hadn't gotten through to her in Chicago?"

“That’s right. Neither her nor the old man. With the funeral over, they’ve gone to a summer cottage they got up on Lake Huron. No phones. His company in Chicago’s not cooperating. He’s some kind of executive bigwig there and told them to leave him alone until he comes back when the old lady’s doing better in a few days.”

“An executive biggie in Chicago? So what’s the Alabama connection?”

“Double my salary and I’ll tell you.”

“Mag, are you prepared to believe that somehow this Jeffrey Stanton learned that Frank Kadinsky was making inquiries about that property in Buncombe County and it was worth stuffing him for it?”

“Yeah, and to make it worse, we’ve got to believe that Stanton—if that’s his real name—is some kind of closet lute freak, or at least knows enough to grow his nails to throw us off.”

“Why do you say ‘if that’s his real name’?”

“I think it’s possible Jeffrey Stanton and Jubal Symcox are one and the same. Remember, their initials are identical,” said Johnson.

“But why would he have a letter addressed to him by both names?”

“Maybe he’s living here under one name—Stanton—and he gets his mail under the other name, Symcox.”

“We can’t push him on that. He’ll know we went through his mail. That’s a violation of mail security regs. He could raise a stink. Or he might spook and split.”

“We may have to take a chance on it.”

Skoda sank further down into the cruiser. “Wish Frank Kadinsky had been run over by a bus. Make our job a lot easier.”

“Think of the reports we’d have to write for Traffic.”

The two men were silent and watched the glass doors at 1716. The street was quiet.

“You know,” said Johnson, “Hudlow may be right. This could be some kind of cult thing. That’s why it’s so hard to get a handle on it.”

“Hudlow is not dumb. Noisy but not dumb.”

"Remember that fantastic blue shaft or whatever it was we saw in Stanton's hallway? It keeps coming back to me. I keep imagining that it's some kind of idol. But then I think, no, it's probably just a piece of junk he picked up at J. C. Penney's, and our eyes were playing tricks on us in the light. Just like with his tongue."

"Hudlow should have been with us, Mag. He would have taken his usual subtle approach and said, 'Mr. Stanton, I see you have a big blue dick in your hallway. Mind telling us about it?'"

"Dewey does have a way with words," said Johnson, not bitterly. "I can't say I'm always ecstatic about them."

"That's the understatement of the century," said Skoda.

"But there's more there than just the words. I have to give Hudlow his due. Don't ever tell him I said so."

"What is his due?"

Johnson stretched in the car seat. "Hud's a sort of romantic oaf, a leftover eighteenth-century American primitive who speaks with the openness of the frontiersman."

"You being charitable?"

"Only slightly. He's a surviving archetype, the yeoman adventurer who sought the freer life on the edges of society in the outback of the South. The backcountryman was a man of action. He had harsh appetites, 'the driven slave of the belly,' W. J. Cash once put it, living close to the soil with every act related directly to his survival. It was a life of violence, but there was also an odd kind of love for politics and rhetoric among the backcountrymen. Believe me, Nestor, I knew some myself, a few bedraggled remnants of them, at least, when I was growing up. Not at all like today's urban man, the 'soft squishy' people Hudlow so despises, people insulated from animal existence by the push-button goodies of the world we're in now."

"We all push buttons."

"Not Dewey Hudlow. His body may be in the late twentieth century, but his soul is in the eighteenth. He still sees everything as direct survival, whether it's locking up people on the street or coming to terms with Ambrose Fairlyte on the floor of Homicide. Think of his foxes, Nestor, his attention to every detail of the slaughter, the disemboweling, the gelding."

"You sound almost as if you respect the man."

"It's not so much that I respect him as I see him as a rare breed, a vanishing one. Whether that's for the good, I don't know."

"The breed is going to disappear whether you like it or not. Progress and all that."

"Well, let me tell you about the new breed, the new back-countryman," said Johnson, settling further down into the car seat. "When I was fourteen years old, I was in east Texas one spring visiting cousins. Ever been to east Texas, Nestor? East Texas is the South writ large. My cousins lived in a rural hamlet there. One day a white man came to the door. He knew my cousins and had an easy way with them. I remember he was very large, large like a Texan should be. But a lot of it was fat, big rolls of fat hanging over his waistband. He worked in a steel rolling mill forty miles away. He drove eighty miles a day. At the mill, he sat in an air conditioned cupola above the production line, in a control room where he pushed buttons and read dials all day, and then drove home again. He came to my cousins' because he was going goose hunting the next morning and wanted somebody to help. I said I would go, and he gave me a friendly tug on my hair and said he'd pick me up next morning at daybreak.

"The next morning came and the big man arrived in his truck. It was a bright blue Chevy pickup. Big, deep-tread tires on it. On the gun rack across the rear window were two twelve-gauge Browning pumps. The man was wearing a fringed leather jacket and a wide leather belt with a huge silver buckle with a buffalo head on it. He had on a wide-brimmed cowboy hat and a pair of tooled leather boots, pointed at the toe with high heels. Struck me as very feminine at the time. But who was I to say? He had a friend with him dressed the same way. The two men climbed into the cab of the truck, and I got into the back with a sackful of decoys and a long-haired retriever. We drove out into the countryside to some marshlands. We parked and got out and walked a few yards to a stand-up blind. I set out the decoys and held the dog. Then we took cover in the blind. After a while, we heard the geese coming in from the south and saw a small formation. The geese pitched into the decoys. The man and his friend raised their shotguns and fired several times. Three birds fell to the ground. The dog ran out across the marsh and brought them back. We waited a while longer, but no more geese came. I collected the decoys, and we walked back to the truck. We drove to my cousins' where the man left me off with the geese. I went behind the house, picked the birds and dressed them. I carried them over to the man's house. He thanked me for them and tugged my hair again and gave me five dollars.

"That was the sum and substance of the day's hunting. Now when you think about it, Nestor, the only physical action of any consequence that that man took during the entire day was to pull the trigger on his pump gun. Just the jerk of his finger. Everything else was done for him. He had his big blue iron horse to get him there. He had a dog to fetch the birds and a fourteen-year-old boy to set out the decoys and pick and dress the birds. He didn't do anything. And the saddest thing of all is he didn't need the birds in the first place. They had nothing to do with his survival. It was just sport, a luxury, with all the nasty smelly aspects sanitized and kept safely away from him.

"This pathetic figure is the new backcountryman, Nestor. The modern world has stripped him clean. He has nothing to do, no frontier to defend, no quarry to kill, not even a real horse to ride. But somewhere deep inside him stirs the lean hard ghost of the original backcountryman, yearning to return to the soil, to violence. But he cannot. He can never retrieve what no longer exists. So what does he do? He compensates. He disguises himself as the original backcountryman—the frontier jacket, the tooled belt, the ludicrous boots—and rides off into the cardboard sunset."

"So where does that bring us?"

"To Dewey Hudlow. In contrast, Hud somehow has remained authentic. He is an anachronism, a boisterous vagabond stumbling around in the late twentieth century. He is enormously unhappy, battling against the destroyers of his world. We have all forsaken him—you, me, Ambrose Fairlyte, Florian Boldt—for a world alien to him. Yet he is a part of that world too, its biological captive, and there is no way out."

Skoda said, "Suppose you were to tell him all this. What would happen?"

"He wouldn't lis—"

The two detectives both suddenly sat up. A tall figure with lusterless silver hair had come out of the building and stood on the steps. He looked eastward down the street toward the detectives' parked car, then jumped down to the sidewalk and began running the other way.

"Holy Batman, it's Stanton," said Skoda. "Think he saw us?" He started the cruiser.

"I don't know," said Johnson. "We better pay him a visit."

Skoda guided the car down the street. They could see the silverish head gliding along the sidewalk above the parked cars ahead of them. At the intersection of Eighteenth Street, the man broke his stride for a moment and looked back toward the detectives' car. Then he darted across the intersection. Skoda goosed the accelerator and the car bolted through the intersection to the curb on the far side and came to a quick halt. Johnson sprang from the passenger side of the car.

"Oh, Mr. Stanton, could you hold on a second?" Johnson spoke politely but firmly. As he stepped toward the tenant, Skoda slipped from the other side of the cruiser. Out of the corner of one eye he saw two silhouetted figures advancing toward the intersection from the north on Eighteenth Street. Then suddenly they were retreating, walking backwards as though watching the intersection. The tenant had stopped at Johnson's request and was catching his breath. His long arms hung loosely at his sides. He was in shirtsleeves.

"Sorry to bother you, Mr. Stanton," said Magnus Johnson.

"Remember me? I'm Detective Johnson. We were just making house calls and happened to see you running here. Everything okay?"

"Oh, yes, there's nothing wrong," the man answered. His voice contained the same alien resonance Johnson remembered from the interview, remote and cool, like a mountain spring whose source is hidden. His deep sluggish eyes showed no emotion. "I was running to get the subway at Dupont Circle. I am late for work."

Johnson glanced at his watch. "It's ten minutes to eleven," he said. "You supposed to be at the GPO at eleven?"

"Yes, that is correct. If you will excuse me." The man started to walk away.

"Just one more minute, if you don't mind, sir," said Johnson, raising his hand. The man halted. "Just one thing we were wondering about and thought you might help us."

"What is that?"

"Happened to see some of your mail the other day in the lobby. You got somebody named Symcox staying with you?" The detectives peered closely at the man. He stiffened for a moment, then seemed to relax again, his dull eyes turned toward them.

"No," he said finally. "He travels. He just gets his paychecks here."

"What kind of travel?"

"I'm not sure that is your business."

"We can make it our business."

"He . . . he is a salesman. Sometimes he doesn't get home for months."

"Where's home?"

The tenant gazed wanly at the detectives. "New York," he said.

"How about Ala—"

Skoda jabbed Johnson sharply.

"Uh, an address. How about a street address?"

There was a pause. The tenant's eyes narrowed. "I don't have one."

Another pause. Johnson glanced at Skoda, who shook his head.

"If you don't mind," said the man, "I really must leave."

"Sure, go ahead."

The leaden-haired man turned and started walking briskly toward Dupont Circle.

"Think we spooked him?" Johnson asked Skoda.

"Christ, I hope not. You damned near spilled it, Mag."

"Maybe you shouldn't have stopped me, Nestor. He might have gone into a clinch."

"Too chancy. We've got to keep this guy cool at least until we hear from Chicago. You know, Mag, you're acting more like Hud all the time. He blew it with Ambrose Fairlyte."

The detectives fell silent. Skoda looked north up Eighteenth Street. The two silhouettes he had seen moments earlier were gone.

"Did you see those two people going up Eighteenth just now?" Skoda asked Johnson.

"I missed them," said Johnson. "I had my eye on Stanton."

"They looked like they were coming toward Stanton but then turned back when they saw us. You suppose they were going to meet him?"

"Let's take a look," said Johnson. They jumped into the cruiser and spun up Eighteenth Street, peering down the side streets at each intersection. They saw nothing.

"Maybe one of them was the guy Stanton met on the subway," said Skoda.

"His ganja man?"

"It's a good guess."

At S Street, Skoda stopped the car. The street was empty.

"I give up," he said. "It was probably nothing. What do we do now?"

"I say drive over to the GPO and see if Brother Stanton shows up for work."

Skoda headed the car east, then south along Sixteenth Street toward Massachusetts Avenue. "I really don't see why we're doing this," he said. "Of course, he's going to work. He was in his shirtsleeves and wasn't carrying anything. No sign he was about to split."

"Let's play sure."

"And he probably was late, and that's why he was running."

"And the two dudes on Eighteenth Street had nothing to do with him."

"And this guy Symcox in New York is legit. Probably has a wife and two-point-three children and an Irish setter in Scarsdale."

They drove in silence, cutting diagonally through the edge of downtown along Massachusetts Avenue until they came to North Capitol where Skoda turned left and pulled over a half block south of the Government Printing Office.

Four minutes later, the two detectives saw the pale figure with pewter-gray hair trot up to the main entrance of the red brick building and vanish inside.

"If he's Frank Kadinsky's killer," said Magnus Johnson, "he sure doesn't spook easy."

31

The single black hair stood stiffly, like an uppity Mexican general, Captain Stohlbach thought, on the side of his nose. He bent over, studying it through a small magnifying mirror on his desk. His fingers pressed against his nostrils. Massive gray appendages and orifices swam slowly in the reflection. He tried without success to grip the hair with his thumb and first finger. "Dadlem," he swore gently. He pushed his nose against his skull, hoping to improve his grip. As he pressed, a blur of new color appeared in the upper corners of the mirror, faint pinks and blues. He heard scuffling and turned to see Dewey Hudlow's frame in the office doorway.

"Didn't mean to bust up your morning toilet," said Hudlow.

"That's okay," said Stohlbach, straightening up and turning the mirror down on the desk.

"Me and Nestor and Mag got to talk to you 'bout Jeffrey Stanton." The three detectives filed into Stohlbach's office and sat down. The Homicide chief cupped his hands over his nose in an attitude of prayer.

Hudlow spoke. "Mag here is all for getting a warrant and going into Stanton's place."

"A warrant?" exclaimed Stohlbach. "Based on what?"

"Based on the coincidence of names," said Johnson. "You have this guy Stanton receiving mail addressed to a Symcox living next door, so to speak, to a murdered man with a file folder in his office overflowing with the name Symcox. It's an unusual name. Not quite like Smith or Jones."

"I never seen a judge issue a warrant on coincidence, Mag," said Stohlbach, "'specially this kind. It's just a first cousin of coincidence. Legalwise, Stanton's the lessee of that unit. Not Symcox."

"Suppose Stanton and Symcox are one and the same? It's really Symcox using the name Stanton to hide his identity from Franklin Kadinsky."

"Then why would he still be getting letters addressed to Symcox?"

"Whoever's sending the letters—a bank or a billing agency—knows him as Symcox, not Stanton, and he wants it that way. To some people, he's Stanton. To others, he's Symcox. He takes care of it by having his Symcox letters sent to 'Care of Jeffrey Stanton.'"

Stohlbach was still dissatisfied. "S'pose a judge bought the notion. What would you say you expected to find in the apartment?"

"Ashtray full of fingernails," chortled Dewey Hudlow.

"I think," said Johnson, "we could say we expected to find letters or other documents linking up to the correspondence in Frank Kadinsky's office."

"Ain't a judge on God's green earth would buy that notion, Mag, nor the U.S. Attorney's office, either. Besides, we been all through that file that John Hero Smith gave you. There's no Jubal Symcox in there. What does it say the full name of the property owner down there in Alabama is, Hud?"

Hudlow opened the folder. "Says here: Nathaniel and Sarah Symcox; three hundred and eighty-two acres with improvements, Section Twelve, Township Twenty South, Range 8 East. There's no Jubal Symcox."

"Maybe Jubal is the son of Nathaniel and Sarah," suggested Johnson.

"No such luck," said Hudlow. "I called down there to that

county seat, Goshen Shoals, in Buncombe County. That place must be the ass-end of nowhere. I talked to their Vital Records. No Jubal Symcox, either a birth certificate or death certificate. I got the sheriff's department, too, and they said it was a family named Symcox lived 'bout ten miles out on a ramshackley farm that kept pretty much to theirselves, strange folks. Sarah and Nathaniel and maybe a child or two, but that was all they knew."

Magnus Johnson raised his hand. "I know nobody thinks much of my idea that Stanton and Symcox are the same guy. But just on the off chance, maybe we could check if Stanton has an Alabama connection."

"We can start right here," said Stohlbach, opening the Kadinsky homicide file. "Let's see. GPO and the L'Enfant Court management both list Stanton's last previous in Washington. Some other apartment on Nineteenth Street. He moved out of there more than a year ago to L'Enfant Court, and the records of the earlier apartment have been destroyed. Routine. No Alabama connection there."

"What about the POB on his government job entrance form?" asked Johnson.

"Just says 'United States.'"

"How can he get away with that?"

"Government never checks those dern applications," said Stohlbach. Now he was looking more closely at the form. "My land, he didn't even put down any personal references here."

"Guy's a zero. Puff of smoke," said Hudlow.

"Wish we'd hear from Chicago and them Kadinsky folks," said Stohlbach, lines of frustration across his face. "We could use a three-point shot from the fifty-yard line right about now."

"There's still a couple of possibilities," said Johnson. "Like I said before, it's possible Stanton set up Ambrose Fairlyte with the fingernail routine. Only now Stanton is Symcox. He's stalking Frank Kadinsky. He moves into the apartment building more than a year ago and spends all this time getting acquainted with the tenants. He zeroes in on Fairlyte and works the setup. No?"

"Listen," the captain said. "I'm ready to try most anything. Mag's made a point. Maybe you all should pay Mr. Fairlyte a visit and ask him if Stanton or Symcox or whatever his name is ever took a fancy to his fiddle. If you can get enough for an affidavit, we'll go for the warrant."

"That's fine, if poor old Fairlyte can take another visit from us," said Johnson. "One more and I think he might have cardiac arrest."

"Maybe this time, Hud ought to stay home and count his toes," suggested Stohlbach.

"All right with me," said Hudlow. "He's your boy."

32

Johnson and Skoda walked toward Dandelion Foods on H Street. Colorful signs in the window heralded a sale on black-strap molasses. The detectives entered and saw Fairlyte standing at a cash register. He looked up and recognized them.

"Am I under house arrest this time?" he said. "What possibly could you want?"

"Believe it or not," said Johnson, "we come in peace."

"I believe it not. Where's your company goon?"

"He's busy biting the heads off chickens at the office."

"His behavior is improving."

"He responds well to therapy."

"Well, I'm sorry he didn't get to see me in my natural habitat here. Do you like the store?"

"It's the nicest natural food store we've seen in the last ten minutes."

"All right. What can I do for you?"

Johnson stepped toward Fairlyte. "In your apartment building, do you know this fellow Stanton? Lives above you in Two-B."

"Just slightly. We say hello in the hall. Haven't you asked me this question a hundred times before?"

"Probably," said Johnson, "but we're slow learners. Can you recall any specific times when you've talked with him at length, not just to say hello in the hall?"

Fairlyte pondered the question. "Not really," he said. "I know we met at a couple of the building security meetings, and it seems to me we talked a little bit."

"About what?"

"I don't really remember. At those occasions, it's usually just chitchat."

"Did you ever talk to him about your lute or guitar playing?"

Fairlyte thought again. "You know, I think I did. I mean, I love to talk about ancient instruments any time I get the chance. But maybe it wasn't Stanton. Maybe it was somebody else I talked to."

"Try to remember."

Fairlyte looked down at the floor. "I think you're right. I think I did talk to him, but I just can't be absolutely certain."

"Do you remember specifically what you discussed about the lute?"

"Oh, God, no. I mean, sometimes I talk about music theory. Sometimes string tuning, sometimes wood and construction."

"What about fingernails?"

"Oh, yes, I talk about that, too. But that's usually with other players, people who grow their nails, too. We talk about length and how to take care of them, things like that."

"Did you ever talk to Stanton about that?"

"I doubt it. He doesn't play any of the instruments. At least, as far as I know. The only way I would have talked about fingernails with him would be if he brought the subject up."

"Maybe he noticed the long nails on your right hand and asked about them. Is that possible?"

"It's possible, yes. But I don't have a specific recollection. People do occasionally notice my nails and ask about them."

"Was Stanton—"

"I'll tell you this," interrupted Fairlyte, "Mr. Stanton is an inquisitive person. It seems to me each time I talked with him, he asked me a lot of questions. He did most of the asking, and I did most of the talking."

"What did he ask you about?"

"About what I did, what kind of work I was involved in."

"So maybe you did tell him about teaching and playing the lute."

"The more I think about it now, the more I think you may be right." Fairlyte looked suddenly at Detective Johnson. "Oh, my God, don't tell me," he said, "you guys think Stanton copied my fingernails and tried to set me up?"

"We're not saying that. We're just looking at possibilities."

"You sound desperate. Like I said, I may have talked to Mr. Stanton about lutes and ancient instruments and possibly even fingernails. But I can't be certain."

"Not certain enough for an affidavit to that effect?"

"An affidavit? For what?"

"Just an official sworn statement."

"Oh, heavens no. I couldn't do that."

Johnson turned to Skoda. "You got any other questions, Nestor?"

"No." Skoda took a long breath.

"Well," Johnson said, turning back to Fairlyte, "sorry we had to bother you again."

"Oh, no bother. It's nice not being a suspected killer for once."

Johnson looked at Fairlyte. "There's one thing. We'd appreciate it if you wouldn't speak to Mr. Stanton. Just go about your business in a normal way."

"That won't be difficult. I rarely see him."

The detectives left Dandelion Foods.

"Damn," said Skoda.

"Know what you mean," said Johnson. "Lot of gray ambiguous crap. Why can't we come up with a nice clean witness who can point to somebody and say, 'That's the guy'?"

"Only happens on television."

Johnson and Skoda were walking west on H Street. They picked up two hamburgers at McDonald's and wandered absently past the New York Avenue Presbyterian Church toward Franklin Park.

"Know what I'm thinking?" said Johnson.
"War council?"
"Right on the money. This is getting serious. We've just about run our string. Stohlbach is getting antsy. We're all about half dead from the surveillance. If it is Stanton, it's just a matter of time before he splits. In fact, I can't understand why he's still hanging around. We've got to move."
"I'm for that," said Skoda. "Let's go see Hudlow."
"Not in the office, Nestor. Call him landline. Right now. Tell him to meet us in Franklin Park. At the Thirteenth and I corner."
Skoda stepped into a telephone booth on Thirteenth Street. A moment later, he was out again. "He's on his way. What about the cruiser? It's still down on H Street."
"Let Traffic tow it. We got other fish to fry."
The detectives crossed I Street and walked into Franklin Park, a spacious square of stately willow oaks and Japanese zelkovas. Discarded newspapers blew along the walkways. Two young black men were perched on the back of a park bench with their feet on the seat, talking to three other men facing them. A large silver boom box sat on the bench, yawping with resolute frenzy. The men eyed the two detectives as they walked by.
"Ever wonder how many deals go down here every day?" said Magnus Johnson. The two detectives sat down on a bench. They looked up at the soft tracery of green above them and waited. The boom box played on. Within minutes, a cream and blue Metropolitan Police scout car pulled along the curb on Thirteenth Street and stopped. Dewey Hudlow opened the passenger door and pulled himself out. The scout car swam back into the traffic. Hudlow walked across the grass toward his partners. The group of blacks stared at Hudlow and the scout car disappearing into the traffic. Then, like a flock of pigeons rising simultaneously on an unseen signal, they fled from the park.
"That was quick," said Johnson to Hudlow.
"Express service. Boy from Two-D give me a lift." Hudlow looked around him. "How come here, Mag? Couldn't you tone

this meeting up and have it in Lafayette Square by the White House?"

"Only the CIA and KGB allowed over there."

"Oh, just us riffraff here. What's up?"

"Fairlyte gave us a lot of mealy mush about maybe he remembered, maybe he didn't, on Stanton. There's not enough for an affidavit."

"So, what do we do, hit him over the head with a lute?"

"This thing's getting to the breaking point. Nestor and I were just talking. Stanton could split any time. It's not going to do any good to talk directly to him. He'll just play possum. He'd never consent to a search, not the way he's been acting, and a warrant's a joke. We need more."

Johnson took a breath. "I'm talking out of school, Hud," he said, "but I think we got to go into Stanton's place without paper."

Hudlow was stunned. "Shitjimpiss, Mag, you can't mean that."

"What choice is there?"

"I can't believe you. Mr. Prim and Proper. Go in there without a warrant? You're flat crazy. How you going to put that down later?"

"Fudge it. Maybe we won't find anything. Then it won't matter."

"Goddamn, Mag, here you been lecturing me on all this mickey-mouse courtesy with the witnesses, and then you come up with this world-class dingbat invasion of a man's whole goddamn house. You fucking with the Fourth Amendment, Mag, or Thirteenth, whichever it is."

There was a long silence. Johnson kept his head down, toying with a pebble on the sidewalk with his toe. "Jeffrey Stanton is involved in this thing up to his armpits. You know that way down in your gut, don't you? We have run out every lead, looked under every stone. We have evidence, but it's odd evidence, the kind that makes judges roll their eyes. But at the same time, you know it's right. You know to amoral certainty."

"Well, I ain't going into nobody's house on a moral certainty."

"Going in will be easy and clean," insisted Johnson. "Quaver will give us the key. Straight down the gangplank. No Watergate stuff."

"It's too dangerous," said Hudlow.

"Do you want to see Jeffrey Stanton get away?"

"Keep surveilling him."

"All he's got to do is walk across the Fourteenth Street Bridge into Virginia, and he's gone. No other jurisdiction will go along. FBI would laugh."

Hudlow studied his hands for a moment. "Look," he said, his voice lower now. "I been on this force for seventeen years, Mag, and I ain't stepped on my dick yet. I ain't about to do it now, not for this case nor any other."

"You never fudged on a warrant, never bent things a little? You've skated pretty close to the edge before, and it didn't seem to bother you."

"Different stuff," Hudlow said stubbornly.

"Yeah, like nearly beating the life out of Ambrose Fairlyte on Captain Stohlbach's floor."

"You know that was strictly office. Strictly him and me—"

"And while we're at it, there's the little matter of fraternizing with informants. You know the policy on that."

Hudlow whirled on Johnson. "You leave Quovadis Logan out of this, you sorry bastard. She ain't got nothing to do with this case nor no damn policy!"

Nestor Skoda slid between the two detectives. "Hold on, guys. There's lots more important things to do here."

"Sure, Nestor," said Magnus Johnson with surprising vehemence. "It's okay for Hud here to be punching some nigger preacher on Ninth Street, but God forbid that we search the house of the man that killed Franklin Kadinsky, faithful employee of almighty Congress."

Skoda stepped back. The three men fell into silence. Each looked away from the others. The drone of traffic was heavy in the early summer air. Finally Skoda spoke. "Look, can't we all kiss and make up. I'm sorry this happened. We've got a lot on us. What do you say?"

Silence fell around them again. Then Hudlow spoke. "Okay, ya'll go ahead. But I just want you to know I think you're letting Stohlbach and the rest of them stampede you. Nothing scares me more than a bad search or a bad arrest done in a hurry."

Hudlow got up from the bench and walked off. His massive figure diminished among the trees and finally disappeared.

"Why did you do that, Mag?" said Skoda.

"Do what?"

"Hit him with Quovadis Logan. That was a little low, wasn't it?"

"Yes, but it was calculated. He's so schiztsy about us going into Stanton's place, I'm afraid it might get back to Stohlbach or Freeman. Not that Hud would report it, but he might talk around. He's a loose cannon, to say the least. I just wanted him to know that we have some ammunition, too."

"You are a schemer, aren't you?"

"Yes, and an immodest one, too. I think I bought our way into Jeffrey Stanton's apartment."

"When do we do it?"

"Tonight."

33

Johnson slid Quaver's passkey into the lock, turned it and the door swung open.

The detectives stepped inside. A short inner hallway gave onto a living room, which to their surprise was illuminated. It was furnished with three or four large square wooden chairs. The walls were bare, the windows hung with thick gray drapes. In the center of the room on the carpeted floor sat a plain shallow dish, and in it were four squat candles burning, each casting a faint light to the ceiling. The odor of ginger hung in the air.

A profound silence enveloped the room. The two detectives found themselves tiptoeing and speaking in hesitant whispers as they studied the unadorned walls and floors. Johnson motioned for the two of them to go deeper into the apartment. In the hallway leading to the kitchen and bedroom, they passed the table bearing the blue stone shaft they had seen from a distance on their earlier visit. Two candles flickered dimly at its base. Tiny flecks of yellow glinted on its cool surface. The two men lingered, staring at the object.

"Let's get back to this after we check the other rooms," whispered Johnson, pulling himself away. A doorway on the left side of the hall opened into the kitchen. Johnson flicked a light switch, and a dim bulb in the ceiling showed a small room almost bare of furniture. There was no table in the center, no appliances on the counter. The cupboards contained a few rudimentary dishes and simple flatwear. In the refrigerator were three or four unmarked boxes. Johnson opened them. Each contained a gray paste that smelled faintly of sour milk.

They moved on to the bedroom. Again they found little. Heavy drapes hung across the windows. A plain wooden chair sat in one corner, a chest of drawers in another. In the center, filling much of the room, was a neatly made mattress lying directly on the floor. Johnson opened the chest of drawers. From the dim light in the ceiling, he could see a stack of handkerchiefs and plain white undershirts and shorts in the top drawer, neatly folded shirts in the second, a sweater or two in the third. He felt through each drawer, pushing the stacks of clothing aside and then replacing them carefully. In a closet hung two pairs of trousers and a lightweight topcoat. Nothing else.

A small bathroom off the bedroom also yielded little. A single toothbrush rested on the side of the basin. The medicine cabinet was empty except for a razor and a vial of gritty white powder.

"Christ," murmured Skoda. "No medicine, no aspirin, no Band-Aids, no toothpaste. What is this guy, the invisible bionic man?"

"At least he shaves," whispered Johnson. "And he does use a toothbrush. The bristles are still wet."

"What about the candles? He leaves them burning all night? Isn't that taking a chance?"

"His choice."

"And the rest of the place," said Skoda. "No telephone, no radio, no TV, no stereo, no clothes, no pictures on the walls. My God, it's like a monastery."

"Maybe that's what it is. Let's go see the thing on the hall table. It's the only thing left."

The tapering shaft rose perhaps three feet from its pedestal, glistening faintly in the light of the candles, its cerulean surface almost metallic in its hardness. Magnus Johnson reached toward the shaft. Its touch was cold. It seemed to have a much greater weight than its size suggested, as though it were rooted deep in the foundation of the building. At its base lay a large conchlike shell the color of alabaster with an overlay of tiny brown spots. Encircling it was a ring of smaller, conical shells, all pointed to the center, painted in delicate bands of claret and cream. The entire assembly rested on a large elaborately carved base of grayish wood.

"Just as I thought," whispered Johnson, peering closely. "Lapis lazuli. Almost certainly from Burma. It kind of jibes with the other things. The big shell at the base is some kind of chank, like the ones found in Indian waters. The little shells look like volutes from Sri Lanka. The wooden base is sandalwood. It's got a kind of Indian feel about it."

"Yes," said Skoda, "but what does it add up to?"

"Remember what you said about a monastery?"

In the dark table beneath the pedestal were two shallow drawers. Johnson pulled them open. Both were filled with papers: GPO pay stubs. "These are what he showed us when we came here the first time, remember, Nestor?"

"Yeah, but is that all that's in there? No letters, no bank checks?"

"That's it," said Johnson, pulling all the papers out and probing the recesses.

"He must have other papers here somewhere," said Skoda. "I can't believe this is it."

As he spoke, the two detectives heard a muffled tapping against one of the windows in the living room behind them. "What the fuck?" whispered Skoda. Both men dropped to their knees and turned toward the windows. The thick gray drapes across them admitted no light. There was another series of tappings, like pebbles hitting against a window.

"That's deliberate," whispered Johnson. "Somebody's throwing something."

He crept across the living room floor around the large candle-lit dish to the windows. Slowly he parted the drapes an inch and looked out. He remained there on his knees for several minutes, motionless. Then he closed the drapes and stood up.

"What's going on?" asked Skoda.

"Jeffrey Stanton has a couple of cohorts. Two guys standing in the alley looking straight up at the window. Little Mediterranean-looking guys. They just left."

"Could you hear them talking?"

"Yeah, but I couldn't make out the words. Mumble-jumble. The light's not very good out there, but I could swear one of them was that guy Hud and I saw on the subway with Stanton. The bald spot."

"Not too swift coming here now," said Skoda. "Don't they know Stanton works nights?"

"No phone, remember?"

"What time is it? Maybe we should get a move on."

"It's eleven twenty-five," said Johnson. "Let's check out the table under the stone statue."

The detectives stooped in front of the table. Below the two shallow drawers was a broad panel of dark wood. Johnson tapped it with his knuckles. There was a quick hollow echo. He felt the surface and edges of the panel.

"There's a compartment behind that panel," he said, "but I don't see any way to open it."

Johnson got down on his knees and felt underneath the table. "Nothing here," he said. "Let me try the back." He wedged his arm between the wall and the table. His fingers ran over the smooth back of the table. Then he felt a slightly raised surface. He pushed down on it gently. At first it did not move, but with more pressure, it suddenly slid downward, leaving an aperture large enough for his hand. He reached in and felt two spoollike objects side by side. Both were loose and seemed to turn on threads. He began turning one clockwise, and after several revolutions it locked flush against something. He began turning the other spool. It turned more slowly than the first and with greater difficulty. But as it turned, he could hear other pieces inside the table beginning to move.

"Hey, Mag," said Skoda in an excited whisper, "the front panel is starting to open." In a few more moments, Johnson completed turning the spool, and a large drawer now lay fully open in the front of the table.

They looked inside. It was empty except for what appeared to be a leather-bound cover of a book. Gently, Johnson lifted it from the drawer. Holding it like an offering, he carried it to the candle-lit dish in the living room. He placed it on the floor, and the two men examined it. The leather cover was embossed in extravagant geometrical designs, like a family Bible. It bore no words. Johnson opened the cover, and inside lay a thin sheaf of papers bearing a firm, disciplined handwriting.

The two men settled down on the floor of the apartment and began to read.

Buncombe County, Alabama

WE, Nathaniel Symcox and Sarah Symcox, brother and sister, commence this undertaking in the name of darkness. That for the preservation of our posterity and honor of our forebears, we are commanded to create a new people, a family-nation above all others, free from taint, pure in purpose and sanctified in its own blood. This family-nation, conceived from our own loins, shall fend itself from all intrusion, provide for seclusion in perpetuity and maintain its blood within itself, bound by the holy vows of Nirriti. Above all, it shall pledge utter fealty before the altar of dark ecstasy on which our commandment was first ordained, revealed in a blinding obsidian light—a Dark Epiphany—that illumined the passage of our union. It is a union that shall forever be the signal fire of our future. In the name of Kali, let no man cut us asunder.

To assure fruition of our dream, we set down these injunctions:

THAT the family-nation shall live and remain in perpetuity

upon the Symcox property in Buncombe County, Alabama. There shall be no commerce with others outside the family and property, and no member shall leave therefrom except for extraordinary cause.

THAT absolute secrecy be maintained. False records purporting to show adoptions or marriages of persons outside the family shall be maintained, and all female members shall remain in isolation during periods of pregnancy.

THAT as soon as practicable, arrangements shall be made to obtain small arms, ammunition and other ordnance from private stocks to assure protection from intrusion.

THAT the labyrinth of caves under and about the Symcox property shall be a sacred ground and the place, if necessary, of final defense. Any known entrances on the property shall be concealed from public view.

THAT the welfare of the generations shall be maintained by the Symcox estate trust, administered in a prudent and discreet manner by the Northern Alabama Mercantile and Safe Co. in Birmingham, Ala.

THAT Alba Symcox, our once beloved sister, who renounced the family-nation and fled against our will, removing with her the family ring, shall be hunted down and brought to justice.

THAT the family-nation shall be known as Dark Epiphany, and that name shall not be uttered beyond the family.

These then are the commandments.

Nathaniel Symcox
Sarah Symcox

Johnson and Skoda peered at each other in the candlelight.

"What the hell we got here," said Skoda, "the Third Reich South?"

"Looney Tunes."

"Small arms, weapons. I don't like that kind of Looney Tunes."

“Forget the weapons. Look at that name: ‘*Alba* Symcox, our once beloved sister.’ ”

“Alba?”

“Yeah, that’s the Symcox-Kadinsky connection! Alba Kadinsky, mother of Franklin and Monroe Kadinsky. She must also be Alba Symcox, sister of Nathaniel and Sarah Symcox.”

“Jesus,” said Skoda, laboring with the thought. “But she’s in Chicago married to a respectable millionaire.”

“Exactly. She couldn’t take the kinky stuff down on the farm, so she split.”

“With the family ring.”

“Something to remember them by.”

“And who the hell are Kali and Nirriti, an Italian law firm?”

“Some type of Hindu gods. I’m telling you, Nestor, this job’s been wrapped in off-brand Indian stuff from the beginning. The tongue, the blue shaft, now this.”

Skoda looked at the papers again. “This must have been written a long time ago.”

“Probably. No date on anything.”

“So where does Jubal Symcox fit in?”

Johnson pondered a moment. “Must be the son.”

“Son of Nathaniel and Sarah?” Skoda’s eyes widened. “Yuck.”

“And like I said all along, Jubal Symcox is in fact Jeffrey Stanton. Now you know why he looks so—unusual.”

“All for the noble ‘family-nation’?”

“It also explains why there’s no birth certificate for Jubal Symcox in Alabama. It was never recorded.”

“We’re playing with an awful lot of loose pieces here. How do we put them together?”

“Alba Kadinsky. We’ve got to get to her.”

“She ought to be back from that place they went to up on Lake Huron by now. Try again tomorrow.”

Johnson looked at his watch. “We got to take this document out of here.”

“If he finds it missing, he’ll split.”

“Come on, Nestor. This stuff is hot. Suppose he destroys it?”

“It’s a chance we got to take.”

“I say take it. We can fudge something later.”

“How?”

“God, I don’t know. I’ll dream up something tomorrow. Invention is the illegitimate child of necessity, quote, unquote.”

“We’re playing with fire.”

“Nothing new for us, Nestor. Come on.”

“Well, we’ve gone this far—”

They heard a distant rattle. Someone had entered the lobby below. The two detectives froze. Footsteps ascended the stairway. They stopped at the second floor landing, fifteen feet from Symcox’s door, then slowly passed and continued to the third floor.

Skoda shuddered. “These house calls are starting to get to me. Close the drawer, Mag, and let’s get out of here.”

Johnson rewound the spools behind the table, and the drawer slowly shut.

34

"Hey, Hud." It was the voice of Douglas MacArthur Cheek on the telephone. It lacked the familiar ripple of humor around the edges.

"Yeah, Cheeks, it's me. What's up?"

"Quovadis." There was a hesitation. "She dead."

"Say what?"

"Just now. I seen it."

"Make sense to me, man."

"She killed out here on Ninth Street, in front of her place."

Hudlow turned his back to the office and crouched over the telephone. "Come at me again, Cheeks, straight."

"Like I said. She—I'm sorry, Hud."

"Hold on a second." Hudlow placed the telephone across his stomach and looked up at the fluorescent lights for a moment. He blinked in disbelief. "Vadis?" He clutched the arm of his chair.

"Cheeks, who's up there?"

"Traffic. One-D."

"What the hell happened?"

"Motorcycle. Run up on the sidewalk out of control."

"Where was Vadis?"

"Standing by the lamppost. Hit her up against it."

"What about the sumbitch that did it?"

"Dead, too."

"Who is he?"

"Don't know. Wasn't no jitterbug. D.C. tags. Look like some kind of A-rab."

"Hold on again, Cheeks." Hudlow shook his head and tried to focus on the papers strewn on his desk.

"Hud, you listening?"

"Yeah, go ahead."

"I ain't got much time. Man from One-D letting me use a pay phone."

"You a witness?"

"Yeah, I told you I seen it."

"What you seen?"

"Sumbitch going up and down the street like a house afire. Big ol' Japanese hog with this boy on it. Turn around the block ever' few minutes. Vadis come out and hadn't been there long when he come up on the sidewalk. Like to hit me and three, four other people, too."

"Was he fried?"

"Must've been. Listen, Hud. The reason I call, when she laying there, I went over to her, and she said tell Hud something. Said tell you the Texas Avenue Annex."

"The what?"

"Texas Avenue Annex. Something like that. I couldn't understand too good. She didn't say nothing after that."

"Texas Avenue Annex?"

There was a silence. Hudlow groped toward his desk and rested his elbows heavily.

"Was Thomas there?"

"Vadis' boy? Naw. Ain't seen him lately."

Hudlow released a breath. "Do me a favor, Cheeks. Call his grandmother over Southeast, soon as you can. He's prob'ly over there. Let the boy down slow."

"I already figured that."

"Will he stay with her?"

"Yeah, or go back to Shreveport, one."

"No, get the ol' lady to keep him. Keep him near."
"Okay. You want to see him, Hud?"
"I—no, better not right now."
"I got you."
There was another silence. "He ain't but nine years old, Cheeks."
"The ol' lady, she watch him good."
"Yeah, I guess."
"Listen, Hud. I got to go. The man calling me."
"Okay, Cheeks. Thanks. Oh, just one more thing."
"What that?"
"I'm going to need to get some money to Thomas. You know, thirty, forty bucks ever' couple weeks. Can you carry it over there for me?"
"Sure, Hud. No problem."
"Tell the grandmother he's my—tell her whatever you want, Cheeks."
"Gotcha."
"You a good man."
Hudlow hung up the telephone. He grunted softly and felt the water rising in his eyes.

35

"I want you to know I don't appreciate this business too much, getting up in the middle of the night to come down here. This better be good."

Captain Stohlbach looked at Skoda and Johnson across his immaculate desk. The two detectives stared back, their eyes swollen with fatigue. It was just after midnight.

"Like we told you on the phone, Stanton has split." It was Johnson speaking. "He's not at his place, and his supervisor at GPO says he didn't show up for work."

"We got to move, fast," said Skoda.

"Move?" said Stohlbach. "He's gone. End of the chapter. Close the book."

"No," said Skoda. "Listen to what Mag has to say."

Stohlbach looked skeptical. "Not another theory on the interlocutory corpus of a flagrante delicto?"

"Better than that," said Johnson. "Now that he's gone, we don't need a warrant to get in his place. Just get the building management to declare the apartment abandoned and have his property put out and we can look it over. Probably give us some clue where he's gone."

"Idea's got hair on it, doesn't it, Chief?" said Skoda.

"Abandoned property? In just two days? U.S. Attorney's office might not shoot from the key on that one."

"Doesn't have to be exactly two days. Stretch it a little. S&N Realty will go along. They'd love to get this case closed."

The two detectives looked eagerly at Stohlbach. The captain stroked his unshaven chin. "I don't know. S'pose the sucker comes back?"

"He's not coming back," said Johnson. "He's gone."

"No guarantee."

"Everything but."

"He comes back, your rank in a sling."

"Trust us, Chief."

"You talked to Hudlow about this?"

Johnson glanced at Skoda. "No. He wasn't with us this evening. Where is he now?"

Stohlbach waved his hand. "He took out of here earlier. You hear about that preacher woman been a snitch of his?"

"Quovadis Logan?"

"Yeah. Got killed. Traffic accident. Up Ninth Street. I imagine he went up there."

"That was eight hours ago. He's not at home, either. We tried him."

"Well, he's senior man. I think we want some throughput from him."

"It's got to be soon. We got to get to S&N Realty in the morning."

"Keep trying Hud at home."

"That's why we called you first. We need to short-circuit things."

"What's the rush?"

"Every minute, Stanton's another mile away. Searching his place is our only chance."

"I don't know. You two just strike me as being almighty jumpy."

"Just doing our job, boss."

"Okay." Stohlbach sighed. "Hudlow goes along with it, we do it."

36

By midmorning, Stohlbach, shaven and in a clean shirt, was thumbing through the sheaf of yellowing papers from apartment 2-B. Skoda and Johnson sat in front of him like two retrievers that have dropped a stick at their master's feet.

"Dadlemest business I ever seen," marveled Stohlbach. "'Dark Epiphany . . . conceived from our own loins'? I don't remember that in Sunday school."

"Didn't we tell you we'd find something crazy?" said Skoda, glowing. "Plus the Stanton-Symcox lookalike contest. Mag's theory was right all along. Now we can go after the son of a bitch."

Stohlbach winced. "'White male subject,' Nestor. It's in the manual."

"Made the whole abandoned property thing worth it," continued Skoda. "What's more important, Mag just got off the phone with Chicago. He finally got through to Alba Kadinsky. She's back. Tell the chief what she said, Mag."

"She's exactly what we suspected: a fugitive, an escapee, from the Symcox family. Been away from them since sometime after World War II. She's catching the next flight out of Chicago and will be here this afternoon. Says she's up to doing it now. We need her to identify Jubal's property at the apartment and give us a full statement."

“Glad to hear she’s okay,” said Stohlbach. “I was starting to think ol’ Jubal might’ve slid in ahead of us. Chicago PD got our telex on Jubal?”

“Yep. They’ve put the Kadinsky residence on special attention.”

“What’d Alba say?”

“A lot. It didn’t come easy. You’re going to love the phone bill.”

“Don’t worry. It’s only money.”

“Basically,” began Johnson, opening his notebook, “she confirms that she is in fact Alba Symcox, older sister of Nathaniel and Sarah. Age: sixty-eight. Also confirms that Jubal is the son of Nathaniel and Sarah. Estimated age: mid-thirties. The Symcoxes are an old Alabama family, going back to the early nineteenth century. Lots of colonels in the Civil War.”

“Alba a southern belle?”

“Hard to say. Sounded very subdued on the phone. After her escape from the Symcox place forty years ago, she said she found her way to Chicago. Says she used several disguises and did everything she could to cut off ties with the family. She ended up marrying Jerome Kadinsky. He’s executive vice president of Fancher-Drysdale investment bank in Chicago, and she’s stayed put there ever since.”

“What about the Symcoxes?”

Johnson examined his notes. “Okay, like I said, the family goes way back, but somewhere around the turn of the century they lost their original estate on the Gulf Coast and moved to a farmhouse on that property in Buncombe County. Sort of faded, eccentric gentry living off a trust fund one of the colonels set up after the Civil War. They were solitary people and apparently withdrew more and more from mainstream society, with the farm becoming the center of their lives. When World War II came along, Nathaniel Symcox got drafted and went to the Far East. He was with Stilwell in Burma. Got captured by the Japanese. He escaped and apparently got lost in the boondocks, some remote region of the Burma-India border. Alba called it the Naga Hills. This is where things start getting flaky. She says he was discovered starving and delirious by some off-beat commune of Hindus. They took him in, nursed him back to health. But then they started keeping him to themselves, like some kind of exotic pet. They were involved in some pretty kinky stuff, a Hindu practice called Tantrism. Left-handed Tantrism—"

"Left-handed who?" asked Stohlbach.

"Tantrism. It's a kind of worship where your regular values are reversed—black is white, evil is good. They were into stuff like human sacrifice, drinking their own urine, indiscriminate sex—"

"And cutting their tongues," added Skoda. "The good things in life."

"Nathaniel fell under their spell and stayed for several years. It was not until after the war that an occupation patrol came through and found him. But by then he was completely wigged out. He came away kicking and screaming, lugging a huge blue stone statue with him. No doubt the one Jubal had in his apartment here. He was brought back to the States, boarded out of the service and hospitalized for some time. He was eventually released, but according to Alba, he never really recovered. He came back to the farm in Alabama, carrying on about his newfound religion. He had a strong, magnetic personality and gradually instilled in the others this idea of creating a perfect race of people from the remnants of the Symcox family. He appealed to all their old southern pride and bitterness. Here was their chance to reestablish the old order, the glory of a hundred years ago."

"Sort of an uptown Klan," said Skoda.

"Exactly. Except they weren't interested in converts. Just themselves. They were already pretty flaky and allowed themselves to be pulled into Nathaniel's web, a sort of loose tribe of sisters and cousins and aunts, about a dozen in all. It was all built on this concept of reversed values, rejecting society. His proudest moment was when he 'married' his sister, Sarah."

“His own sister.” Stohlbach gasped. “Why would he do that?”

“What greater reversal of values could you have, Cap, what greater scorn for tradition? That’s what he was doing.”

“Yeah, but punching your own sister. If you have children, don’t their molecules come unwrapped or something?”

“Basically, that’s right. I don’t know if Nathaniel thought that through, or cared.”

“Alba say anything else?”

“She was pretty distraught on the phone, so I didn’t push her too much. She’ll give us a complete fill when she gets here this afternoon. Apparently she was the only member of the family that had any qualms about anything. She was turned off by Nathaniel from the beginning but was afraid to leave for the longest time. Nathaniel had created a kind of internal dictatorship and ruled the roost. Alba was only in her twenties and had hardly ever been off the farm, like most the other Symcoxes. In a way, it’s a miracle she got away at all.”

Dark furrows crossed Captain Stohlbach’s brow. He turned to Johnson. “You mean to say, Mag, when she gets here this afternoon, we’ll be looking across the desk at somebody who their uncle or brother was—” Stohlbach stopped, his hands gesturing futilely.

“I don’t know,” said Johnson. “It doesn’t show on her driver’s license.”

37

The door to Captain Stohlbach's office opened. The Homicide chief rose uncertainly as Alba Kadinsky entered. She was slender, almost thin, in a dark suit, clutching a small purse.

"This is Mrs. Kadinsky," announced Magnus Johnson.

Stohlbach stared at the woman. There was a pause. Then: "Ma'am, I'm Hubert Stohlbach, commander, Homicide Branch. Hope your trip from Chicago was pleasant and . . . and without negatory effect."

"It was quite all right, thank you," said the woman. Her voice was toneless. She brushed a strand of loose hair from her face, and her wide vulnerable eyes fastened on Stohlbach. Through her fatigue, she bore a faded stateliness.

"We've been talking from the airport," said Magnus Johnson. "She came without her husband. Said she wanted to talk to us on her own."

"Yes, ma'am, we understand," said Stohlbach.

"She was reviewing her brother's hospitalization and other things," Johnson said, turning to the woman. "Captain Stohlbach here has been briefed on your family. Do you mind continuing, ma'am?"

"No, no," she said, taking a seat. "It's just difficult to know exactly where—"

"The hospitalization, ma'am," said Johnson gently.

“Yes.” She took a handkerchief from her purse and blew her nose.

“Take your time, ma’am,” said Stohlbach.

“All right,” she said, drawing a short breath. “After the war, Nathaniel was in Atlanta for more than a year. No one visited him. We all stayed on the property. Then one day he came home. He brought all his books and sandalwood antiques from India with him. The doctors had told him to stay on medication, but he ran out of it and never got any more.”

She stopped and reflected a moment. “He began teaching us his ‘revelations’ from India, the visions, the ceremonies, the nighttime feasts—always at nighttime—the ‘dark convulsions of joy,’ he called them, where we would learn the Tantric secrets.”

“Tantric,” interrupted Johnson. “Could you tell us a little about that.”

“Yes. It is one of the many forms of Hinduism, based on a body of literature called Tantras. In its dark or ‘left-handed’ form, it seeks to honor everything that ordinary people consider unworthy or evil. Like other Hindus, its followers have many gods, but left-handed Tantrics most honor Nirriti, deity of darkness, and Kali, goddess of destruction.”

“What secrets did Nathaniel teach you?”

“Secrets of prayer and discipline to help put aside the distractions of ordinary day-to-day living. This allowed us to focus on what he said was the true vision of reality—a series of cycles of life and death. Reincarnation, some would say. Circles of misery within misery, inverting all our values so that we saw joy in death, grief in birth, darkness in light. Who were we to challenge Nathaniel? We were ignorant children, isolated from the world. He was the traveled wise man returning with the Truth. He had a terribly compelling effect on us.”

Stohlbach raised his hand, his face clouded with confusion. “I’m sorry, ma’am, we can’t submit a report on that. Can you be more specific? I mean about what Nathaniel did.”

Alba Kadinsky moved to the edge of her chair, her shoes primly together on the floor. “The potions, the mandalas, we learned those from his books. But Nathaniel's greatest secrets were never written down."

"What were they?"

"They started with his marriage to my sister, Sarah. Their first night was called 'Dark Epiphany.' There was a feast. It was in one of the caves beneath the house. There was a huge obelisk, some kind of cave formation, lit with candles. We were forced to do things—"

"Things?"

"Goats, they were sacrificed. We ate their brains, their . . . their organs. The men forced themselves on us."

"Couldn't you leave?"

"I was terrified. Nathaniel and my other brothers kept a tight grip everywhere. There were more marriages. Children were born. Many died. We buried them in the caves. With each marriage, there was a feast. Nathaniel made us drink home brew mixed with our—" She stopped again.

"Yes, ma'am?"

"I'm sorry." She was sobbing now. "The children were forced to watch the newly married couples. Nathaniel said it made them stronger, more fit to perpetuate the family. Once Nathaniel asked a mother to sacrifice her baby. The baby was deformed. Nathaniel said it would prove her strength. She couldn't do it. So her uncles did it for her. I heard the baby crying in the next room, and then it stopped—"

"Yes?" said Stohlbach.

"Nathaniel's rule went on. Blood, drinking, threats. Finally, Nathaniel said he wanted me, he wanted a second wife. I . . . I complied, but only long enough for him to relax his guard. And then one night I escaped. I took the family ring with me. I could not bear the thought of the ring being a part of his new order."

There was a long silence. The woman snuffled into her handkerchief. The detectives watched her as the shadows deepened in the office.

“Ma’am,” said Magnus Johnson softly, “if we could ask you one other thing.”

“Yes.” She nodded.

“About the arms and munitions. There was a reference to them in the letter we found in Jubal Symcox’s apartment. Did you ever have any on the farm?”

“No. At least not while I was there. Nathaniel talked a great deal about getting some. But we were so isolated. It was difficult to make contact. Also, no one ever bothered us, we were so far out in the country. There was no feeling that we needed anything. Although, I remember now he said that when he died, he would authorize his first-born son to leave the farm and obtain arms.”

“Who would that be?”

“Jubal. There were two other brothers, and several who died. Jubal would be at least in his thirties by now. Have you found him?”

“No, ma’am,” said Johnson. “We’re working on that.” He paused. “Mrs. Kadinsky, could you tell us why you never went to the authorities about this before?”

The woman turned her eyes to the floor, twisting her handkerchief in her fingers. “I . . . I couldn’t,” she whispered. “There was so much fear and—”

She looked up at the detectives. “Shame.” Her head dropped again, and she wept into her hands, her narrow shoulders shaking.

Johnson went to her side, attempting to comfort her. “I think that will be enough for now,” said Captain Stohlbach.

38

The blinds had been pulled in the Homicide office, and the fluorescent lights hissed softly. Most of the desks were empty. Dewey Hudlow entered. He stared at the floor, his face drawn. He ignored Johnson sitting nearby.

"Anything new in the second interview?" Captain Stohlbach asked Johnson.

"Well, we got a better line on Franklin and Monroe," said Johnson. "Alba married the banker guy, Jerome Kadinsky, and they had just the two children, Franklin and Monroe. No daughters."

"What about Jerome? He know about the Symcoxes?"

"Says she never told him. Sounds weird, I know, but I guess some men accept huge blank spots in their wives' past and let it go. She was swank enough and had enough of that old southern charm to keep him pacified, I guess. But when Franklin and Monroe came of age, she decided to tell them all about the Alabama connection. Swore them to secrecy. But telling them was a mistake, especially Monroe. He became extremely curious about the Alabama family and Nathaniel's strange experiment."

"That's why he made that trip to the caves?" asked Stohlbach.

"Right. He knew the location of the caves from descriptions she gave him. That's how he was able to link them to the I-59 engineering project when the paperwork on it came across his desk at the Federal Highway Administration."

"And then he wangled a spot on the crew that went to Alabama."

"Exactly," continued Johnson. "He wanted to see for himself. Remember that letter he wrote to Franklin about going down there against his better judgment? He was going partly out of curiosity and partly to offer an olive branch, if he actually encountered them."

"He took the ring with him, didn't he?" said Stohlbach. "The family ring."

"Exactly. That was his olive branch. Remember, Nathaniel and Sarah were pretty angry that Alba took the ring in the first place and said they'd hunt her down to get it back. Symbols of that sort are big with loonies."

"What kind of ring was it?"

"She said it was a large silver alloy band, no stone, with a crest bearing a sun and a crescent moon under a rampant lion."

"What's that mean?"

"Beats me. Maybe the lion, he's on top. He's the king and runs the show."

"So Monroe goes off to Alabama ten years ago with the ring and doesn't come back. What does that prove?"

"Nothing," said Johnson. "We don't know how he died. The bodies of the highway party still haven't been found."

"The Symcoxes offed them?"

"Possible. Nathaniel and Sarah attached great value to the caves. What did they say? It was their 'sacred ground.' They would tolerate no intrusion. The darkness of the caves made a perfect fortress. It's all consistent with their notion of reversed values, of darkness being preferred to light."

"So why did Monroe go with the highway crew? Why couldn't he go just by himself?"

"Like his letter said, he wanted cover. Maybe protection, too. My feeling is both Monroe and Franklin had a lot of mixed feelings about being associated with the Symcox family. Dishonor, of course, but also a blood tie. They were bound by their mother's secret and knew she lived in fear of Nathaniel."

“That letter was ten years old. Why you s’pose Franklin sat on it all this time and didn’t take his suspicions to anyone?”

“Maybe fear. Maybe shame. Like his mother. I don’t know.”

“Sounds thin to me, Mag.”

“Maybe he didn’t think much of it at first. Just his brother getting carried away. Then after a few years, he begins to have second thoughts and starts nosing around privately.”

There was a pause. “Look here,” said Dewey Hudlow, getting up slowly from his chair nearby. It was the first time he had spoken. “All this talk about rings and Hindus and praying with your left hand on your nuts is fine. But there’s still a lot of holes in this thing.”

“Name some,” said Johnson.

“Okay. You got this sap-brained hillbilly that goes for indoor poontang, and you made the family connection with Symcox and Kadinsky. All that’s fine. But you tell me how in the world Jubal Symcox ended up in the exact same apartment building as Frank Kadinsky. Especially with rental space hard as it is to find in downtown D.C. Ain’t that a pluperfect coincidence?”

“No, it was not a coincidence,” said Johnson. “He was stalking Kadinsky. He comes up here eighteen, twenty months ago, bides his time and then jumps at the apartment when a vacancy comes up.”

“But why’d he have to be in the same building? Couldn’t he kill him just as good from Swampoodle?”

“He wanted to get into the building to see Kadinsky and his neighbors up close. For the setup. Ambrose Fairlyte. Remember?”

“But how did he know to come to Washington in the first place?”

“When that highway crew with Monroe Kadinsky was killed down in those caves, the Symcoxes must have found the family ring on Monroe. That baffled them. Monroe’s ID showed he lived in Washington and his last name was Kadinsky. They couldn’t figure what in hell he was doing with the family ring. But they suspected the worst. Somebody was after them. Then Franklin Kadinsky, Monroe’s brother, starts making formal inquiries at the county court about the Symcox property. Some clerk in the courthouse tells Sarah or Jubal or somebody, and now they're really freaking out. Franklin has the same last name as Monroe. They're both from Washington. Something's got to give. So Jubal Symcox leaves the farm and comes to D.C. Simple as that."

Hudlow was still not satisfied. "So once he gets here, what made Frank Kadinsky spook just before he was taken out?"

"He found out he was being shadowed," said Johnson. "Remember, Jubal was using an assumed name. He was invisible. But Kadinsky must have picked up on him somehow, maybe something in a chance conversation. Maybe he saw some of his mail in the lobby addressed to Jubal Symcox, 'care of Jeffrey Stanton,' just like we did."

"One more thing," said Hudlow. "All this stuff about small arms and ammunition. Were they going to have theirselves some kind of Dark Epiphany Army?"

"Mostly protective stuff, self-defense, going by Nathaniel's letter," said Johnson. "Don't forget, Jubal was under orders to get the stuff when Nathaniel died."

"God only knows what kind of arsenal they might have by now," said Hudlow. "Maybe we should run that Dark Epiphany name by the FBI. They keep a lot of kooks."

"Check that bank in Birmingham, too, where Nathaniel said the family trust fund was at," said Johnson. "See where the disbursements went."

There was another pause. Then Captain Stohlbach spoke. "Where you think Jubal's at right now?"

"Either still here, or split for Alabama," said Johnson.

"That means a fugitive warrant," said Stohlbach.

"Not just that," said Johnson. "We need a search warrant for that farm."

"Wait a minute, Mag. You suggesting what I think you're suggesting?"

"Yeah, couple of us need to go down there. Help with the warrant."

"I can't let you do that. I need all my troops here."

“Those yo-yo sheriffs down there don’t know a search warrant from a sack of salt. They’ll be tripping all over each other.”

“I can’t get the travel allowance.”

“Captain, this is a serious matter.”

“How you going to justify the travel?”

“You know the routine: ‘MPD has peculiar and unique knowledge in reference to the captioned subject,’ et cetera and et cetera.”

Stohlbach looked helpless.

“You want Jubal to get away?” Johnson asked.

“Oh, land’s sake, go on down there,” said Stohlbach.

Johnson’s face broke into a massive smile.

“But only the two of you,” the captain added. “Just you and Hud. Nestor stays here to mind the shop.”

“There’s a couple of loose ends, Captain,” said Johnson. “It’s possible we may have to go down into one of those vertical pit caves on the Symcox property.”

“Whatever for?”

“Property search. The good stuff may not be in the house.”

“Jubal keeps his extra socks in a cave?”

“Maybe. If we do it, we’ve got to have the equipment, ropes and maybe cable ladders, I don’t know what all—”

“Homicide’s not paying for that, Mag.”

“Split the cost with the county and the state or whoever’s there. It won’t be much. And we’re going to need a couple of guides, some kind of trained cave climbers.”

“This ain’t no expedition to Mount Everest, Mag.”

“No, but going down into a vertical pit cave a couple of hundred feet deep is not exactly child’s play. We’ve got to have some experienced people with us.”

“And pay their insurance, too, I s’pose,” groaned Stohlbach.

“Come on, Chief, cave crawlers love this kind of stuff. They’ll probably do it for nothing.”

“I’m going to have to think on that one.”

“Well, you think. I’m packing.”

39

Dewey Hudlow wedged himself into the telephone booth and called Washington. Beyond the hinged doors he could hear the subdued clamor of the airport concourse and the occasional thunder of a jet taking off.

"Hey, Nestor. That you? This Hudlow. In Atlanta."

"Yeah, Hud. Good trip?"

"Never did like airplanes. Ain't natural for man to fly."

"Or swim, either. Strictly a land animal, right?"

"Far as this boy goes, I clue you."

"Mag there?"

"He went to rent a car. We driving up to Goshen Shoals this evening."

"How far is it?"

"'Bout a hundred and fifty miles, by way of South Overshoe. Sumbitch ain't hardly on the map."

"Hey, you'll be in your element. Lots of rednecks."

"Yeah, but they talk funny."

"Listen, couple things. FBI blanked on Dark Epiphany. Also nothing on the Symcox name. But they're sending a resident agent from Huntsville to hook up with you on the fugitive warrant in Goshen Shoals."

Hudlow grunted. A large pregnant woman with bulging eyes approached the phone booth and looked in at Hudlow.

"Hud," said Skoda over the line, "you and Mag doing all right?"

"Yeah, you know." Hudlow pulled out his notebook and pretended to pore through it, glancing up at the woman. "Not a whole barrel of laughs coming down on the plane."

"Why you suppose Stohlbach sent you two?"

"See if Alabama is big enough for both of us. D.C. ain't."

"I'm not sure he thought that one through."

"Yeah, you won't be here to keep the peace, Nestor."

"How does somebody like Stohlbach get to be chief of Homicide? Sucker never worked a real case. Came over from Files and Distribution. How'd he do it?"

"Signed all the right forms."

The pregnant woman had folded her arms menacingly across her chest. Hudlow bent over his notebook.

"Look, Hud," said Skoda. "Go easy on Johnson while you're down there. If it wasn't for him, we wouldn't be this far along. All that hifalutin knowledge of his has some use."

"Don't take no Ph.D. to break into a man's house."

"That was my thing, too. Don't lay it all on him."

"You got to understand, it's hard to work with a man that does that. What's he going to do next time? It's the ol' trust thing."

"All I'm saying is just try to go easy. Maybe he will, too. Show all those deputy sheriffs down there how warm and cuddly you two can be."

"I been thinking 'bout that, Nestor. They just going to love it, a chicken bone detective."

"This is the new age, Hud. They see them all the time on TV."

"Uncle Ben in bib overalls 'bout all they can handle."

"Well, then it's your job to protect him. Show them he's a regular guy."

The woman was glaring at Hudlow through the hinged doors. "Hey, Nestor," said Hudlow, "there's a pregnant frog out here wants this phone. She's about to sit on my mouth if I don't hang up. Any other news from up there?"

There was a pause. "Uh, yeah. One of your snitches, guy named Cheeks, called. Said Quovadis Logan's little boy hasn't showed up. Cheeks asked me to tell you."

"Thomas not at his grandmother's?" said Hudlow, his voice tightening slightly.

"That's what Cheeks said. Missing Persons has it."

"Keep on them, would you, Nestor?"

"You bet."

"And Nestor. Check something out for me."

"What's that?"

"Texas Avenue Annex."

"Texas Avenue Annex? What in hell is that?"

"I don't know. Might have something to do with Kadinsky."

"How so?"

"Tip. Somebody said it might be a connection."

"That all you got?"

"Yeah, they didn't tell me anything else."

"Your snitches usually talk a lot more."

"Not this one."

40

Buncombe County Deputy Sheriff Benny Guy Gomillion held the Pyrex coffeepot up to the window. An umber sludge rolled across the bottom of the glass.

"See you struck oil this morning, Tabard," said Gomillion.

"Good for what ails you," came a voice from behind him. Gomillion continued to study the coffeepot. The liquid lapped in minuscule waves against the side. He shook the pot gently. The sediment rose like storm clouds, darkening the upper levels, and then slowly settled again. As he studied the pot, he saw a dark red Chevrolet Impala pull into the courthouse parking lot. A thin drizzle was falling.

"Company," Gomillion announced. "Must be them boys from Washington."

He heard the doors of the car slam and the rasping tread of feet on the wooden steps to the office. Two figures in pale raincoats entered, one behind the other. The room, bare except for a few low pieces of furniture, seemed fixed in permanent twilight.

"Hi, I'm Dewey Hudlow, detective, Washington, D.C., Metropolitan Po-leece. How you this wet Alabama day?"

"Dry for now," said Gomillion, smiling. "I'm Benny Guy Gomillion. This here's Sheriff Jones. Tabard Jones." A muscular man with a sleepy face rose from a darkened recess of the office and came forward. The three men shook hands around.

“Oh,” said Hudlow. “And this here is Magnus Johnson. Detective Magnus Johnson. He’s with me.” Johnson stepped from behind Hudlow.

“Good morning,” he said softly. Gomillion’s eyes widened for a fleeting moment.

“How you, Johnson?” he said. He took Johnson’s extended hand briefly. Sheriff Jones stepped forward and surveyed the detective. He seemed to be forming words with his mouth before he spoke. He glanced at Hudlow, who gave him a barely perceptible nod.

“Welcome to Goshen Shoals, Johnson,” the sheriff said at last.

Johnson peered through thick glasses. “Thank you,” he said.

“This is new country for me and Mag,” said Hudlow. “Never been here before.”

“Not many folks have,” said Jones. “It’s kind of at the end of ever’thing. But we like it that way.”

“Seems so quiet. Sorry we have to come in here and bust it all up for a while.”

“You mean the Symcoxes? That ain’t nothing. Their place is ten miles out in the country. Won’t nobody hardly know we was there.”

“You got the search warrant?”

“Yeah, Judge Tatem. No problem. Also, State Police called about the fugitive warrant on this Jubal Symcox. I don’t know no Jubal. Do you, Benny Guy?”

“No, sir. Let’s see. Who’s up there at the Symcox place now? There’s Sarah. I know she’s up there. I seen her a few times in Goshen Shoals. Come in here for her mail or the bank now and again. And ol’ Nathaniel. I believe he’s up there. Or maybe he’s dead by now.”

“How about children?” asked Hudlow.

“Children?” Gomillion scratched his head. “All these years, I ain’t seen a child one. But it’s people say there’s some up there.”

“Well, our information is that Jubal is Sarah’s son,” said Hudlow. “Be in his thirties by now.”

"Like I say, I never heard anything 'bout no Jubal."

"Real spooky-looking boy. Got silverish hair and this weird-shaped head."

Gomillion and Jones shook their heads gravely. "The fugitive warrant says homicide," said Gomillion. "Jubal whupped up on someone in Washington?"

"You bet," said Hudlow. "Strangulation."

"Law', we ain't had a homicide or anything close to that here in, what is it now, Tabard, six, seven years?"

"At least."

"And y'all think he's back up on that farm hiding out?"

"That's our guess."

"FBI in Huntsville called up here yes'day. Said they sending somebody up here, too. What in hell is this, World War Three?"

"Don't worry about them. They just candy asses."

"So what's the story?"

"More tangled than a weasel trying to milk a bobcat."

"Well, could you fill me and Benny Guy in?"

"No problem," said Hudlow. "You got a couple of years?"

"Before you do that," interrupted Magnus Johnson, "do you mind if I use one of your phones, Sheriff? I need to check with our people in D.C. They're expecting to hear from us."

Sheriff Jones gave Hudlow another quick glance. "Certainly, Johnson." He led the detective to an inner office, then came back out, closing the door behind him.

"What it turns out is this," said Hudlow. Jones and Gomillion pulled chairs up close to the detective. All three men were more relaxed now. "It was this boy that works for the House of Representatives in Congress named Kadinsky. Franklin Kadinsky. He was strangled in his apartment in D.C., couple, three weeks back. We couldn't make head nor tails of it for the longest time. Wasn't no reg'lar killing. No jitterbugs or dope or nothing. Well, we got to interviewing this guy that worked with Kadinsky, which he gave us some papers showing Kadinsky was trying to find out about a accident where a bunch of highway people, including his own brother, was killed or disappeared in some kind of cave situation back up here in Buncombe County. You know what I'm talking about?"

"Oh, yeah," said Jones. "Ten, eleven years ago. Engineering party on Interstate 59. Disappeared up in the northeast corner. Never found a trace of them, except their truck. Remember that, Benny Guy?"

"Yeah, that was the last time there was some excitement around here. State police, helicopters, highway folks, dogs. I thought *that* was World War Three. This must be World War Four now."

Gomillion pulled a foil packet of Red Man plug tobacco from his shirt, opened it and proffered it to Hudlow with a clasp knife. Deftly, the detective cut a small square for himself, put it into his mouth and then passed the remaining plug around to his companions. For a few moments, the three chewed solemnly, letting the wads soften, a ceremonial warmth filling the room.

"So this guy that worked with Kadinsky give us the highway papers and all," Hudlow continued, "and the name Symcox popped up. Turns out they got property round I-59 somewheres. That right?"

"Yessir, that would be right," said Jones. "Don't the Symcox property run clean over to the county line right near where the interstate comes through, Benny Guy?"

"I believe so. It's all pretty close in there."

"Well, it turned out that this Jubal Symcox was living under a phony name in the same apartment building in Washington as where Kadinsky was killed. That seemed like too much for coincidence, so Mag"—Hudlow pointed toward the inner office—"him and his partner, they went into Symcox's apartment and found the damndest bunch of shit you ever laid eyes on."

"What was it?"

"Mainly this letter, like a ol' timey testament, by Sarah and Nathaniel Symcox, saying how they was setting up this purebred type pedigree nation-state thing of just Symcox family members, nobody else, out there on the farm property, all secret, and guns to keep folks out, and how ever'body in the family swore allegiance except this one sister Alba, which escaped, and the rest of them under orders to revenge her. Well, we found Alba in Chicago. She's the mother of the two Kadinsky boys. She spilled ever'thing, about how she left the family and took off for Chicago and disguised herself and married some big shot banker and how Nathaniel was a prisoner in the Second World War up near India somewhere and escaped and took up with this off-brand bunch of Hindus that got him started on all this weird bidness, standing on their head, eating yak puke and whatever. He flipped out pretty heavy, and when he come back to the States, he got this notion of starting up the pure race thing with his family, punching his own sister Sarah and getting the other members—"

"Oh, come on," said Jones. "You dreamt all that up."

"No, ask Mag in there. He knows more 'bout it than I do. And at the end of Sarah and Nathaniel's letter, they laid down a bunch of commandments which the family s'pose to follow and not tell nobody and stay on the farm. Then this guy Kadinsky, the one that had the brother killed down here with the highway group, he steps right in the middle of it, suspicioning that the disappearance of his brother had something to do with the Symcoxes. Best as Mag and me can figure it, the engineers stumbled over something that the Symcoxes didn't want them to see, maybe down in one of them caves, so they offed them. Next thing you know, Frank Kadinsky is smelling around, writing to the survey office here and all, so Jubal goes to Washington and takes him out. He tried to lay it on another tenant in the building and then took off. That's why we think he's back here now."

Gomillion whistled softly. "Them caves," he said. "The northern end of the county is honeycombed with them. You never find somebody hiding up in there. Some of them's three, four hundred feet deep, maybe more. Ain't hardly nobody been in them."

"Symcoxes s'pose to keep their religious stuff in there, according to the letter," said Hudlow.

"What kind of religious stuff?"

"I don't know. Maybe idols and all. Mag in there, he would know."

"How come he knows so much?" asked Gomillion, a trace of querulousness in his voice.

Hudlow paused and then looked at Gomillion. "Mag? He's got more information jammed in that burr head of his than any six of us put together. Don't ask me where he got it."

Gomillion looked blankly at Hudlow. "These Symcoxes. What you s'pose they pray to, the fatted calf?"

"Up in D.C. at his apartment, ol' Jubal had this tall blue stone thing he prayed to. Mag says it was like a stone dick."

"Pray to a dick?"

"Hey, listen, I ain't no sociologist. It's just this blue stone thing stands about three foot high. Come out of Burma, is what Mag said, way back in the mountains."

"What kind of people live up in there to do that?" asked Sheriff Jones.

"Burma people, I guess," said Hudlow.

"I had a uncle over there in the war," said Gomillion. "He seen them."

"What were they?"

"Well, they call them aborigines," said Gomillion, "but they mostly niggers."

"Whatever they are, I don't want no parts of them," said Hudlow. "Now these Symcoxes, when's the last time you seen any of them?"

"Like I told you," said Gomillion, "only one I seen recently is Sarah. Maybe six months back. She must be getting on. Years ago, seems to me I heard people saying they did have some kind of commune-type hippie thing up there. S'posed to had their own school to keep the truant officer out, you know. But I heard it all kind of fizzled. Tell you the truth, I never even been up there. No one goes there. S'posed to be all run down, no electricity, no road, got to walk in three, four miles."

"I guess we'll be paying the place a visit shortly—"

The door to the inner office opened, and Magnus Johnson walked out. The three men stopped talking. Hudlow removed the wad of tobacco from his mouth.

"Excuse me," Johnson said. "I didn't mean to be on the phone so long. There's a lot of new things."

"Was that Stohlbach just blabbing," asked Hudlow, "or Skoda telling you something real?"

"Detective Skoda."

"Well, what we got?"

"First, FBI got to the bank in Birmingham. There's a Symcox trust account with an excess of two million dollars in it. It was terminated two or three years ago and regular distributions of the principal have been going out to Sarah and Jubal. Ten and twelve thousand dollars a clip, sometimes more. Nathaniel, the old man, apparently is dead."

"Two million dollars," blurted Gomillion. "They ain't that much money in all of Buncombe County."

"About half of it is still there. All the canceled checks to Jubal are coming back from D.C. Now we know what the plain brown envelope we saw in the apartment lobby was all about."

"What's he been buying?" said Hudlow. "The Washington Monument?"

"Next thing," continued Johnson, "it turns out the Texas Avenue Annex you told Nestor about is one of these mini-storage warehouse type places in southeast Washington. It's where you can rent a self-contained shed or storage space. Seems Jubal has several sheds there rented in his name. We don't know what's in them, but Skoda's getting a warrant and going down there tonight with Six-D."

"Texas Avenue Annex," muttered Hudlow. "Much as I been over D.C., I never heard of that one."

Johnson turned to Gomillion and Sheriff Jones. "My partner, Detective Skoda in Washington, asked that if it's possible, we hold off here on executing the search warrant at the farm until they check the mini-storage place. Then we won't be going into the farm quite so blind. Does that sound all right?"

Sheriff Jones looked at Gomillion and nodded. "No problem."

"How many deputies do you have?" Johnson asked.

"Four full-time."

"No county police, right?"

"That's right."

"Well, depending on what comes out of Washington and how big a thing we think we have, we may want to ask for assistance from the state police. That okay?"

"Fine with me."

"Just in case it comes up, Detective Skoda also has arranged for two professional speleologists to come in here from Chattanooga. They're guys experienced in cave climbing. Probably tomorrow or—"

"Hold on there, Johnson," said Sheriff Jones. "You saying we might go down in one of them caves?"

"Why, yes," said Johnson, a note of caution in his voice. "It could become necessary."

"You ain't getting me to dive into one of them holes, no, sir."

Johnson took a short breath and looked at the sheriff. "It's your jurisdiction and your warrant. You or one of your men has to execute it."

"It don't cover under the ground. Just the premises."

"Look at the language again, Sheriff. It's in the specs we sent you."

Jones opened a metal box on his desk and took out a sheaf of papers bound by a rubber band. He unrolled the papers, turned back the top sheet and moved his finger slowly across the second page. "'. . . and any open areas lying under said property.' Yessir, there it is."

"Look," said Johnson, "it may never be necessary. Let's hope so. It's just that we want to be covered."

---o---

Jones was only partially mollified. "Seems to me you all making the World Series out of the Little League."

"We don't know which it is, yet," said Johnson.

"Sheriff," said Hudlow, raising his hand in a conciliatory gesture, "why don't Mag and me take off now. We ain't going be doing anything the rest of today while they work that warrant in D.C. We might as well go down to Gadsden and take in a picture show or something. When we know more, we'll be back. How's that?"

The four men shook hands. Johnson and Hudlow moved toward the door and stepped out into the rain. From the parking lot, the courthouse was dark and forlorn. Rivulets of pearly water ran down the tin roof. No one was in sight.

41

"Hey, Mag. You're not going to believe what we found." Skoda's voice had risen an octave.

"Slow it, Nestor," said Johnson into the telephone. "Mother Stohlbach's paying for the call." Johnson sat on the edge of the motel bed, a yellow legal pad on his knees. Hudlow hummed tunelessly in the shower a few feet away.

"At the Texas Avenue Annex. Goddamn shed was full of rifles, magnum ammunition, even some kind of plastic explosives. Bunch of free-lance Lebanese making the deliveries. Connections in Cyprus and Lisbon. Intelligence is talking to them right now."

"Christ, what was Symcox getting ready for, invasion of Normandy?"

"Looked like it. Bunch of three-hundred-caliber Mauser rifles with scopes on Buehler mounts and a half-dozen Dutch-made mortars. Jubal must have been using D.C. as a transshipment point."

"What about the explosives?"

"Bomb Squad said it was some kind of gas-enhanced plastic, like the stuff the crazies in Beirut use. Hard to get outside military channels."

"The Symcoxes must be known in high places."

"All those Civil War colonels. What you think they were really up to?"

"Nothing," said Johnson. "They're just crazy, what few of them may still be around. Nathaniel's dead. Nobody here seems to know much about them. Any sign they shipped any of that stuff down here?"

"No. Shed manager said nothing's gone out."

"Everything pretty well buttoned down?"

"All the ordnance is impounded. No sign of Jubal. You probably got him down there."

Johnson pondered a moment. "Lebanese," he said. "So the little dark guy with the bald spot that Hud and I saw on the subway with Symcox, maybe he wasn't selling dope."

"Same with the ones we saw outside his apartment window. And the ones running up Eighteenth Street."

"We sure misfired on that one."

"There's more, Mag. You know the tip Hud got on the storage shed? I think he got it from Quovadis Logan."

"How you figure?"

"Turns out the manager at the storage shed is her cousin, guy named Spriggs. When we went in with the warrant, he started talking. Said Quovadis had told him little bits about the Kadinsky killing, stuff I guess Hud had passed on to her, like it was on L'Enfant Court. He noticed one of his sheds was rented out to a guy on that same street. He said it was unusual, a white guy giving him business. He checked the address with Quovadis, and it turned out to be the same building as Kadinsky's. It's that simple."

There was a brief silence. Johnson stared at the telephone.

"Anything on Quovadis' boy Thomas?" he asked Skoda. "Hud told me about him."

"Not a thing. Missing Persons still looking."

There was another pause. "Oh, one other thing," continued Skoda. "Remember the motorcycle that killed Quovadis? That may not have been an accident."

"How do you mean?"

"The guy on the machine. He was a Lebanese national."

"Oh, come on, Nestor. You know all these rag heads look alike."

"Yeah, but this one had the address of the Texas Avenue Annex in his pocket."

42

A warm mist hung in the air. The cruisers, their fishing pole antennas swaying gently, pulled onto the shoulder of the dirt road. Muffled thumps and thuds echoed against the wall of hickories and chestnuts to either side of the road as the men began assembling in a loose swirl of hats and shotgun barrels.

Sheriff Tabard Jones rested a muddied boot on the front bumper of his cruiser, unfolding a survey map. Several state troopers marched up and stood stiffly beside him. Benny Guy Gomillion reached into the backseat of the cruiser and pulled out a large nervous Doberman pinscher on a choke chain. Two other deputies, dressed in striped beige trousers and curl-brim straw hats, joined Sheriff Jones. Each chewed gravely. Dewey Hudlow and Magnus Johnson stood in the circle of men, eyeing the alien wall of trees around them. Just outside the circle stood an FBI agent, dressed in a baby blue jumpsuit, and, beside him, two ragged pale men with coils of rope and metal tackle piled at their feet. They were the speleologists from Chattanooga.

Magnus Johnson looked at them and the FBI agent—the tidy federal protector and the tattered crawlers of caves, thrown together in common cause. The cavers' bony faces reflected fatigue, as though they had just emerged from weeks underground. Jack Farthing, at thirty-five the older of the two, had the look of a battered hawk, his tired eyes scanning the earth ceaselessly. Jesse Lamont, the younger, nursed a bruise on his face from a recent fall. The FBI agent, in contrast, was all ruddy wholesomeness, his placid good looks so flawless as to be unmemorable. There was no uneven feature, no crag or fissure for the eye to grasp. The perfect federal agent. Even his name—was it Eliot Todd, or Todd Eliot?—was appropriately uncertain, though Hudlow and Johnson privately had opted for the latter.

"The house lays back in there three or four miles," said Sheriff Jones, pointing to a faint path disappearing into the forest. "It's kind of rough ground. Hope ya'll ain't brought your city shoes."

The men, fifteen in all, formed a single file and entered the forest, Sheriff Jones at the lead, the speleologists bringing up the rear, each lugging a tangle of harnesses, helmets, ropes, sleeping bags, food. A dusky light enclosed them. Mist clung to the tree branches, and the leaves above vanished into a silent gray vault.

Johnson stopped to remove a stone from his shoe, falling behind the others. He signaled to Hudlow to stay back with him.

"There's something you should know, Hud," he said slowly. "It may have been one of Symcox's people that got to Quovadis."

Hudlow's eyes narrowed. "Quovadis? How you figure?"

"Nestor told me on the phone last night. Said the guy on the motorcycle had the address of the Texas Avenue Annex on him."

"Goddamn Lebanese? How'd they make the connection between Quovadis and the po-leece?"

"Must have overheard her and her cousin talking about it at the Texas Avenue Annex."

Hudlow said nothing. A distant storm gathered on his face.

"I just thought you should know, Hud, before we go into this place," said Johnson. "I'm sorry." The two detectives scrambled to catch up with the other men.

They walked in silence for an hour. At length, they heard a

distant rush of water and after climbing down a shallow ravine, crossed a swollen black stream. Several more ravines followed, and then the floor of the forest flattened out. Within minutes, the trees began to thin, and the men came out onto a broad overgrown meadow. In the distance set against a hill stood a large frame house.

"That's it," announced Sheriff Jones, glancing at his map. The men stopped. Nothing stirred in the darkened windows of the house. Its unpainted clapboards were weathered dark brown, the once silvery tin roof turned to rust.

"Y'all get down and stay here," Jones ordered the two speleologists. Farthing and Lamont promptly sat down amid their ropes and stared quizzically at the law officers.

The sheriff surveyed the house seventy-five yards away. "Ain't no way to go up there without them seeing us," he said. "Open ground all the way."

Jones cupped his hands around his mouth. "Sarah! Jubal Symcox!" he shouted. His voice echoed briefly against the house. "Ya'll in there? It's me, the sheriff. Step out on the porch, would you? Real easy."

Silence. A small dark bird fluttered from under the eaves of the house and darted away. There was no other movement.

After a minute, the sheriff said, "Okay, let's go." The men began walking slowly toward the house. The morning mist was thinning now, and the sun shone through faintly. "Heads up," said Jones. The state troopers and a deputy sheriff broke off and circled toward the rear of the house. Jones continued his forward march, flanked by Gomillion with the Doberman and a second deputy holding a shotgun at port arms. Hudlow, Johnson and the FBI agent followed.

As they neared the raised front porch, they passed a garden with irregular rows of bush beans and new lettuce. The porch was bare. Sheriff Jones mounted the wooden steps while the other men stood back in a loose semicircle. He rapped on the door sharply.

"Sarah. Miz Symcox. You in there?" he shouted. No response. "Hey, Sarah. It's me. Tabard Jones. You hear me?"

More silence passed. "Maybe she's getting hard of hearing," said the sheriff. He banged on the door again.

"Don't you think we might as well go on in now, Sheriff?" said Hudlow.

Jones gave Hudlow an impatient look. "I'm not sending a man into this house first off. Benny Guy, bring Skip up here."

Gomillion climbed the stairs with the Doberman. The animal's ears flattened as it strained against the choke chain.

"Hold on," said Hudlow, looking at the Doberman. "Is that the only way you have to soften this place up?"

Gomillion turned on the detective. "This is what we got. Skip's my personal dog, my responsibility. You mind?"

"It's other ways to flush somebody."

Sheriff Jones stepped toward Hudlow and looked down from the porch. "Now there's no reason to get worked up," he said softly. "I told you, I ain't sending a man in there first. It's y'all says this Symcox boy is a cuckoo. He might do most anything. But if he's in there and behaves himself, Skip won't harm him. As far as the ol' lady, if she's sitting in there deaf or asleep, he won't bother her, neither. Do we understand each other now?"

Hudlow fell silent. Johnson leaned toward him. "Let it go, Hud. It's his show."

The sheriff and Gomillion turned toward the door and tried the latch. It was locked from inside. The two men leaned against the door, and it gave way easily. Gomillion unleashed the dog, and it bounded inside. For several moments they heard its nails clacking in a furious staccato over bare wooden floors as it raced from room to room. Finally, it returned to the doorway, tongue hanging, stub tail aloft. Gomillion slipped the choke chain back over its head.

"Okay, fellas, let's go in," said Sheriff Jones.

The house echoed with their heavy feet. Inside, they found a few pieces of rudimentary furniture scattered about the ground floor. Shelves and tabletops were bare. Windows stood curtainless. A handful of primitive utensils was strewn in the kitchen. A faint smell of wood smoke hung in the room. Magnus Johnson studied a vast arched fireplace across the back of the kitchen. Its charred logs were cold, but the stones under the mantel still held a lingering warmth.

Upstairs, several bed frames with thin horsehair mattresses were pushed together in different rooms. Tattered blankets and graying sheets lay in heaps. A few shapeless garments hung in the closets.

The searchers reassembled on the porch. "Don't look like anybody been here a good while," said Sheriff Jones. "What do you make of it, Benny Guy?"

"Hard to say, except look at that garden patch, Tabard. It's fresh. Looks like the bush beans just been stripped."

"Fireplace stones inside are still warm, too," said Magnus Johnson.

As he spoke, two state troopers came round from the rear of the house. "Better look at this, Sheriff," said one, pointing.

The men stepped to the side of the house. The trooper pointed to a small tree near the back porch. Suspended from one of its branches by the rear legs was a large gray sheep. It was headless, the fleece at its neck red with drying blood.

"Jesus," muttered the sheriff. "What kind of Brand X stuff is this?" The men ran to the tree. Random splatters of blood appeared on the ground beneath the animal. The body turned slowly on the branch. There was no trace of the head.

"Got any ideas what the hell this is?" said Hudlow, looking to Johnson.

"Not exactly a marshmallow roast."

Silence fell over the men again. Flies were beginning to gather on the sheep's open neck.

"Ain't this a little off the subject?" said Dewey Hudlow. "We s'pose to be looking for Jubal and them. Is there a cellar under the house maybe?"

The men reentered the house and in a few minutes discovered a rough-cut square of paneling in the kitchen floor. With some prying, it lifted from the surrounding hardwood boards. Beneath it was a small dark hole. A wave of cool musty air issued from it. Gomillion released the Doberman again, and it darted into the hole.

Screams suddenly burst from the hole, human shrieks mingled with the savage barking of the Doberman.

"Hold, Skip! Hold!" shouted Gomillion. "Who's down there?" The dog's barking stopped, but waves of high-pitched screaming continued. One deputy jammed his shotgun into the hole, while another flashed a light. "Anybody got a weapon down there? Throw it out!" Gomillion ordered. The screaming continued. "Stop that hollering, goddammit, or I'll put the dog on you again, you hear?"

The screaming diminished to whimpers. "Gimme another light," said Gomillion. He flashed it into the hole. The lawmen peered into the darkness, and in the shallow cellar, huddled among the shadows, crouched a half-dozen children and adults, strange, dazed figures in ragged flowered dresses and faded trousers. They gibbered among themselves, their eyes exploding with fear. Hollow soiled faces framed in nests of ashen hair squinted into the officers' lights.

"Okay," said Sheriff Jones. "Get 'um out one at a time, men." Slowly, hesitatingly, the group—two men, a woman and three children—scrambled out into the kitchen. They stood mute, bunched, clutching each other.

"Sarah's not with them," said Jones, scanning the faces. "These females are too young. Where's Sarah?" he demanded.

The faces were motionless, yielding nothing. "And Jubal," snapped Dewey Hudlow. "Where's Jubal Symcox?" The adults pulled the children closer to them and remained silent.

"Shit fire," said Jones, scratching his head. "I don't know what kind of circus this is, but I'm glad it don't come to town often."

43

The afternoon sun was starting to fall toward the western trees, and the farmhouse became darker. The two speleologists had built a fire in the backyard and were preparing supper.

"Well," said Sheriff Jones, taking a deep breath, "it's a cinch they ain't going to talk anymore this evening."

"Shoot, if they said two words, it would double what they told us already," said Gomillion. "Wish Sarah was here. She'd talk. But them others." He looked at the group huddled in the grass nearby under the eye of several troopers. "I never seen nor heard anything like them in my life. Some of them must not ever been off of this property. Act like scared rabbits."

"And Jubal," said Magnus Johnson. "Since they won't give us any answers about him, we better find some answers of our own."

"Jubal?" said the sheriff. "He's split, if he ever was here at all."

"And leave these people behind? He's the only adult besides Sarah that seems to be able to deal with other humans. These people are helpless. I don't think he would leave them. Neither would Sarah. I think they're still around somewhere on this property."

The sheriff's eyes narrowed. "You still suggesting they maybe went down in one of them cave things?" Several of the other men now gathered in a circle around the sheriff and Johnson.

"I'm saying it's a possibility."

"Don't make a whole lot of sense, Johnson," said Sheriff Jones. "In the first place, the state troopers searched everywhere the last three hours and ain't found nothing. Even that hole under the house don't go nowhere. And in the second place, you'd think that with the law after them, ol' Sarah and Jubal be gone as far away from here as possible."

"Bottom of a cave is about as far as you can get," said Johnson.

The sheriff shook his head. "People round here say some of them pits run six hundred, eight hundred feet deep. What makes you so sure they could even get down in there?"

The ring of faces around Johnson and the sheriff tightened. Johnson looked toward Hudlow, but Hudlow was staring at the ground.

"Look," Johnson said at last, "I know this is kind of hard to appreciate, but we're dealing with a one-track mind here. Like you said, Sheriff, Jubal's a cuckoo. And if we just accept that and try to see things in a cuckoo way, we can begin to see why he would come back here. There is nothing else for him. He was born here and grew up here. He was taught all his craziness here. The only person he knows and trusts is his mother, Sarah, and she's here. This is his home base. It's his whole life, his religion and all the trappings that go with it. He's got it all underground here somewhere. He figures he's safe there. We'll never go down and find him, and eventually we'll go away, and then he's free again."

Sheriff Jones looked dissatisfied. "If all that's true, then maybe he'll just die down there. He can't last forever."

"That's possible," said Johnson. "But it's more likely he has some kind of easy exit, maybe a series of short ladder climbs, so he can come out for food and water. The problem is we don't know. Maybe we'll get lucky and find it. But don't count on it."

"You're trying to make it sound like we ain't got much choice," said the sheriff.

"Well, we do have a fugitive warrant to serve," Johnson continued. "And don't forget that highway engineering party that disappeared down here ten years ago. They're still not accounted for."

"This ain't no holy crusade, Johnson. This is a property search. Seems to me we pretty much done our duty."

Johnson looked helplessly at the faces surrounding him. The men stared back. All except Hudlow, who kept his head down.

"Then I guess there's really only one thing left to do, Sheriff," said Johnson. "It's your warrant, but if you won't take it down in there"—Johnson's voice dropped for an instant but suddenly lifted—"then Detective Hudlow and I will do it."

The air was thick with silence. The men turned toward Hudlow. Slowly he raised his eyes and looked at Sheriff Jones. "Sheriff," he said in a hoarse whisper, "Detective Johnson is right. We'll do it ourselves."

"Count me in, too," came a voice from the edge of the circle. It was Eliot, the FBI agent. The others turned to him in surprise. It was the first time he had spoken since they had left Goshen Shoals.

"Well, look here," stammered the sheriff. "It's not like we can't do it, Benny Guy and me. I didn't mean to suggest that we . . . it's just that, well, do you think them two little boys, them speleo-whatchamacallums over there, you think they know what they're doing?"

"They're professionals," answered Johnson. "They don't have to look like Charles Atlas to be good at this. They're going to give us instruction and then go in with us."

"Yeah, but they so skinny and raw-looking. Look like a rat terrier could shake the cotton wadding out of them."

"It's technique, not muscle. Be thankful we have them."

o

Just before supper, one of the state troopers found a hole about a half mile from the house. It was a modest aperture, perhaps seven feet across, fringed with bushes. A shaft of fading sunlight fell across its yawning darkness. The men gathered at its edge.

Farthing picked up a stone and dropped it into the darkness.

He cocked his head and listened. There was a single, distant *plop*. "Three and a half, four seconds," he said. "Maybe two hundred and twenty feet deep. Muddy bottom."

"One thing's for sure," Johnson said. "This is not a regular entrance that Jubal Symcox or anyone else ever used. There's no path to it, no trampled underbrush. Let's just hope it leads to the cave he's in."

"If he's here," said Jones.

Farthing cleared his voice. "We can't go down today," he said in clipped tones. "It's too late. Jesse and I will do the climbing instruction tomorrow morning."

"How long will it take?" asked Sheriff Jones.

"A few hours. Probably the whole morning. How many are going down?"

The sheriff looked around at the men. "Let's see. It'll be me and Benny Guy. And Johnson and Detective Hudlow. Is that right?"

"And me," said Eliot, the FBI agent.

"Okay," said Sheriff Jones. "The rest stay up here and hold these Symcoxes. We go down tomorrow."

44

The pearl gray rope was wrapped neatly several times around the tree at the rim of the hole and disappeared into the darkness. The mists and weakling sun of the previous day had given way to brilliant skies, and the weight of summer fell heavily on the officers. They watched in silence as Farthing and Lamont checked over the equipment and made last-minute adjustments. Farthing would be the first to go down, then the five law officers, one by one, and finally Lamont.

Since the instruction session that morning, Farthing had assumed nominal command. He no longer deferred to Sheriff Jones. The sheriff and other officers stood docilely amid backpacks, helmets, carbide lamps, seat harnesses and an alien array of steel carabiners and friction-release ascenders.

Farthing, lean and ascetic in a light wool sweater and parachute harness, quickly threaded a braking rack onto the rappel rope and clipped it to his harness. He gave the rope an experimental tug. It was snugly anchored. Then with his back to the pit and the rope trailing loosely through his hands and around his waist, he stepped rearwards, leaned into the pit and vanished.

Several minutes elapsed. Lamont crawled to the edge of the pit and waited. The rope, which had been taut, suddenly went limp. A faint shout followed.

“He’s off the rope,” said Lamont. “He’s reached bottom.”

With a second rope, Lamont and the other men then lowered their backpacks into the pit, along with additional coils of rope, two 410 Mossberg Cruiser shotguns, several four-shot speed loaders and an extra pouch of No. 4 shot 12-gauge shells. Sheriff Jones handed over his prize black-framed Franchi S.P.A. pump rifle.

“Expecting Godzilla?” asked Hudlow.

“Never know what might pop up down there,” said Jones. “Most acc’rate weapon in Christendom.”

“Okay,” said Lamont. “Who’s first?”

Eliot stepped forward. Lamont tied him into the descent rope and hitched a second, belaying line to his harness. The FBI agent, his blue jumpsuit now torn and soiled, waved jauntily to the other men and backed slowly over the side into the pit, mimicking the movements he had been taught that morning. Lamont sat down facing the pit with his feet chocked against two large stones and slowly paid out the belaying rope as Eliot descended.

In turn, Sheriff Jones, Benny Guy Gomillion and Dewey Hudlow followed and within an hour had completed the descent. Only Lamont and Magnus Johnson remained at the top.

“Remember, keep your descent slow but steady,” said Lamont as he buckled Johnson up. “If anything happens with the main rope or you lose control, I’ve got you on the belay line.” They were the same words he had given the other men.

Johnson buckled himself into the webbed harness. Next he rolled the striker wheel of his carbide lamp with the heel of his hand, and a thin acetylene flame leaped from the ceramic tip. He adjusted the water release and seated the lamp on his helmet. He picked up the rope and edged toward the rim of the pit. He hesitated for a moment and then leaned backward into the dark maw.

His toes bounced lightly against the stone wall and sent flurries of dust into the sunlight across the top of the pit. The soft birr of the rope feeding through the rack was reassuring as he lowered himself below the lip of the pit. In the next instant, the wall suddenly angled away from his feet, and he found himself dangling free in space and enveloped in darkness. His breath caught for a moment. He began looking for a point of reference, some tangible piece of the world around him, as he turned on the rope. Below was only blackness. Above was the mouth of the pit, a swatch of bright gray light. To his sides he saw nothing at first. Then gradually with the aid of his lamp he began to discern dim uneven surfaces flickering among the shadows of the barren karst. The surfaces formed a crude but gargantuan slit in the earth, a vast Triassic wound, at once dark and unrelentingly vivid.

His descent continued, the rope humming through the rack. The patch of light at the top of the shaft gradually diminished. His arms ached from feeding the rope, but he felt that he could not stop.

Now he began to hear voices below and saw occasional spurts of light.

"That you, Mag?" It was Hudlow's voice, echoing up the shaft.

"None other," shouted Johnson hoarsely. "How much further?"

"Mile or two."

Johnson sped up his descent. He could now hear the feet of the men below as they stumbled about. Moments later, their lamps began playing across his face. Several arms reached up toward him, and he was pulled down to the floor of the cave.

Hudlow was at his side. Sweat dripped from his face. His eyes were small and unhappy. "Next time, man, I'm taking the Greyhound. How 'bout you, Mag?"

"That was a booger."

"Going out's got to be worse. You have to fuck with gravity."

Johnson stripped off the seat harness and looked about him. The other men were sorting through equipment and readying their backpacks. A scree of boulders and tree branches lay at the base of the pit. The air was cool and still, filled with the sweet stink of carbide. The walls glimmered with a veneer of pale brown mud.

"This is not a beautiful place," muttered Johnson.

"Typical of around here," said Farthing. "Limestone land-form. At one time, water ran through here. That accounts for the mud."

"Is it coming back any time soon?" asked Hudlow.

"No, no. You can tell by the scree. There's been no water here in a long time."

"Anything else been in here?"

"Doesn't look like it. When I first got off the rope, I saw no footprints of any kind, human or animal. This is a virgin pit."

At that moment, the men heard the low thrum of the rope, and the legs of Jesse Lamont suddenly appeared from the obscurity above. He landed lightly on the cave floor and un-buckled his harness. All seven men were in now.

Farthing opened a small pocket compass. "The house is roughly northwest of the pit," he said. "Is that the way you want to go?"

"Yes, ain't we agreed on that?" said the sheriff. The other men murmured assent.

Farthing scouted the perimeter of the room and returned to the base of the pit. "There are three ways out of here. One is sort of northerly. It's the closest to what you want."

"We'll take it," said Sheriff Jones.

The men shouldered their packs and formed a rough single file behind Farthing. Jones slung the Franchi on one shoulder and carried a shotgun loosely in front of him. As they started, Johnson took a last look up at the pit opening above them, a minuscule prick of light suspended in a limitless vacuum of black. He lingered, his face upturned, not wanting to leave the life-nurturing light. For an instant, like the single frame of a motion picture, he saw another light—a vivid curved streak suddenly obliterated as the lid of the abandoned car trunk in Orangeburg slammed down around him, imprisoning him in blackness. He shuddered and turned to follow the men in the cave ahead of him.

The cave narrowed but soon broadened into another room, a low-ceilinged chamber filled with chilled, humid air. The men's breath came in quick gray puffs. The room narrowed again, but its ceiling rose and disappeared into the gloom. It was like being encapsulated, Johnson thought, in a vast elastic tunnel that was squeezed and reshaped constantly by an unseen hand. At every turn there was a new configuration, a new grotesquery of slanting facets and mud-caked petromorphs. Bulbous mounds and toadstools erupted from the floor. Crevices opened and closed. Walls fell away and suddenly reappeared, closing in on the loose litter of boulders along the pathway. The men walked in silence, their lamps casting vague shapes around them.

For an hour they marched in what seemed a gradual descent ever deeper into the earth. Johnson tried to concentrate on the practical task of maintaining balance and watching his footsteps, but a faint forboding began to come over him, a realization that with each step he was removed further and further from the base of the pit and the life-promising flicker of light, his last link with the world above.

Farthing called a halt. The men fell gratefully to the ground. They began reloading the carbide reservoirs of their lamps.

"There's a squeezeway just ahead," announced Farthing. "No way of knowing how long it is or whether it dead-ends. I'll try it first and then come back." He got up without his pack and disappeared.

Magnus Johnson stared at the men around him, admiring their composure. Or was it fatigue? Gomillion and Sheriff Jones dozed, shotguns cradled loosely in their laps. Eliot gazed at the ceiling. Hudlow stepped behind a stone buttress and urinated.

Johnson felt a faint tingling in his fingers and tightness across the chest. But the tightness was more than a simple limitation within himself. He felt the impenetrable immensity of stone and earth above him crushing down. He imagined a pebble somewhere in the immensity that had withstood the eons of wind and waters pinioned between massive stones now suddenly shattering and bringing the whole tenuous underworld down in collapse. It would hardly be observed from above, just a brief grinding shift in the crust of the earth. But there would be no escape, even if he found temporary refuge under an arched stone, only the slow dissipation of oxygen.

He shuddered again. A commotion near the front of the group interrupted his thoughts. It was Farthing, returning from the squeezeway.

"Looks all right," he said. "About thirty feet long. All horizontal. Like a road culvert. Opens up into a very large room at the other end."

"How do we do it?" asked the sheriff.

"On your backs, knapsack hooked around your ankle, drag-fashion. It's like a worm hole."

The men reassembled and followed Farthing toward a narrow recess. Their lamps flashed across a short vertical wall. In its center, about knee-high, was a smooth, nearly circular opening the width of a man's shoulders. Farthing slipped in, dragging his pack behind him. The others followed.

At Johnson's turn, the detective peered into the hole. He could see the disembodied feet of the man ahead scuttling toward the other end, tugging his pack. Johnson strapped his own pack to his right ankle and slid in on his back, his arms and hands stretched ahead of him, clawing at the ribbed surface of the hole for locomotion. A new ominous constriction crept into his chest. The yellowish flame of his lamp illuminated the hole and magnified its features, bringing the curved surface pressing down on him, an entombing weight forcing the bile of fear into his gullet. The quick-frame image of the abandoned car trunk flashed before him again. Nausea swept over him. He needed desperately to raise his knees or his head, to assert some feeble measure of freedom, but could not. His breath came in short jerks, and he knew he was edging toward full frenzy. He tried turning his attention to something, anything, else: the pack on his ankle, his helmet, the muffled voices ahead of him. He scrabbled along, seeking the end of the squeezeway. At last he felt cooler air around him. His head suddenly fell free at the end of the squeezeway. A moment later he tumbled onto the floor of the cave and then stood up with relief.

The searchers were in an enormous vaulted room. Farthing shined a six-cell flashlight toward the ceiling. Strange fluted columns loomed in the darkness. Silence filled the room.

Then Farthing spoke. "It should be easier going now." His voice echoed dully. "Seems to have leveled out. We're probably about three hundred feet down."

"We ought to start thinking about Symcox, seems to me," said Sheriff Jones. "We been in here a good while."

Jones and Gomillion took the lead, and for the first time, Farthing fell back toward the rear.

Jubal Symcox was surely ahead, Magnus Johnson agreed, but he was also thinking of what was behind them: the squeezeway, the confusion of muddy trails, the precious pinpoint of light now lost in the folds of the earth. He thought of the trees and sunny rocks at the top of the pit and had a fleeting portent that he would never see them again.

45

The clink and scrape of men eating had ceased; the Primus stove had been extinguished and the bottles of white gas put away. The last Thermos was sealed and returned to its pack. Johnson became starkly aware of the withdrawal of sounds and sights. The other men had dispersed, seeking level ground to lay out their bed rolls. He could hear only an occasional muffled word. Light squirted faintly here and there beyond the stony bulwarks of the room where the men had eaten.

Hudlow busied himself next to Johnson, like an enormous brood hen tidying its nest. The uneven ceiling of the cave hung a few feet above their heads. A candle burned on a tin can top, casting uncertain shadows across their bedding.

"Ain't exactly the Waldorf," mumbled Hudlow.

Johnson lay on his back, fully clothed, his legs thrust stiffly into the sleeping bag. He stared at the ceiling, still wearing his glasses.

"Mag, you ain't said word one since we come in here. You don't like these Boy Scout jamborees?"

"Tired, I guess."

"I reckon you tired. We been in here near 'bout fourteen hours. You know it's two o'clock in the morning?"

"Morning, night. What's the difference down here?"

Hudlow grunted and burrowed down into his sleeping bag. He turned away from Johnson and pulled the sleeping bag cover

over his head, grunting again softly. Johnson took almost childish comfort in having Hudlow near him. His thick form rose and fell with his breathing. He seemed oblivious, like all the other men, to the suffocating tomb in which they lay. He was also oblivious to the deep and darkening terror that had begun to grip Magnus Johnson.

I must sleep, Johnson said to himself over and over again.

o

He lay in complete blackness, rigid and unmoving, eyes wide open, seeing nothing. He did not know how many hours had passed. Element by element, he had witnessed the world vanishing around him. First the human murmurs had ceased, then the glimmering lights of the other men. For a long time, he could hear Hudlow's heavy, uneven breathing close to him, but it too had softened with sleep and vanished. Then only his candle remained. It too began to dwindle, slowly, silently, the flame sinking into an ever widening pool of wax. The flame, as if in answer to his silent pleas, burned faithfully far longer than he thought possible. It remained erect and almost without motion in the breathless cave. Then suddenly the wick tilted. It lost its foundation in the molten wax and started to fall. The flame shrank and guttered in a final reach above the wax and then vanished altogether.

The car trunk.

He lay in complete blackness, a blackness beyond the darkest night, a blackness without sight or sound or movement, without time or direction or space. His eyes, his ears, his skin registered nothing. It was more than the blackness of ancient continents. It was the blackness of the center of the earth. While there had been light and human murmuring, he could keep the fear at bay, but now with the blackness, the unfathomable bulk of the earth moved over him and was beginning to crush him. He saw himself an insect sealed in a darkened crevice, waiting dumbly for death.

The car trunk.

He lay in complete blackness, listening in the silence. The terror seized him, immobilizing him, yet urging him to move, to react. He wanted to bolt down the broken corridors of the cave, to scream for liberation. But he knew nothing would help, nothing could remove the suffocating blanket of blackness. There was nothing to reach out to.

And then the silence stopped. Or was it that there never had been silence? Yes, there was sound. But it was within him, not outside, a faint constant ringing within his head, suffused with a thin distant roar, like cataracts of a mighty river leagues away. The roar was deep inside his skull, the engines of his brain. He could hear his brain, so total was the void around him. It churned away, driving blindly, drawing energy from itself. Then from deep within he began to see an expanse of misty water. Its surface was still but dull, yielding no reflection. A dark broad-winged bird wheeled silently over the water. It turned its head from side to side, as though looking for a place to land. There was nothing, not a rock, not a piece of driftwood. The bird circled and circled. The gray water stretched endlessly. Slowly the bird descended toward the surface. Its wing beats now came in faltering jerks. It tried to gain altitude but fell. One of its wing tips cut into the water. The bird tilted steeply, and collapsed into the misty darkness. Water poured into its lungs, leaving it to struggle impotently in that terrifying moment between the certainty of doom and unconsciousness . . .

Johnson heard himself screaming—desperate, mechanical ululations splitting the humid air.

"What the fuck!" Hudlow scrambled in the darkness. The screams tore into his ears like a Klaxon. He grabbed a flashlight. Magnus Johnson was sitting bolt upright, shaking uncontrollably, his mouth opening and shutting in rhythm with his screams. Spittle hung from his lips.

"Mag, wake up! It's me. Stop this shit!" The screams continued. Hudlow shook Johnson by the shoulders. Other men began stumbling toward Johnson and Hudlow, their flashlights criss-crossing in the darkness. Farthing rushed up and knelt by Johnson.

"Hey, stop it!" He slapped Johnson sharply across the jaw. The screams stopped for an instant, then resumed as short, barklike whoops. Johnson continued looking straight ahead, his eyes unfocused.

"What's he having?" yelled Hudlow over the clamor.

"Claustrophobic reaction," shouted Farthing. "He may have hyperventilated, too."

"What do we do?"

"Slap him again. If that doesn't work, punch him real hard in the stomach."

"Goddamn, I ain't doing that, and you ain't either."

"He could become convulsive."

Hudlow turned menacingly toward Farthing. "Come one step closer, Farthing, and I'll slit your bag and step through it."

The shouting continued, a hoarse rhythmic chant. Hudlow knelt protectively over Johnson. Farthing backed away while the other men looked on.

"You all get back," snapped Hudlow. "Just get back and give him some air."

He turned to Johnson, who had a look of uncomprehending torment on his face. His barks came in quick succession. Hudlow reached toward him and drew him slowly to his chest. He hesitated for a moment, looking up at the ring of men around him, and then began patting Johnson tentatively on the back. The men continued to stare.

"One of you light me a candle"—Hudlow spoke over Johnson's shouts—"and then get out of here. Git!"

Eliot propped a lit candle near the two huddled men and withdrew. The others followed.

Hudlow looked down at the shuddering face at his chest. The eyes were still unfocused, the mouth rimmed with white paste. Hudlow continued to stroke Johnson's back.

"Hey, it's me. Ol' Hud. Can you hear me?"

There was no response. The barking shouts went on ceaselessly. Hudlow pulled the trembling body closer to him.

"It's okay, Mag. Take it slow. Nothing to worry about." He looked down again at Johnson and in the wavering light of the candle began to rock him gently.

The shouts continued but gradually transformed to sustained weeping. The body quivered and jerked, heedless at first of Hudlow's heavy comforting hands, but with time, the tension began to ease. The weeping slowed and descended in pitch, becoming an intermittent moan.

And then there was silence.

Johnson's head hung loosely against Hudlow. For a moment, Hudlow thought he had fainted or fallen asleep. But after several moments, Johnson slowly lifted his head and looked up at Hudlow. His eyes were ringed with fear. But deep within, amid the turmoil and disorder, Hudlow saw a confused glimmer of trust.

"Damn, you give me a start there, Mag," said Hudlow softly. "Thought you was trying to call Captain Stohlbach long distance."

Johnson nodded his head, but did not speak.

"Just take your time," said Hudlow, "take your time. I ain't going nowhere. Want some water?"

Johnson nodded again. Hudlow pulled a canteen from his pack, opened the top and put it to Johnson's lips.

"There, that's good," said Hudlow. "I always say a man who can drink is a man on the road to health."

Hudlow leaned back against the cave wall, cradling Johnson in his arms. Then he saw Johnson's lips began to move. "Just don't say anything right now," Johnson rasped.

"Sounds good to me," said Hudlow. He closed his eyes. He fell into a light sleep. When he awoke, the candle had shrunk to half its size. Johnson still lay against his chest. He was looking intently at the candle.

"Doing better now?" Hudlow asked.

"Some," said Johnson. His glasses were still on.

"Want to talk about it?"

Johnson stirred against Hudlow's bulk. "I can't."

"No sweat. This ain't Twenty Questions."

Several moments passed in silence. Then: "One thing, Hud."

"What's that?"

"Don't go away."

46

The room soared a hundred feet to its scalloped ceiling, dwarfing the men below. They threaded their way along the boulder-strewn floor. It was the largest room they had entered yet and appeared to be several hundred yards long.

Farthing stopped to take a compass reading. "We're running more in an east-west line than I thought," he said. "It's hard to say where we are in relation to the house."

"Them compass things any good down here?" Gomillion asked Farthing.

"Usually, although you can get some deviations if there are magnetic elements in the bedrock." The speleologist studied the compass with a puzzled look on his face.

Hudlow approached Farthing. He looked over his shoulder toward Magnus Johnson who was sitting some distance away, his head between his knees.

"Look," said Hudlow, lowering his voice. "You suggesting we might be lost?"

Farthing looked surprised. "No. I was just taking a routine reading."

"Yeah, but the deviations and magnetic jimwhistles and all."

"There's no problem. Even without a compass. We can always follow our tracks back to the pit opening. Lamont's left reflector tape at the major turns and junctions."

“Well, okay. I was just a little concerned about Mag. I don’t want anything to touch him off again. He’s still got a feather on his asshole.”

“I’ll be cautious about what I say.”

“What exactly went wrong with him? I never seen anybody act like that before.”

“Chronic phobic reaction, CPR. Probably combined with fatigue.”

“He didn’t have any control over himself. It was like somebody else was inside him.”

“He may also have been starting to undergo sensory deprivation.”

“Okay,” said Hudlow, “but no more talk now about being lost or the fucked-up compass. Got it?” Hudlow walked away.

The men resumed their march. They walked the length of the massive room and entered a rocky defile that careened left and right and then descended steeply to a small stream, the first water they had seen. It glittered in the light of their lamps and disappeared into a crevice. Magnus Johnson looked into the sandy shallows. Not a sign of life, not a minnow. At least that’s consistent, he thought. The entire cave was devoid of life. They had seen nothing, no bats, no insects, no primitive lichens.

Beyond the stream, they entered a low-ceilinged room from which several other passageways radiated. They chose the largest and continued. The passage veered sharply to the left and narrowed to a low crawlway. They were on all fours now, clambering over and around boulders that choked the passage. Minutes passed. Gradually the crawlway widened and opened into a vaulted corridor.

A faint new smell filled the air.

“Wood smoke,” said Sheriff Jones, raising his hand. He stiffened perceptibly and peered into the darkness beyond the reach of the men’s lamps. He spoke in a half whisper. “Farthing, would you come up here a minute?”

The speleologist edged forward and sniffed the air. “Wood smoke, all right. Damn foolishness to build a fire in a cave.”

"Yeah, but where's it at?" asked Jones.

"No way of telling. Could be miles away, or just around the corner. Depends on the ventilation."

"But it could be near?"

Farthing looked at Jones. "That's right."

The sheriff took a breath. "This calls for a huddle. Can we gather round here a minute?" He beckoned to the other men.

"Anybody got any bright ideas?" he said. "We going into this thing kind of blind. Farthing here says the wood fire could be close or could be far. No way of knowing."

"And we don't know what Symcox's got," said Gomillion, gesturing toward the dark. "Maybe a rifle, maybe shotgun. Maybe there's more'n just him in there."

"And also," the sheriff continued, "if this boy's a cuckoo, he's not going to react normal."

He shrugged. "This situation's a basic bitch." He looked down the darkened pathway. "We got to have light to follow the path, but the light shows where we're at. We're sitting ducks."

"I would suggest," said Farthing, "that you just use one small flashlight in the lead. Keep it close to the ground, just so you can see immediately in front of you. Kill the carbide lamps. If we come into another room, use a six-cell light to scan it first and then move on."

The men reassembled in a line and began moving forward behind Sheriff Jones. His shotgun was poised in front of him now, but the Franchi remained on his back. The pathway underfoot was smooth. Each man held onto the pack of the man in front of him, their feet sucking softly in the mud.

The path descended and turned, first to the right, then to the left, before entering a tall narrow chamber. Sheriff Jones quickly played the six-cell light over the room and saw nothing. The searchers continued, moving slowly. The odor of wood smoke seemed to diminish.

They crept in rough monotonous lockstep. Slowly, subtly, the smell of smoke returned. At the same time, the muffled steps of the men began to echo more distantly. They had entered a new and much larger room.

Gomillion tugged at Sheriff Jones. "How much more of this we got to—"

A sudden flash split the blackness, followed by a deafening explosion. Another flash, another explosion, and then four more. The men fell to the ground, mud and gravel raining on them. The roar of the explosions echoed and counterechoed.

"Cover!" shouted Jones. Momentarily dazed and blinded, he squeezed off two rounds from his Mossberg toward the flashes. His own blasts ruptured the darkness, revealing momentary glimpses of an immense cathedrallike room with a grotesque stone obelisk in its center. The thunder of his gunfire, magnified a hundredfold in the cave, reverberated wildly through the room, cross-crossing from one height to another and rumbling off into the recesses. The men were thrown into black silence again.

"What's the sumbitch got?" yelped Gomillion. "A howitzer?"

"Hush it down," ordered Jones. "We don't know what's between us and him. We may be laying wide open."

The men listened. Hudlow and Johnson lay rigidly side by side, each with service revolver drawn. They strained every sense in the darkness. At length they heard a dry rustling. It stopped, then resumed.

"It's a ways off," muttered Hudlow. "Maybe twenty, twenty-five yards."

The sounds stopped again. The men peered into the void. They waited.

"Let him make the first move," whispered Jones.

Minutes passed. Johnson began to squirm. Hudlow drew closer to him. He was about to speak when both men saw a dim, wavering light appear ahead of them. It was obscured in shadows, but in the next moment blossomed into a blinding incandescence. Now they could see the obelisk, a massive stalagmite tapering toward the ceiling fifty feet in front of them. From behind it stepped the wraithlike figure of Jubal Symcox. He held a highway flare in his hand. Leaning back, he hurled it toward the law officers, and in the same instant Sheriff Jones fired at him in another shattering blast. The flare arced through the air, landing in a shower of sparks midway between the law officers and the obelisk. In the shadows beyond, the men saw Symcox hesitate for a moment and then vanish behind the obelisk again.

The flare continued to burn on the mud floor, illuminating a moonscape of boulders and shallow escarpments. The men scurried for cover. Symcox suddenly reappeared at the edge of the obelisk, kneeling, a rifle raised to his shoulder. A fusillade burst from the barrel, raking across the floor of the room and shattering the stillness yet again. The men returned fire, pumping round after round, as Symcox retreated behind the obelisk.

The air was thick with smoke and the reek of gunpowder. The men reloaded. They waited and listened, blood surging in their ears. Through the thickened air they heard a low confusion of grunts and murmurings. Vague shadows moved behind the obelisk. Then silence.

Symcox appeared again, this time unarmed. The leaden hair hung over his forehead. His hands were extended in front of him, empty, palms turned out in a gesture of—what was it?—supplication, defeat? He lurched forward one or two steps and then fell face first into the mud.

The men waited. There was no movement, no sound. Jones rose cautiously to his knees. "Anybody else back there come out!" he shouted. "This is the sheriff. Throw any weapons out first."

No response. "Give it another minute," said Jones. "I thought I saw another shadow back there." He turned to the men sprawled on the ground around him. "Anybody hurt?"

"Nope, don't think so," said Hudlow. The other officers grunted in agreement.

"Goddamn miracle," said the sheriff. "How about you two boys back yonder?" he called to the speleologists. "You still here, or gone back to Chattanooga?"

Lamont raised his head from behind a stone twenty yards to the rear. "We're still here," he said, "but Farthing's hit."

"Damn. Where?"

“Upper chest. Near the right armpit.”
“Is he conscious?”
“No. He’s bleeding from the mouth.”
“You got the medical kit?”
“Yes. I’m trying to plug the hole.”
“Shit! Anyone here know about gun wounds?”
There was a pause. “I do.” It was the FBI agent.
“Good. Slide back there and help out, would you, Eliot? The rest of us will mind things up front.”
Eliot turned and crawled toward the speleologists.
“Don’t like the sounds of that,” said the sheriff, lowering his voice. “We need that boy.”
He looked out toward the burning flare. Still no response. “Okay, let’s move.” At the sheriff’s signal, Hudlow, Johnson and Gomillion stood up and took a few tentative steps toward the obelisk, weapons poised.
At that moment, new scuffling sounds came from behind the obelisk. The men scurried back to cover. There was a pause, and then into the light emerged a tall, withered figure, a woman. It was Sarah Symcox. She held a boy in front of her, the mouth of a blue-barreled pistol pressed against his temple.
Hudlow rose from the ground. “That’s my— That’s Quovadis’ boy, Thomas,” he blurted. “What the fuck?”
Johnson pulled Hudlow down again. “No, Hud! Wait.”
The officers crouched frozen, peering across the flare at the woman and child. She wore a loose faded print dress and heavy leather shoes, a pathetic, menacing specter. Slowly, still gripping the boy, she sidled around to the front of the obelisk, pressing her back against it. She dropped to her knees so that the boy shielded her almost entirely. The child’s face was filled with uncomprehending terror.
“Invaders!” The woman’s voice filled the cavernous room with unexpected power. “You have trespassed, and you shall know the consequences.” The voice, guttural and commanding, contained the same alien formality as her son’s.
“In the name of Kali and of all that is sacred here, I com-

mand you to cease. You have taken my son, but you shall never take me nor this child." The pistol remained at the boy's head.

"I can't believe it," whispered Hudlow hoarsely, looking toward Thomas. "How'd they do it?"

"Listen to me!" commanded Sarah Symcox. "I shall tell you only once. You are to put your arms down and, one by one, come forward to me."

The men were silent.

"Sheriff Jones," the woman called. "You are first. I'm surprised to see you a part of this. Please come forward."

The men looked at each other. "Better do it," said Benny Guy Gomillion.

"Now!" demanded the woman.

Sheriff Jones scrambled to his feet. He dropped his shotgun and unslung the Franchi from his back, placing it on the ground next to Gomillion. He began walking unsteadily toward the obelisk, his hands held out from his sides.

Hudlow turned to Johnson and Gomillion. "This ain't no surrender," he whispered. "This is a execution."

Johnson squinted at the woman almost hidden from view behind the boy. "Can't take her out with anything we got here. Except"—he looked at the heavy black rifle Jones had left on the ground—"except maybe the Franchi."

"Shot pattern risky with the Mossbergs," agreed Gomillion, nodding toward the obelisk. "The boy."

The men watched as Sheriff Jones approached the highway flare midway to the obelisk.

"How long is that flare good for?" asked Johnson.

"They last thirty minutes," said Gomillion. "It's about half gone."

There was time. On impulse, Magnus Johnson felt for his backpack and jerked it in front of him. "Look," he said quickly to Hudlow and Gomillion, "keep her busy. Talk to her. String it out. I've got something here."

They heard Sarah Symcox speak again. "Halt!" she ordered Jones, who had come within a few feet of the obelisk. "Now lie down, Sheriff, your head at my feet." Jones dropped to one knee, then the other, and placed himself prostrate before her. Keeping the pistol pressed closely to the boy's head, she looked out toward the remaining officers. "Mr. Gomillion," she said. "You are next. Please."

As Gomillion started to rise, Johnson grabbed his arm. "No! Wait," he whispered. "Tell her something. Tell her you're wounded. You can't walk." Johnson lowered his voice further. "And get the Franchi. Put it on her. You've used it before?" Gomillion nodded. "Good," said Johnson. "She probably can't see enough to know what you're doing."

Gomillion nodded again. He raised his head. "Miz Symcox," he called. "Your son, he got me. In the leg. I can't get up."

"How am I to believe that?" the woman answered. "Perhaps you should try a little harder, Mr. Gomillion. My patience is wearing."

Johnson jabbed Dewey Hudlow. "Talk to her, Hud. Use your silver tongue. Anything. Keep her going."

Hudlow got on his knees and looked toward the woman and the child she held. He cleared his voice. "Miz Symcox," he said, "Deputy Gomillion's telling you right. He's hurt. How 'bout me? Can't I be next instead?"

"Impossible! That would—"

"I don't s'pose you know me, ma'am. I'm Detective Dewey Hudlow, Metropolitan Po-leece, Washington, D.C. I could—"

"That is not my interest. My interest is Mr. Gomillion."

Hudlow looked frantic. "That boy you got there," he said. "He ain't harmed nobody. Any chance of you turning him loose—?"

"You take me for a fool?"

"No, ma'am. I was just thinking if one of us might could take his place maybe—"

"Impossible!"

"Well, ma'am, I know how you feel . . ."

As Hudlow talked, Johnson dug frantically into his pack. He found his Thermos and a cannister of white gas. Shielding himself behind a rock, he quickly unscrewed the bottom of the Thermos, removed the glass filler and drained the few remaining drops of coffee from it. He opened the gas cannister and poured its contents into the filler and capped it. Next he yanked the carbide lamp from his helmet, strapped it to the glass filler with reflector tape and ignited it with the striker wheel. A pale yellow flame spurted from the lamp tip. He looked up and saw Hudlow's arms stretched solicitously toward Sarah Symcox, his voice droning in oddly polite repartee. Gomillion lay flattened against the floor, the Franchi trained on the woman.

Quickly, Johnson loosened the carbide-filled bottom compartment of the lamp, causing it to flame out. He juggled it cautiously.

"Get ready," he said to Gomillion. "You'll know when to open up."

Johnson looked out again and took a deep breath. Then he sprang to his feet and hurled the flaming bomb toward a wall to one side of the obelisk. It shot through the air and shattered against the surface, exploding in a sudden shower of light. The woman whirled at the diversion, swinging the pistol from the boy's head and exposing her own to the sights of the Franchi. Gomillion fired. The shot rent the air, piercing the woman's skull and sending up a spray of splintered stone behind her as she slumped to the ground without a word.

The child ran yowling from the obelisk, the echoes of Gomillion's blast in the air. Sheriff Jones rose from his prone position, rushed to the fallen woman and kicked away the pistol still clutched in her hand. He rolled her body over. Blood pulsed slowly from the wound above her eye. Her head wagged in animal convulsions, and a few weak gurgles issued from her mouth. Then she was still.

The flare continued to sputter in the mud, hissing faintly. A pall of smoke hung over the obelisk.

The boy ran to Hudlow, who scooped him up and held him whimpering as Johnson and Gomillion surveyed the room cautiously.

“Better check back here,” said Gomillion, circling behind the obelisk and shining his six-cell light into the darkness.

There was nothing.

“Hallelujah!” Gomillion hooted. “It’s done over.” Relief spread across the faces of the men. “Amen,” said Sheriff Jones.

From behind the obelisk, Gomillion retrieved a rifle. “Lookey what Jubal had back here,” he whistled. “A Ruger Mini-Fourteen. Looks like a two-twenty-three caliber with a forty-shot banana clip. No wonder it sounded like the end of the world in here.”

Remnant flames from Johnson’s firebomb licked the wall adjacent to the obelisk. Gomillion examined the broken pieces of the detective’s carbide lamp littering the cave floor.

“Farthing and Lamont got a couple of spares in their gear,” said Gomillion. “Not a bad shot, Johnson. You ever throw for Atlanta?”

Johnson walked to Jubal Symcox’s body and stood over it. With his toe he flipped it over and gazed down at the pale face. Muddy water trickled off the forehead and into the lead-gray hair. A dozen small reddened holes appeared in tight shot groups across the chest. Then Johnson noticed Symcox’s lips and chin glistening oddly with a swirl of grayish red smears. A small gelatinous pulp, like partially digested food, protruded from the open mouth. The elongated tongue, freed by the severed frenum, lay stretched underneath in the mud. Johnson knelt over the body, signaling Sheriff Jones. The two men looked more closely. Oozing in the grip of Symcox’s right fist was another pulpy wad, similar to the one in his mouth.

“What in hell is that?” asked the sheriff.

“His last supper?” muttered Johnson.

“And lookey what we got here,” said the sheriff, pointing at the obelisk. At its base amid the charred remains of a fire was a ring of human skulls, perhaps twenty in all. Several were the size of tennis balls.

“My God,” muttered Johnson. “Like an open grave.” He

stooped and looked more closely. "The little ones, those would be Symcox infants."

And at the center of the ring of skulls, mounted on a stake, was a sheep's head, its eyes bulging in vacant terror. The top of its cranium had been sheared off, and a large metal spoon rested in the opening, like a ladle in a preposterous ceremonial tureen.

"Jesus, that's what he was eating," said Magnus Johnson, looking back at Symcox's body.

The sheriff drew close. "Eat that? What for?"

"Don't know. Expanding his animal wisdom maybe?" Johnson pointed upward. "He left the best part hanging on that tree behind his house."

Johnson turned away. For the first time he noticed that the obelisk was encircled by garlands of what appeared to be thin white bones strung end to end with wire. They lay in contrast against the brown surface of the obelisk.

"Finger bones, that's what they look like. Human finger bones," said Johnson.

He stepped back from the obelisk. Its surface was chipped here and there from the gunfire. "You know what this whole thing is?" he said. "It's a *linga*. This is their sacred ground. The place Alba Kadinsky described for their ceremonies."

"But how come the finger bones?" said Jones.

"Don't know. Some kind of symbolism, I guess. Hands guarding the sacred possession maybe."

Johnson continued to look at the brittle white garlands. A glint of metal caught his eye. He stepped to the base of the shaft and looked more closely. On one of the bones dangled a ring. He held it between his thumb and forefinger and shined a flashlight on it. Dimly he saw a minuscule image: a lion, its foreclaws raised, standing over the sun and moon.

"My God," he muttered. "Hud, come here. Look at this."

Hudlow stepped toward the obelisk, still carrying the child. He peered at the ring.

"Jumping Jesus." He turned and looked down at the circle of skulls at his feet. "Then Monroe Kadinsky's in there somewhere."

“And the highway crew,” said Johnson.

The men stared at the diadem of eyeless sockets.

“You know,” said Johnson, “we’re going to have to bag all this stuff and bring it back for identification.”

At that moment, Eliot, the FBI agent, appeared. “Farthing’s dead,” he said.

47

The fleck of sunlight shone distantly at the top of the pit, remote but beckoning. Magnus Johnson looked up the darkened shaft with gratitude and longing, his fear now faded into fatigue.

The men, spent from the return trip to the base of the pit, moved about slowly, gathering their belongings. The three corpses lay side by side, legs lashed together, hands tucked into their pockets. Each body had several thicknesses of cloth bound over the head.

"Nice to see that piece of daylight again, isn't it?" said Johnson, still looking upward.

"Nothing like a little sunshine in your life," said Hudlow. He cradled Thomas in his arms. They both looked up.

"We going home to Mama?" the boy asked.

Hudlow hesitated. "Mama's . . ." He swallowed. "Thomas, first we got to get out of this place. Go up a rope here and get out. Then we'll worry about going home. Understand?" The boy nodded.

Johnson spoke. "How's Lamont holding up?"

"He's hurting," said Hudlow. "Won't go near Farthing."

"Can't blame him. Eliot's really come through. Carried Farthing most of the way."

"I had half a mind to leave Jubal and Sarah back there. Pus bags."

Hudlow looked toward the top of the pit again. "Sure wish we didn't have to climb that rope," he said. "It's so close, but so far." He shivered. "Thomas, you sure you don't recollect how they brought you in here?"

"I told you I was blindfolded. But it wasn't no ropes. It was ladders and walking."

"Well," said Hudlow turning to Johnson, "Lamont said there was other passages into that place that the Symcoxes might have used, but with the bodies and all, we didn't have time to check them or take the chance of hitting a bunch of dead ends."

"There had to be another entrance," said Johnson. "A simple walk-in one. I mean, they were coming in with food and firewood. It had to be a walk-in."

Lamont summoned the men, his face drawn. "We're going to start ascending out now," he announced. "Who wants to go first?"

Eliot volunteered.

"Okay," said Lamont. "The way it works is this. Since there's only me now, I'll go up first ahead of Eliot and belay each of you from the top. I'll take the boy out with me, piggyback. The state troopers should still be at the top. I'll have one of them take the boy down to the road and get him checked out at a hospital. You guys all remember how to buckle up with the Gibbs ascenders and use the rollers?"

The men nodded.

"Good. Then you should be able to handle it down here on your own. Figure a minimum of twenty minutes each to do the climb. With more experience, someday you'll do it faster. Once you're all out, I'll call Chattanooga and get a couple more cavers to come down and help get Jack and the other two bodies out."

He looked briefly toward the corpses, then strapped himself and the boy into his seat harness and attached the small metal ascenders on the climbing rope for his feet and shoulders. He gripped the rope and began a slow ascent, vanishing in the darkness above.

The end of the rope oscillated lazily just above the floor of the cave, like a cobra standing on its tail. After several minutes, the rope stopped moving. The men heard a faint shout from above.

"Guess he's out," said Eliot. A second, belaying rope hurtled down the pit, landing in a loose coil at the FBI agent's feet. He tied himself into the lines and, like Lamont, disappeared up the shaft.

Several more minutes passed.

"Benny Guy and me going to flip to see who goes last and stays alone with the bodies," said Sheriff Jones.

"Anybody got a two-headed nickel?" asked Gomillion.

Twenty-five minutes later, the rope went limp, and the men heard another shout from above. The end of the belaying line came whirring back down the shaft.

"Okay, guess it's me now," said Hudlow. The same small, unhappy look when he had first rappelled into the pit two days earlier returned to his face. He completed tying the belaying line and tested the climbing rope. It stretched under his weight. He began the ascent and soon was out of sight.

Johnson sat down and leaned against his backpack, his head upturned. He tried to keep his eyes fixed on the point of light above, but found himself dozing in fatigue. His head rolled to the side. Slowly a limitless arch of blue came into his view, at once brilliant and soft. He floated upward through it in serene silence. He felt no encumbrances and at the same time was secure in his weightless journey. It seemed a journey without end, comforting and full of hope. Then he sensed an unwanted intrusion. The images around him began to sink. He tumbled between sleep and consciousness and snapped awake in a babble of voices. He saw Gomillion and Sheriff Jones standing rigidly in front of him, their heads tilted upwards toward the point of light. Vague but urgent shouts cascaded down the shaft.

"What's going on?"

"Can't tell," said Sheriff Jones. "Some kind of trouble up there. Can't make out any of the words."

The men listened. They could hear Lamont's bell-like

shouts, impatient and rushed, interspersed with a lower and more weary voice.

"That's Hud," said Johnson, scrambling to his feet. "Something's happened to him."

They waited. The shouting stopped. Moments later, they heard the whirr of someone descending a rope. It was Lamont. In the next moment, he was at the bottom and dismounted.

"Detective Hudlow has frozen on the rope," he announced. "He won't move."

"What do you mean frozen?" asked the sheriff.

"He's panicked."

"Panic? From what?"

"The height. The open space. I don't know."

"Can't you talk him out of it?"

"Tried. He won't listen."

"How far up is he?"

"About a hundred and forty feet. He's got another eighty or so to go."

"He didn't do this coming in. Why's he doing it now?"

"No rhyme or reason. It can happen any time."

"Maybe he'll climb down if he won't go up."

"He won't go either way," said Lamont.

"Can't you and Eliot and all those state troopers up there pull him out on the rope?"

"The troopers have gone. They took all the Symcox people to some social service agency for observation. There was only one trooper left when I got up there just now, and he left with Thomas for the hospital. Hudlow's awful heavy. Even if we try to move him, he may panic and break out of the harness."

"What about the other passageway? You know, the easy one the Symcoxes s'posed to used. The troopers ever find it?"

"Yes. A lateral entrance with a series of ladders and gradual inclines. But they don't know where it ties in with this pit. Even if we could use it, Hudlow refuses to climb down. He's so near the top, we might as well stay where we are."

“Why can’t we all go out on your rope now and then pull him out together?”

“Take too long. Be at least sixty minutes for the rest of you to climb out. I’m not sure he can last that long.” Lamont looked up into the darkness.

“What do you mean not last that long?” asked Magnus Johnson.

“Look,” said the speleologist. “You know he’s overweight. He’s hanging there paralyzed. His face is puffed up like a balloon. When I got to him, he was having some kind of seizure. His pulse was up around two hundred. He’s vomited all over himself. His adrenaline has screwed up. I don’t think he can take much more.”

“What’s likely to happen next?”

“He’ll eventually get exhausted. He could lose his hold or go unconscious.”

“And fall?”

“No, the belay line will hold him. Eliot has control of that. But it’ll make rescuing him harder.”

“What do we do?” asked the sheriff.

“Can one of you talk to him?” Lamont implored.

“Talk to him? You can’t understand anything hollering up and down this hole. It’s like a baffle box.”

“No, I mean climb up there and talk to him, side by side.”

“I don’t know. Benny Guy, you think you could talk sense to him?”

“I could try.”

Magnus Johnson turned toward Lamont. “I think I should do it.”

Sheriff Jones raised his eyebrows. “You want to do it?”

“Why not?”

“I mean, I guess it’s all right, except, you know—”

“He’s my partner. I think I know him.”

“But all that trouble you had back there in the cave, Johnson. You sure you up to this?”

“This is a different situation.”

"How different?"

"I don't think you would understand, Sheriff."

"I just asked a simple question."

"Look, we've got a man in trouble up there. Is there some reason why I have to be cross-examined this way?"

"I just think we ought to be sure."

"Sure about what?"

"About, well, about you."

"What's the problem with me?"

"I'm just wondering will he be willing to listen to—"

"Sheriff." Johnson fixed his eyes on Jones with cold ferocity. "He will listen to me more than any other person standing here, I guarantee you. I suggest that you let me go ahead, or do I have to be more direct?"

The sheriff looked stonily at Johnson, then turned with a shrug toward Lamont. "That sound all right to you?"

Lamont fingered his harness uneasily. "Yes, I suppose. He is his partner. Perhaps he'd have the best chance."

"Then be my guest," said Jones, bowing gravely to Johnson.

Lamont, a look of relief in his face, readied Magnus Johnson's ascenders and buckled him into a seat harness. "You'll have no belay this time," he said, "but just work the ascenders the way we showed you. You'll have no problems. Good luck."

Johnson began the upward climb. The grip and release of the ascenders were awkward at first, but gradually he developed a rough rhythm, hugging the rope as he worked his arms and legs. The men below disappeared from sight, and once again he dangled free in the unmeasured emptiness. A few tentative tremors shot through him, but he found himself able this time to ignore them largely. A quarter of an hour crept by as he progressed slowly. He looked up. The dot of light was larger now, becoming a jagged but distinct shape. He lowered his head again. The light of his helmet lamp fell on the rope next to him. His eyes followed it up. Soon he made out the dim bulk of Dewey Hudlow. In a short while, he was next to him, panting lightly.

Hudlow's face was red and swollen, his eyes almost closed. His mouth was a defiant, frightened slit. His hands gripped the rope like the coils of a python, holding his trembling body tight against the line. His shirt and rigging glistened in the lamp light and gave off a sour smell.

Their bodies swayed gently against each other in the darkness. Hudlow's eyes, now only pinpoints of light between folds of skin, yielded nothing. Johnson did not know what to say. Finally:

"Hey, Hud, we can't go on meeting like this. You okay?"

There was no movement of the mouth or eyes.

"What's going on? This is supposed to be my act, not yours."

Several moments passed in silence.

"Hey, I want to help. How about it, Hud?"

Hudlow's body turned slowly on the rope.

"Silent treatment. Is that the way to treat friends?"

Hudlow's eyes widened slightly, then narrowed again.

"You really look wide awake. Want to run a few laps and shower? Then maybe you'll feel like talking."

"Talk." The word suddenly shot from Hudlow's mouth between tightened lips, a low growling command.

"Well, good. That's progress. Just don't hit me with too many things at once."

"Not me," rasped Hudlow.

Johnson thought for a moment. "Why did you decide to do all this now?"

"Save the best to last, I guess."

"Well, first I went and did it. Now it's your turn, I suppose."

Hudlow nodded again.

"Jones and Gomillion must think we're a pair of city sissies." Johnson chuckled.

"Fuck Jones and Gomillion."

"That's more like the old Dewey Hudlow we love and admire."

"Talk to me about here," ordered Hudlow.

Johnson gave a quick look of surprise. "This situation we're in?"

"Yeah. Cut the cute shit."

"You sure? I'm not your therapist, you know."

"I don't want no therapist. I want to know what's going on."

"Well," said Johnson, groping slowly, "how about you telling me first what you feel."

"I can't move my hands."

"Why?"

"Because I'm . . . I'm . . . I'm flat scared," Hudlow blurted. A faint crease of relief crossed his face.

"There, you said it. You're scared. Maybe that's a start. Get some of this macho hang-up stuff out of the way."

"Been thinking of that jumper I lost at the Gramercy Building. The rope snapping and seeing him slip, just getting smaller and smaller till he hit."

"Totally different situation, Hud."

"I'm afraid if I stay here this rope will go, too, especially with my weight. But at the same time I can't *move*." Tears were now spilling out of Hudlow's tightened eyes.

"The rope snap? You've already been down it once and halfway back up, and it's served you well. These things are made to hold an armored truck."

"One other thing, Mag."

"What's that?"

"I got to piss."

Johnson paused. "Why you asking me? Miss Manners' not around. Go ahead."

The two men looked at each other. Hudlow's eyes remained motionless for a moment, then slowly widened. Traces of tension along his jaw softened.

"That was down good," he said hoarsely.

"Doctor's orders."

"At least that's one muscle that's relaxed."

"How's your pulse doing now? Let me feel it."

Johnson reached toward Hudlow's left arm clinging to the rope and put his fingers on the wrist. He counted.

"About a hundred and twenty or thirty."

"What does that mean?"

"Means good. Lamont said it was up a bit more earlier."

"Tell me what's going on, Mag."

"You mean what's going on inside you, physically and all?"

"Yeah, like that."

"I'm not sure that would be too good, Hud. I don't think these things are supposed to go this way."

"No, I mean it. I want to hear it. I think if you explain it, I might whip it."

"It might do the opposite."

"No, you good at making sense out of a mess."

"Might be one of those uppity lectures you jump on me about all the time. It might not be down in the sewer."

"Mag, I want to get out of here." Hudlow's eyes flooded with desperation. "I . . . we can work it. Like back in the roof-and-alley days."

Johnson glanced down into the depths below. He looked back up. "Hud, what you got is a thing called acrophobia. It's a temporary fear of heights. Just temporary. No big deal. Happens to people all the time."

"Phobi—what?"

"Acrophobia. But it's more than just fear. It's a kind of emotional disorganization. You have this feeling that you're going out of control and you're at the edge of going crazy. It's a little more severe with you here because of the situation. Not everybody gets to hang on a rope in the middle of a two-hundred-foot pit like you."

"Yeah, that idea come to me."

"But in fact thousands of cave climbers do this very thing all the time all over the world, and never have a problem. It's safer than trying to cross Pennsylvania Avenue at lunchtime."

"Now you trying to scare me again."

"You got so many ropes and pulleys and sling-whistles all over you it would be impossible to fall."

"I know that in my head, but not in my . . . my belly."

"What's going on in your belly is this. When you decided halfway up this rope for no damn good reason that it was dangerous, your fear caused a lot of juice called adrenaline to get squirted around inside you. It redirected your blood supply in all different directions to make you feel dizzy and nauseated and shivery and your breath come harder and your heart beat faster and whatever else you're feeling."

"Like a goddamn headache in the back of my head and chest pains and I can't get enough air."

"And you think you're having a heart attack, don't you?"

"You damn right."

"Well, you're not. You're hyperventilating. Imbalance of oxygen and carbon dioxide in your blood. Nothing serious. It's straightening out on its own right now. Just stay with me."

Hudlow hung silently on the rope. "You went through this same bidness down there in the cave, didn't you, Mag?"

"Yes, I did. Only it was the darkness, not the height. Everybody's got their thing."

"You knew what was going on then but couldn't help yourself?"

"I was a mess. You saw me. I needed help. I knew all the time it was a physical-psychological thing, but I still couldn't control it. There was a fear in my stomach sharper than any knife on this earth. But you took care of it, Hud, slow but sure. A practical meat-and-potatoes man to help shrink back my imagination. That's what it took."

"Did you believe me?"

"Yeah, slowly I came around. I said if this place doesn't spook Dewey Hudlow, then it must not be too bad."

"I got to admit it wasn't my favorite garden spot."

"But you had—I don't know what to call it, Hud—some kind of solidness or . . . certainty that everything was all right. You transmitted that certainty to me."

"That shit doesn't usually work with phobias."

"It did that time."

"How?"

Johnson hesitated. "Your voice, your hands." He stopped again. "These things are hard to say, Hud. It's girl talk. Different league."

"How you think I felt down there? I must've looked like a wet nurse with you. And Jones and them staring at us."

Hudlow fell silent. Then: "Mag, remember Ambrose Fairlyte that took a lick at me at Homicide that night? I wonder how he'd manage in a situation like this?"

"No way of knowing. Maybe a champ, maybe a chump."

"It's hard to judge a guy from outside." Hudlow hesitated a moment. "I been thinking 'bout ol' Ambrose. Maybe he was okay, in his own off-brand way."

"Would you buy a used yogurt stick from that man?"

"Mag, you were right to stop me when I was scrambling around with him on Captain Stohlbach's floor. I want you to know that."

The two men swung almost imperceptibly in the darkness. "You know, Mag," continued Hudlow, "we must look ridic'lous swinging around out here in the middle of nowhere and me with vomit and pissed myself. Hope didn't nobody get hit below."

Johnson was silent. He sensed a slight relaxation in the body next to him. Neither man spoke for several minutes.

Then Hudlow stirred on his rope. "I think," he said softly, "I'm ready to go."

Johnson smiled. "Try loosening your hands a little."

Hudlow slid both hands up and down on the rope. Tentatively, he raised his feet and readjusted the ascenders. He nodded to Johnson. "Keep in tandem, would you?" said Hudlow. "Stay close." They started the ascent.

Slowly, the opening above them grew larger. Johnson longed to touch it, to hold the life-giving light in his hands. They could see the parallel climbing ropes and belaying line now stretching toward the gap. Foot by foot, hand by hand, they ascended, watching the ropes grow shorter. The opaque gray light at the top turned a faint blue. Now they could see the outline of bushes hanging over the lip of the pit.

“Hey, Eliot,” Johnson called up. His heart pounded.

There was a brief rustling above and a shower of gravel and leaves fell noisily on the climbers’ helmets. Eliot’s unshaven face appeared at the rim of the pit twenty feet above them.

“Hallo!” he called. “I’ll be here to pull you.”

Sunlight danced across the top of the pit, casting faint, promising rays in the dark where the two men climbed just under the lip. As they neared the top, Johnson turned to Hudlow. “You go first. I’ll be right under you.”

He watched as Hudlow pulled himself up and grasped at the rounded stone of the lip. Eliot, tied to a safety rope, leaned over and gripped one of Hudlow’s trembling wrists. He pulled, but Hudlow’s upward motion suddenly ceased. His body slumped, becoming a dead weight again, and Eliot did not have the strength to pull him over the top. Hudlow squirmed at the rim of the pit, his body halfway out, like a man struggling in quicksand. Quickly, Johnson maneuvered himself below until Hudlow’s boots rested on his shoulders. Then with a grinding thrust of his ascenders, Johnson jerked himself upward under Hudlow, lessening Hudlow’s weight for a split second so that Eliot was able to yank him over the lip with a final heave and drag him onto the ground.

Johnson watched Hudlow’s feet disappear over the rim. Then he began ascending the last few feet himself. Moments later he felt the warm stone of the lip under his own hands. His head burst into the sunlight and Eliot hauled him onto the rough dry earth at the edge of the pit.

He lay there, filled with a joyous release, his starved senses devouring the world around him, the blinding sunlight, the roaring breeze, the deafening chirrup of birds.

He sat up and threw off his harness. Hudlow lay sprawled nearby. Both men were immobilized, catching their breath, savoring the newfound earth. Then they stood up and walked unsteadily toward each other.

“Tell me,” said Magnus Johnson, his face suffused with relief and exhaustion, "that rope trick you just did down there: did you really think you were going to die?"

"Well," answered Hudlow slowly, "I didn't see no angels, but I could hear 'em singing."

Hudlow placed his arm on Johnson's shoulder. There was no resistance. The two men walked away, talking quietly.

EPILOGUE

In the weeks that followed, the Symcox family members, children and adults alike, were placed under foster supervision in Buncombe County, while authorities, never before confronted by such circumstances, pondered their permanent fate. Eleven of the sixteen adult skulls removed from the cave were identified, through dental charts, as those of the highway administration team members. Each bore a small ragged hole at the center of the occipital bone near the base of the skull. Official cause: small-caliber bullet or pointed instrument. No identification could be made as to the remaining five adult skulls and several infant skulls. Authorities assumed they were those of Symcox family members who died at birth and from other natural causes.

Alba Kadinsky buried an urn containing Monroe's remains under a simple stone next to Franklin's in the Kadinsky family plot in Chicago. At the service, she was accompanied by Jerome, an unquestioning, loving husband who accepted the deaths of his two sons with a kind of stunned equanimity. Florian Boldt flew to Chicago, again, offering what comfort he could. When he returned to Washington, he gave up the apartment in L'Enfant Court, taking the Roxbury clock with him to a sunny condominium in West End overlooking Rock Creek Park.

Metropolitan Police released the Symcox family ring to Alba Kadinsky. At first, she considered returning it to Washington. Then after holding it a day, she drove north from Chicago and threw it into Lake Michigan.

Quovadis Logan was buried in Shreveport at the family church. Thomas went to live in Southeast with his grandmother. Once a month, Douglas MacArthur Cheek would take the long bus ride across town and leave off $40 from Detective Dewey Hudlow.

Detective Nestor Skoda, after brief deliberation, joined the folk Mass in Arlington. He agreed to play the tambourine, but also began studying classical guitar. His teacher: Ambrose Fairlyte.

Dewey Hudlow bought a new she-fox. But he would be on his own for next winter's hunt. Cheeks had had to give up running the fields.

Magnus Johnson returned to his garden, nursing the jewelweed and summer yarrow, digging and shaping. He visited the cemetery every Friday.

Captain Stohlbach signed PD Form 73 in triplicate, assigning Mag and Hud to the same section in Homicide. They were partners now.

About the Author

PAUL W. VALENTINE, a reporter for *The Washington Post*, lives in Baltimore, Maryland, with his wife. They have five children. He is working on his next novel.